Three Years on Doreen's Sofa is an ou~~~~~~~~~~~~~~~, touching, clear~~~~~~~~~~~, raunchy, and hilarious tour of the dark side of today's Maui. It's amazing just how much happens to the main character Bobby, as he encounters a huge cast of characters every bit as memorable as the folks you've met in Longs. Bobby has to learn that stupid isn't funny but Lee Cataluna knows it from the start, so the most ridiculous moments ring true, showing that even at their worst, most people are just trying to handle. An endlessly inventive and engaging story by one of Hawai'i's favorite writers.

    —Craig Howes, co-producer of *Aloha Shorts*

Lee Cataluna wants her readers to meet Candide's distant cousin: Meet Bobby, who sleeps part-time on his sister's couch—he's local and native fauna of Kepaniwai Park—or maybe you'd rather not. Panglossian, eternally optimistic swimming in the ebb tide of Hawai'i post diasporan tsunami, Bobby leaves a trail at the foamy edge of the receding surf, slurpy cups, chicken bones, the familiar Styrofoam detritus of paradise lost. Displaced cuckoo birds gargling in palm shade groves, napalm fueling bbq smoke, a rising curtain to Paradise sunset, paradise lost, the littoral an Edenic wasteland. If you're local, you won't laugh. Laughing inside these pages is for tourists. For all its humor, the narrative is excoriating and relentless.

    —Jeffery Paul Chan, author of *Eat Everything Before You Die*

With her recognizably distinctive local voice, Lee Cataluna's first novel may open up a whole new era for Hawai'i literature.

    —Ryan Senaga, *Honolulu Weekly*

Lee Cataluna

THREE YEARS ON DOREEN'S SOFA

Lee Cataluna

THREE YEARS ON DOREEN'S SOFA

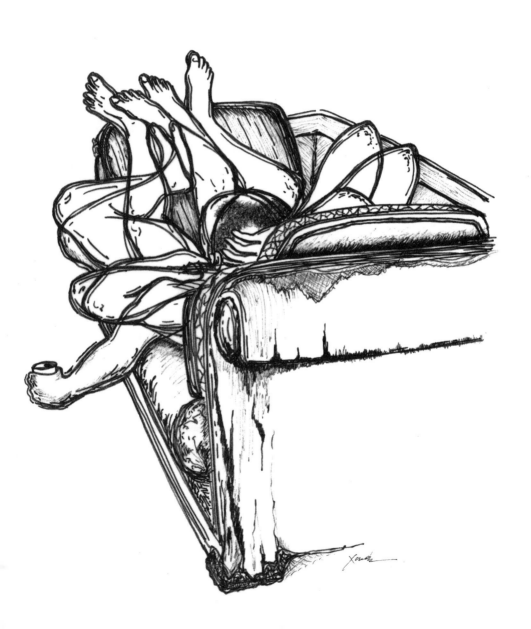

ISBN 978-0-910043-85-4

This is issue #99 (Spring 2011) of *Bamboo Ridge, Journal of Hawai'i Literature and Arts* (ISSN 0733-0308).

Published by Bamboo Ridge Press
Printed in the United States of America
Indexed in the Humanities International Index
Bamboo Ridge Press is a member of the Council of Literary Magazines and Presses (CLMP).

Typesetting and design: Wayne Kawamoto

Cover art: "Sofa So Good," © 2011, by Xander Cintrón-Chai, pen and ink on paper, 27.8 x 21.2 cm
Title page: "Bobby's Sideways Mohawk Surprise from Ricky," © 2011, by Xander Cintrón-Chai, pen and ink on paper, 20 x 17.6 cm

Bamboo Ridge Press is a nonprofit, tax-exempt corporation formed in 1978 to foster the appreciation, understanding, and creation of literary, visual, or performing arts by, for, or about Hawai'i's people. This publication was made possible with support from the Mayor's Office of Culture & the Arts (MOCA) and the Hawai'i State Foundation on Culture and the Arts (SFCA), through appropriations from the Hawai'i State Legislature (and by the National Endowment for the Arts [NEA]). Additional support for Bamboo Ridge Press activities is provided by the Hawai'i Council for the Humanities.

Bamboo Ridge is published twice a year. For subscription information, back issues, or a catalog, please contact:

Bamboo Ridge Press
P.O. Box 61781
Honolulu, HI 96839-1781
(808) 626-1481
brinfo@bambooridge.com
www.bambooridge.com

HAWAI'I
STATE FOUNDATION on
CULTURE and the ARTS

ART WORKS.
arts.gov

HAWAI'I
COUNCIL
FOR THE
HUMANITIES

5 4 3 2 1   11 12 13 14 15

To JKL

CHAPTER 1

FRICKEN DOREEN DIDN'T EVEN STOP THE TRUCK. I had to run on the side in the dead weeds and beer cans while she just slowed down a little bit.

I caught up to the passenger door and tried to pull the handle. Doreen yelled at me to get in the back. She had piles of dog blankets under the camper shell. Stink, damp towels with fleas and ticks and hair. The dog was riding in the front. I figured I was lucky she picked me up at all. I stuck my head out the back window for fresh air. Deep breath. Lungs filled with exhaust. At least it cut the doggy stink from the blankets. I could see the dog staring at me through the glass to the cab like, "Eh, no touch my stuff." I showed finger to the dog. Doreen saw in the rear view mirror. I made like I was fixing my hair.

Maui changed plenty in 37 months. All look-alike houses came up where cane fields used to be. Ooka's Supermarket closed. Dairy Queen is called something else now. I hope they still get slush float. And the secret mayo-mustard action on the fries. I gotta get me some. I almost knocked on the glass to tell Doreen to stop and grab lunch but nah, she look like she super pissed at herself for picking me up in the first place. Better not chance 'em.

Doreen, she get one good heart, her. That's her best thing and her worst thing at the same time. She get one fast mouth and one faster arm. That's what saved her all these years. That, and she like one nice life for her kids. She get dreams, her. Even now. I give her credit.

She came pick me up because she thought I could fix stuff. I used to make like I could fix car high school time but that was twenty-something years ago when cars could fix with wrench and WD-40. Now, need all kind fancy computer EKG hookups. I kind of told her in my letter that I learned some skills in prison. Car stuff, carpentry stuff, computer stuff. I kind of told her I could be the man around the house for a little while, help her out, at least until I found my own place.

I did learn plenty stuffs on the inside, but mostly stuff like how to make my own ukulele and how to throw in big words for when you gotta go court. I could fix her hanging side mirror with some duct tape, though. I can do that. I would. For her.

Me and Doreen is brother/sister and we cousins at the same time. Same father, different mothers, but our mothers is sisters. Made on the same day, born on the same day, forty weeks after a Youth Rehab graduation party at Kepaniwai Park. We have a half-sister who is a week older, but she's just a sister because her mother not related to our mothers. As far as we know, but, she was made around the same time in the same car in the same parking lot up Iao Valley.

I met my father when I was inside. First time. I seen him in the yard and I recognized the upepe nose that I get and Doreen get and our other sister get real bad. Me and Dori got some wide noses but sister Taysha, hers is like one airplane hangar. She had pierce 'em and put diamond. Look more big. Sad.

When I told him I was his son, he acted like he didn't know me. But he took a good long look at my fat nose and smiled like yeah, that thing gotta be from me.

My father had rank around the prison. Twenty-something years in and about that much more to go. Stuff got easier for me when I spotted that nose across the yard. I got all the cigarettes I wanted because of that big hand-me-down nose. My father had to be cool, but. Mostly he acted like he didn't know me. But I knew I had his protection.

Doreen parked the truck by some brown apartments by Puuone. She must be doing good these days. Section 8 and working at the airport. She can afford one apartment by herself. No need another boyfriend to pay her rent, drink her beer and slap her around for exercise. Doreen had plenty of them before time. But now, look like she only get the truck, the dog, and her kids.

When she got out of the truck, I tried make the aloha hug to tell her thank you but she was already on me about the rules. She get rules, her. Always. Who knows where she picked up that habit because it ain't from the grandmother who raised us and as far as I know, Doreen never did have to do no time in rehab or juvy.

"No smoking inside the house. No swearing in front the kids. You cannot go around wearing only bebadees in front the kids—gotta always put shorts and T-shirt. Cannot eat the kids' breakfast cereal. That's only for them and fuckin' expensive and no drink no milk neither 'cause that cost money, too. No television shows with violences in front the kids. No bragging about jail in front the kids. No talk too loud, no breathe too loud, no piss me off when I tired. No steal, no argue, no bullshit in the house."

She was going for twenty minutes.

I got stuck on the rule about wearing shorts and T-shirt. I only had with me the clothes on my back, my AA, NA, Al-Anon bookmarks and the glued-together ukulele I made in woodshop. I guess I can score some clothes from Salvation Army or something if I gotta make decent in front the kids.

Dori, she one good mother, strict mother, but her kids is monsters. I not supposed to say that because I'm the nice uncle and nice uncles supposed to think the kids is angels. Liko, the small one, he kinda cute but when he don't get his way, he go off. The girl, Jorene, she sassy. The oldest, Kennison, he thick like Maalaea mud. Cannot get any of them to follow directions. I no mind play good fun uncle with them, but only for like ten minutes at a time. After that, I like them go someplace else make noise so I can drink beer and watch what I like on TV.

Except Doreen says I cannot drink beer in her house. Leave it to her to actually read all those rules the social worker sent her. I pictured her reading all those do nots, do nots and coming all happy.

Her place is small and hot but she made 'em nice as she can with Pepsi mirrors she won from the county fair and color crayon drawings from Liko taped over the places where one of her exes punched the walls.

"Nice," I told her. She had her hand on her hip. "You get two bedrooms?"

"You sleeping your broke ass on the sofa," she said. "And no put your feet on the pillows. That's Kenji's pillows."

By the look of the pillows, Kenji must be the name of the dog.

"And no put your feet on the coffee table." The other hand came up on the other hip. "I just got that thing new from the second hand store."

"Eh, like I said in my letter, it's just for a little while. A week, two weeks. That's all."

"Better be."

If she had another hand and another hip, the two would have connected right then.

"For real, Dori. I got a lead on one good job. I go tomorrow go check 'em out."

"That's right you going tomorrow go check 'em out. I don't want no ex-con sitting around my house doing nothing but eating and scratching. You had three years to eat and scratch. Now you gotta work."

Just as she said the stuff about eating and scratching, I all of a sudden got hungry and itchy.

"No worry, Doreen. I going get one job tomorrow. Stuff is all different now. I had plenty of time to think about my life, you know? Where I going, what I like do. I get goals now. I get direction. Not going be like before when I was just drifting. I know what I like do and I going do 'em. One day, another day, one foot in front the other, my hard work and the guidance from a higher power. Every day is a new beginning."

"Fuck, you talk like you been to too many Twelve Step meetings run by drinkers who still drinking."

Fricken Doreen. She was right.

Afternoon time, Doreen went to pick up Liko from his preschool and the two older kids came home on the bus. I heard them coming so I had time to fast-kind put on shirt. Jorene came through the door first. She stopped when she saw me, one hand on the rusty doorknob, the other hand flying up to her hip. She blocked the brother from coming in, but instead of pushing her on the side, he just stood and waited for her to tell him what she was looking at.

"Eh! Long time no see! How you, baby girl?"

I tried to make my best Good Fun Uncle voice.

"Mommy said don't put your feet on her coffee table." Kennison stood behind her like one robot on pause waiting for someone to hit his go button again.

"Oh, sorry. I never know."

The other hand went from the doorknob to the hip, heavy book bag and all.

"You did know. Mommy told you all the rules. Every single one. And the biggest rule is no bullshit in her house."

"I thought you cannot swear in the house."

Jorene popped her hip to one side. She had found her own version of wahine pissed-off-ed-ness, like one riff on Doreen's theme.

"YOU cannot swear in the house. Me, I can do what I like because I get good grades and I not trying to straighten out my screwed up life. I the good girl. You the fucked-up uncle."

She picked up her book bag and went to the kitchen table. Kennison blinked back on and came inside the house.

"Howzit," I told him.

"Eh," he said, making the casual high school boy wave.

"You heard your sister talk to me like that?" I was looking for some manly back up. His eyes went down to his shoes as he pulled them off without using hands.

"Nope."

He put his books on the kitchen table across from Jorene, who was already heavy into her math homework. He went to the icebox and made two cups of Kool-Aid. I took notice he gave the bigger cup to the sister. Then he sat down and cracked open a book.

I turned the TV back on. Dr. Phil was giving one fat lady dirty scoldings for blaming her ass on her husband's bad behaviors. He was telling her just because the husband is a loser don't mean she gotta eat every damn thing in sight. The husband was looking relieved he was off the hook, even though he just got called a loser on national television.

Jorene snapped off the television.

"No TV until homework is pau," she said.

"I no more homework."

"We get."

Ho, that girl is her mother times ten. She had the mean stare down. I felt my ass moving off the couch with just her eyes. I grabbed my cigarettes and went outside.

Doreen-them lucky. They get one nice apartment they no gotta share with nobody. Maui coming so crowded and rent so expensive, plenty people gotta move back with their parents or take in roommates or live couple families to a three-bedroom house. Coming like Mainland already. Ah, worse than that even. Maui coming crowded and expensive like Honolulu. Doreen and the kids lucky only get them. Them and whatever boyfriend Doreen get at the time, which, judging by the four toothbrushes in the bathroom, was currently nobody. At least not nobody with good teeth. I had to laugh at that one. Like Doreen would ever kiss one guy with bad teeth hygiene. Not no more. She all liberated now.

I gotta remember to get me one good toothbrush. The kind the kids get, the kind look like small sneakers. Mines from jail is pretty had-it. Only good to clean the grout around the bathroom tile.

I leaned off the railing and looked down at the sand dunes and the hollow-tile apartments and the kiawe trees. Broken beer bottles, twisted shopping carts, small pieces of a two-by-four with the nails still stuck inside.

Time to make some plans.

I was going go check out this job that this guy on the inside told me about. I was going that very next day. But all I had was my jeans and my slippers and my wrinkled aloha shirt that was donated to the Job

Connections program from the family of some dead old Japanese guy. Still had his name on the inside collar tag. This my Fujinaka shirt, I call 'em. I got so fat in prison, the clothes I had when I came in no fit no more. Mr. Fujinaka must have been a hefty dude because I fill out his mothball-smelling XL pretty good.

Maybe someday I can buy clothes that didn't used to belong to a dead guy.

My first step before that, but, is I gotta get some money.

I had money from my account at MCCC from when I worked in the laundry and stuff, but that was my cigarette money. Daily essentials come before luxuries. I learned that in my Household Budgeting class.

I could ask Doreen to spot me some cash.

I peeked inside the apartment and Jorene caught me looking. She showed me the finger, like she knew what I was thinking. No, no asking Mama Dori for no money. Not if I like live to see next week.

I just going have to make do with dead guy clothes and a couple less smokes. I looked down at my feet. Had butts all around my rubber slippers. Hard to imagine I only started smoking when I went in. Never had money when I was in high school. Never had the urge when I was on the outside. Nothing else to do when you locked up. I was screwed up before I went inside, but it was just a random thing. Now I get all these permanent screwed-up habits all ingrained inside me.

That night, Doreen made chicken with cream of mushroom soup gravy. She put little bit canned peas and carrots for fancy. I was careful to only take three scoops rice. No like take food outta the kids' mouths. They still growing. Kennison watched me eat but didn't say nothing. Liko made a line of peas on one side of his plate. I acted like good-fun uncle and snatched one pea from the line and ate 'em. Liko started crying. Doreen's eyebrows started climbing up her face. I scooped up as much peas from my plate as my fork could carry and put 'em all on Liko's plate. He stopped crying like someone pulled the plug.

"Don't eat that, Liko," Doreen told him. She grabbed the plate and tossed it in the sink. "You don't know what kind diseases your uncle get."

Before he went bed, Doreen made Liko one peanut butter sandwich 'cause he said he was still hungry. I just watched. I getting better at watching without them knowing I watching. I thought I had my technique down in prison but this family better than most of the inmates I met. They keep their secrets and hide their weaknesses and they watch you like you up to something.

The sofa was all high hills and rocky valleys. Itchy plaid in shades of orange. Made me miss my cot and scratchy blanket. I lay awake the whole night listening to the strange sounds breaking the strange quiet. Dori grinding her teeth. Jorene scratching the mosquito bites on her legs. Kennison trying hard not to make noise while he playing with his dakine.

I watched the clock on the oven. One o'clock. Two o'clock. Three-thirty.

I probably fell asleep around 5 a.m.

Doreen gotta leave the house six forty-five to drop the kids at school before she go work, so they get up fricken early. They woke me up with all the get-ready noises an hour after I fell asleep but I kept my eyes closed so they wouldn't notice me. Too early in the morning to get yelled at for getting in the way. I had to take a piss super bad, but Jorene was iron-curling her hair in the bathroom and Doreen was standing right behind her putting on makeup. No ways I getting in there any time soon.

I took notice had one big plastic cup hanging off the dish drainer. The dinosaur on the cup looked like he was waving at me.

"Best of friends is what we'll be."

Alrighty, my big purple buddy. Help a bruddah out. I grabbed the cup and pulled down my shorts. The cup was three-quarters full when Kennison walked into the room. I didn't even have to look. I heard him breathing. I just kept going. Couldn't stop even if it was Dori yelling in my face.

"I tell you what boy," I said, soft so only he could hear. "You no tell about Barney and I don't tell about you pulling taro in the middle of the night."

"Huh?"

I cannot tell if Kennison is for real dumb or only playing.

"That ain't poi on your pajamas, you catch my drift?"

Kennison walked out of the room. I had the dinosaur cup emptied and rinsed and back on the counter before Doreen came into the parlor. I even made it back to the couch in time to pretend-sleep, but then I thought, eh, more better if I awake when she come in because guarantee she going slap my head for sleeping late.

"Everybody, eat something," Doreen ordered. "Not you, Bobby." I was expecting that. I just sat still on the couch. The kids grabbed Pop-Tarts and ate them raw, no toasting.

"Everybody, drink milk," she commanded. I put my head down. She started to tell me "not you" but she saw that I knew already. She must be happy her training is sinking in.

Kennison poured milk for the sister and Liko. I made my side-eye as side as I could. I took notice he used the Barney cup for the small brother. I was secretly hoping would go to Jorene.

"Mommy, the milk taste funny!" Liko was wrinkling his upepe nose. I shot a look at Kennison. Kennison was blank as the moon, blank as the ceiling, blank as the hollow tile wall in the hallway.

Doreen took a sip and spat it out. "Damn thing was too long in the hot car."

I couldn't believe I skated out of this one!

"Your good-for-nothing Uncle Bobby as' why. Had to wait so long outside the prison in a car with no AC. If he didn't get into trouble his whole life, we would have good milk to drink this morning. But Bobby ruins everything."

Doreen and the kids each gave me the look as they left the apartment, like I was a stink stain on the carpet they hoped would somehow go away.

"Bye. Have one good day," I told them. The door slamming was their answer. At least I tried.

I was waiting all night for them to go so I could be alone, and after they left, I was waiting all day for them to come back. I try talk story with Kenji but he don't laugh at my jokes.

CHAPTER 2

WARREN, MY PAROLE OFFICER, I THINK SO HE MAHU. Not like I give a shet or anything. Just so long he no make trouble for me and so far, I think so he one straight shooter for one not-straight guy. Ah, I crack myself up when I say stuff like that. I not always so funny when I talk to people. I try hard, but never comes out as good as when it's in my head. In my head, I'm fucking hilarious. In my head, the audience is holding their stomachs and rolling in the aisles. In real life, people only look at me like I'm loaded.

I thinking Warren is from the Mainland but he been Maui couple years so he talk like he one of the local braddahs. His boyfriend must be one local guy. Probably hooked up at Hamburger Mary's in Lahaina back in the day. That's where they all used to go. Now get Hamburger Mary's in Wailuku. I cannot believe. Before, when one mahu wanted a place to go to be all into his mahu-ness, he had to go around the pali to Hamburger Mary's or get his ass kicked in one upcountry cowboy bar by upcountry ass-kicking cowboys. Nowadays they can get their action right in Wailuku town. That's progress.

Not that I get one problem with that kind guys. Live and let live is my thing. Had some in prison that tried really hard to be pretty but how you going make like one wahine when you six feet tall, wide like one Chevy, and are deprived of things like tweezers, lipstick, and high heels? I was sad for them sometimes. All they had was the hair and the walk. In prison, they get plenty time for grow long hair and braid 'em fancy. Plenty time to practice the slow shake-ass walk across the yard during rec time. They looked like fat, hairy cons with lower back problems, but ah, they was cool to me. And me, I sure as hell left those ugly-ass bastards alone. But one time in computer education class, one of them told me he/she was going pray for me and that pretty much made my day. Nobody ever said they was going pray for me before. I thought maybe would help. Cannot hurt. But then he/she crossed the line and did one weird wink thing with his/her eye and that was it. I told 'em no talk to me, no pray for me, nothing. Just leave me the hell alone. I get the upepe nose of the Bull of the jail and my father no like his boy getting winked at. I made 'em sound good and scary. He/she looked like he/she was going cry.

But maybe he/she did still pray for me. Right after that I made parole first try. Not like I was really trying because to tell the truth, being inside was a cruise gig. They bring you food, they let you do nothing all day and there's always somebody to talk to even if nobody really listens. The only downside is that it's fucking boring. Everybody try out-do everybody else coming up with exciting bullshit stories about stuff that never happened. But now I'm out, I'm free, I'm on my way to turning my life around and becoming a successful contributing member of the community. Stuff is happening and I have one religious mahu and my own industriousness behavior to thank for that.

Thank you, Ginger Lei Bonafacio (I think that was his/her name), and thank me. Like the song about Bob Marley, "Bob, Bob, you did a good job." That's me, I did a good job. Bobby, Bobby, you did a good jobby.

And thank you, Warren. Thank you for believing in me. Thank you for your guidance. Thank you for your investment of trust in a lost and misguided guy like me. Where would I be without your mentorship and your parole-manship, Warren? Thank you, Warren, for giving me this chance.

I gotta remember to say stuff like that. Those social worker types eat that shet up. Nobody ever tells them thank you. It's only bitch and moan, bitch and moan. But not me. I can smooth talk with the best of them.

Sometimes.

But it's the feeling that counts and I am definitely feeling thankful today.

Doreen only yelled at me three times before she left the house this morning. Only three times and she didn't even slap my head. I am thankful for that.

Kennison left behind his raw Pop-Tart in the broken toaster because I told him I had fix 'em and he was waiting and waiting and nothing happened and him, he not the kind to check it out or ask questions, so he was waiting for the untoasty toaster to pop back up for 15 minutes before his sister was whacking his head and telling him hurry his ass up, she gotta go school before school start because she running for class seckatary and she gotta put up her glitter posters in the cafeteria.

I am thankful for that raw Pop-Tart, food of the Gods.

I'm thankful for the old man who died and left this sharp Reyn's aloha shirt to the Job Connections program so that I could pick it out of all the other dead man clothes. I am grateful to get to wear his nice inside-out Christmas 1995 Reyn's reverse print aloha shirt to my first meeting with my probation officer. I wonder if that was old Mr. Fujinaka's last Christmas on this earth and if the shirt came from the college grad daughter who work one choice civil service job for the Honolulu City and County? Emily Fujinaka, City Wastewater Division. Made her parents so proud. I bet she brought him manapua over on the plane, too. Maui no more too much good manapua. Get Minit Stop and that's about it. Minit Stop get good potato wedges but the manapua either hard like one rock or soggy like one panties. Maui people know that, so when they go Honolulu, they bring back for us poor manapualess people back here on the Valley of No Pork Bao Island. I can imagine Mr. Fujinaka sitting there in his Wailuku Heights house wearing his Christmas 1995 Reyn's reverse print aloha shirt eating his last manapua ever in this world. Mahalo, Mr. Fujinaka. Can I call you Mr. Fujinaka? Can I call you Fooj for short? Maybe his first name was Larry. Larry Fujinaka of Wailuku Heights. Or maybe was Tets. Yeah, I think so Tets because had three or five Larrys on the inside but never

ever had any Tets in jail. Ever. His name must have been Tets. Thank you, Tets Fujinaka. You my main man.

Goddamn it but my mind wanders like one fly when I nervous. And holy shet I feel nervous. Sitting in Warren's office watching that fucking fucker look through my papers—him, not saying nothing, me, cannot make myself stop talking. The more I talk, the more I hear the quiet in the room. I cannot say enough words even if I don't stop to take a breath. The silence is like a hole in the sand that you can never fill up with water. The words just run through and disappear.

And fricken Warren, he don't help me out. It's all one-side conversations like I talking to myself.

So Warren, you like your job? You like your boss? You like your life? You like everybody? You like anybody? You like me?

Warren is looking at papers he already looked at. What the hell is so complicated about my case that it takes him twenty minutes of reading to figure out how to tell me no drink, no use drugs, no hang with hoodlums, no get into trouble, and try find a job while you at it? He looking, he looking, he turn the page, he turn back the page and look again. You would think I was involved in some heavy international, political, secret spy kind of shet instead of driving one fork lift that wasn't mine into a car that wasn't mine while carrying a bunch of cocaine in one fanny pack that was mine and being generally loaded off my happy ass.

So Warren, you from the Mainland or you just fair-skin Portuguese with highlights from Regis salon?

Come to think of it, I get one mahu uncle in my family. Aunty Georgie, we used to call him. Wasn't blood uncle but he was the brother of one of my mother's boyfriends and after the boyfriend left, him and my mother stayed good friends. When I was a small kid, Aunty Georgie used to come over, drink coffee with my mother, teach her how to make home cosmetics with the achiote plant and Vaseline. Sometimes they would laugh together all night. Sometimes, they would cry all the tears for the whole low income housing community. Aunty Georgie would make a mean Bloody Mary that had something like cinnamon or cough drops inside. He would tell us, "Drink 'em, because it's like that V-8 juice except going make you healthy AND sleep real good." Aunty Georgie was the best. I was sad when him and my mom had beef over Carl Manriques and somebody called the cops and my mom got even more piss off when they showed up and asked, "So which one is da mahu?" and we got kicked out of low income housing because she broke the jalousie window when she threw the plastic tub of I Can't Believe It's Not Butter at the cop's head and I had to move back in with my grandma after that. Aunty Georgie was the best. And did I tell you he taught me how to light a cigarette off a car battery?

So, Warren, you smoke or is your teeth that way from chewing coffee grounds or do you smoke couple packs a day? I didn't mean like your teeth was fucked up or nothing. I was just asking for a cig if you get. You a good looking guy. Even with the fucked up teeth. Not that I give a shet or nothing. But you not bad. You one sharp dresser. You mahus really know how to pick out nice kind clothes. You look hot.

Shet, did I really just say that?

Fuck me.

Oh shet, I never mean that, either! I was just saying 'Fuck me' like I am so fucked—not like I like you do nothing to my ass, OK?

Stop talking, Bobby, stop talking, stop talking, stop talking.

What you mean what I on? I'm clean and sober, Warren! I get 16 months sobriety and I ain't about to throw all that effort down the drain. Why, what you mean what I on? Can't a guy be little bit nervous? Can't a guy be a little bit talkative? I was in the joint for 37 months and not like I found much sterling conversations if you know what I mean. Maybe if I had a cig I could stop talking.

I don't like what you, whatyoucall, accusing. No, wait, get one bigger word. I don't like what you . . . implying. No, wait. It pays to enrich my word power. Insinuating. That's the bugga right there. I no like what you insinuating, Warren. Just because I cannot keep my mouth shut don't mean I'm flying high. Maybe I'm just a chatty guy, ever consider that option? Maybe I'm a guy who has a lot to say and I haven't had too damn much opportunity to say it. How you know? You don't know. You don't even know me. You just sitting there, fake-reading my case record while you thinking of what you and your boyfriend gonna do tonight, you and your local boyfriend, what his name? Gerard? Jerome? Local mahus always get that kind name. Jeremiah? So you thinking of Jerry and you should be thinking about me, not how to fuck me, not how to fuck me over, but how to help me, Warren. That's your job, Warren. Your job is to help me set my course on the path of righteousness and doing-goodedness. Help me Warren, you my main and only man. Except for Fujinaka.

All this stuff was playing out in my head as I was twilighting on Doreen's sofa. I kind of woke up little bit and realized I was only imagining I was in the parole officer's office, but then I told myself nah, relax, I only imagining that I imagining. So go back sleep.

I really did mean to go to the parole office for the meeting, but was for one o'clock in the afternoon, and that raw Pop-Tart went down so good with a chaser of past-expiration-date Nyquil from the back, back, back of Doreen's under-the-sink bathroom cabinet, I just lay myself down to watch some "Price Is Right" and before I knew it I was half-sleeping, dreaming while my eyes was wide open, snoring and mumbling and laughing at how fucking hilarious I was with this guy Warren that I was supposed to meet. Cannot be one o'clock yet. The clock says three-twenty. Wait, what? No, probably still morning and I didn't even wake up yet. The Pop-Tart was just a dream. A happy, strawberry-filling dream.

Doreen hit me so hard I saw satellites. Not stars, because those guys stay in one place. These buggas was blinking and orbiting.

"YOU SUPPOSED TO BE AT THE PAROLE OFFICE!"

Her hands wasn't doing a good enough job so she was heading to the kitchen to check out her weaponry. Frying pan. Butter knife. Broken toaster. She ended up coming at me with a dish towel, which may not sound so scary but Doreen could flick that thing harder than any football player in the locker room. The end of that dish towel was taking pieces of skin off the side of my face.

"Doreen, I going! I not late yet. My appointment one o'clock."

Zing! She got my ear with the dish towel. When she pulled it back to reload I could see had little bit blood on it. My poor ear losing ear blood on Doreen's dish towel. I tried to make wounded face but Doreen don't have no compassion sometimes.

"Your appointment WAS one o'clock. It's three-thirty right now. What you doing on my sofa?!"

I was trying to think fast but the Nyquil was getting in my way, like trying to swim laps in long pants. I was going down.

"No, I went and came back already. It's all good. The guy said."

Three whacks with the dish towel of death for that.

"The guy said? The guy said? The guy said?!" I was losing all my ear blood. My ears going come all deflated and hang off the sides of my head like nut sacks without the balls.

"The GUY had call my working place looking for you!"

Oooh, that's bad. Doreen don't like nobody calling her working place. Not Kennison saying he missed the bus because of after-school detention. Not Jorene saying Kennison missed the bus because of after-school detention. Not Liko's nursery school teacher aide saying he doodoo-ed his pants again. No bad news, no good news, don't tell, don't call. She is a professional woman and she work hard to maintain her professionalism in her career. That's what they taught her at Wahine Imua job training, where she turned her life around from an endless cycle of trying to score a union truck driver so she could marry rich. From there, she dropped her mop bucket and push broom and left behind her career as a school sanitation specialist for a fast-paced, high stress, on-the-go job as a Budget Rent A Car airport shuttle van driver. She the first one in our family to get off assistance. To me, she living life in the fast lane, even if she only driving in a loop from the airport baggage claim to the rental car lot and back again.

She work hard, damn it, and she no like no calls from no fucked up half-brother cousin's parole officer saying does she know the whereabouts of Bobby.

"I'm sorry, Doreen. For real."

"For real you better be sorry. Better than sorry, you'd better be gone. Get your ass off that sofa and go report yourself to your parole officer. Or better yet, don't report. Stay right where you are. Hang out. Enjoy. Don't you move a muscle. I'll just bring you breakfast, lunch and dinner from off my kids' plates while you have yourself a spa day. A week off. And then when you right in the middle of enjoying your goddamn "Price Is Right," I calling the cops and violating your ex-con ass and you can go right back inside for all I care. You think I care? Do you? I don't care nothing. I don't give a shet about you, Bobby, so you just stay right where you are and enjoy your little siesta."

Doreen freaks me out with the reverse psychology thing. Sometimes she reverse the reverse couple times and I cannot tell which is the fake one I gotta watch out for or the real one that is even worse.

I ran out the door with my ear blood crusting on my Fujinaka.

But Doreen does care. That's why she made my ear bleed with the towel. She care about Kennison and that's why she yell at him. She care about Jorene and that's why she tell her, "Goddamn it, Jorene, how much times I tell you no wear bra with one tank top because a lady don't let her bra straps show and I no care if they the see-through plastic kind like Victoria's Secret because that's slutty." She care about Liko, that's why she don't let him meet his father.

I know Doreen care about me and she pulling for me to get my act together.

That's why I ran all the way up Wailuku town from the Puuone part of Lower Main in my buss-up jailhouse rubber slippers. Made my feet bleed but cleared up my head. When I got to the parole office, my Warren was walking out the door.

"I'm here!" I was all proud.

"And you are?" Warren didn't look nothing like I pictured him. He was big, old, definitely not mahu. He had that sad dead look in his eyes, the kind that only one wahine can do to a man. Look like he been married to a chick for a long time.

"I'm Bobby! I was supposed to be your one o'clock appointment but I was crashed and I sorry but I no can tell you how good one real sofa feel after sleeping on one jail cot for three years one month. I was zoning. I super sorry I late."

Warren don't look like he was too offended. He don't look like too much can offend him anymore. He is out of offendedness.

"Let's reschedule to next week." He was jingling his keys in his pocket, the male international signal for "I had a big lunch and now I gotta take a shet so I going home."

"Shoots! Shoots! Anytime, Warren. You not going violate me, right? I mean, I came, even though was late, I came and I saw you. This count as I reported, right?"

Jingle, jingle.

"We'll work it out."

Government workers always say "we'll work it out" when they don't have the energy to actually work it out. It's state worker talk for "fuck, whatevers."

"I'll come back. You name the time. I'll be right here, front and center, Warren! You just name the time!"

"Next week, same time."

"You got it. I am here. Right here, front and center. Mahalo, Warren. I really mean it. Mahalo. Mahalo nui. Mahalo nui loa loa loa."

Warren was in his car popping the parking brake during my long list of loas.

No matter. I not the kind of guy who needs everybody's attention all the time. I know Warren care about me. If he didn't, he would've violated me. But no, he gave me a chance. That goddamn Warren gave my sorry ass a chance. Thinking about it, my eyes got all teary. Fucking Warren. I love him.

"I love you, Warren!"

I don't think he heard. He was almost out of the parking lot already, air conditioner blowing, radio blasting.

"Eh, Warren! Warren! Next week when? You mean same time same day or just same time? The same time I was supposed to come or the time I actually showed up? Warren? Warren!"

Gone.

Never mind. I going come every day the same time until I get 'em right. That's how committed I am. That's how thankful I am that this man, this fat, sweaty, teddy bear of a man gave a guy like me a chance.

CHAPTER 3

I WAS ALL READY TO GO TO THE JOB CENTER OFFICE but then I started thinking about how I supposed to get there.

Not like Maui get bus. I mean, Maui get bus, but if you not one small kid, old lady, Japanese tourist, or mental patient, no more bus for you.

Not like I get money to catch taxi, and not like Maui get taxi anyway. I mean, get taxi, but only for tourists who staying in Kaanapali, like eat dinner down the road at Lahaina, and too cheap to rent a car or too scared to drive on Maui roads.

Not like Doreen going let me borrow her truck. Ever. For any reason. No matter what.

So I started thinking OK, I gotta walk down Kahului. Das what, three miles? Five? Thirty? Should I go around Beach Road side or climb up the bridge and head down Kaahumanu Avenue? Which way get the most chances of somebody seeing me hauling my fat sweaty ass down the road and stopping to offer me a ride?

So then I thought about how I going be passing by the high school on the way down to Kahului and maybe I should stop by and say howzit to Doreen's kids. Be supportive and uncle-ly. Those kids don't have no daddy so they depend on me to be the manly role model in their lives. At least I could show up at their school and surprise them once in a while. Kids love that shet, right? I should try to bond. Or something. Maybe they get snacks and they would share. Worth a try. Kids get the best snacks.

Up the bridge, down Kaahumanu, on to snacks.

By the time I got to the high school, was after school already. All the hot rods peeled out of the parking lot and only get the teachers' junkalunka cars parked in the dirt. Eh, try wash your Datsun, Mr. Kinoshita. Me, I was so hot and tired and my feet was all sweaty blisters in rubber slippers, I just wanted to lie down underneath a tree and go sleep in the shade. But all the good trees was gone, cut down to make room for portable classroom buildings that look like the low security dorms at the correctional center.

Kennison get football practice on the down field after school and Jorene get cheerleader practice on the up quadrangle. I figured that's a good time to do the supportive uncle thing, right? I not interrupting them in class or nothing. I remembered from school time that interrupting in class is bad.

Jorene was standing at the top of a pyramid with her feet on two cute girls' shoulders. No mercy, that Jorene. She was yelling at the girls to stop looking so tired and she couldn't even see their faces. She could tell by just the way they felt under her feet that they not smiling. She was yelling at them to smile but she smiling all nice and big even though she yelling. That girl going be mayor of Maui someday. Can just tell already.

She spotted me coming down the sidewalk onto the grass part and gave me the meanest Jorene stink eye she got, which is pretty damn mean and very damn stink. In just that one look she told me, "Fucking Uncle Bobby, don't you come over here try talk to me and check out my cheerleader friends, you fat old loser creepy weirdo uncle! I going call the cops on your ass and you going face all kind freaky freak charges and you know what they do to guys like that in jail, Uncle Bobby!"

All that she said with her mean eyes and the whole time she was smiling.

She going be governor of Hawaii someday.

So I kept trucking on down the campus, down the side stairs, past the cheerleaders, and down to the athletic complex.

Ho, I had some good memories at this school. Freshman year hanging out in the freshman boys' bathroom. Sophomore year hanging out in the sophomore boys' bathroom. Junior year, hanging out in the parking lot in the back by the metal shop. Senior year sneaking back on campus to party with my friends after I got kicked out. Sleeping under the trees. That's about all I remember. OK, not too much good memories, but whatever memories I get left is good. Mostly.

I spotted the football players running drills on the far field.

I could pick out Kennison already, the tall, long-muscle kid who does everything wrong but look real graceful doing it.

He the guy would run the opposite direction of everybody else, but ho, he run nice. Like one long-leg horse. Kennison get the stride. He don't know where he going, but he fucking lope like one loper. Damn that boy can lope.

He cannot catch the ball for nothing but he still get his own wahine cheering section. Every time he fumble, the girls scream and clap and call his name. Sophomore in high school and he already the big man on campus. Local guys with green eyes can do no wrong. Kennison is a chick magnet. Doreen going have to pry the girls off her son like scraping opihi off a rock.

Kennison didn't see me when I walked onto the field. He was too busy trying to figure out what his coach was yelling to him. Somehow "Run left! Run left!" was very complicated to him, and he was stopped down, trying to draw mental pictures in his head. He didn't see the group of girls cheering his number and calling his name. For all he cared, they could be mynah birds eating the seeds from the nutgrass on the side of the field. He was totally focused on football and what he was supposed to do. Just those words "run" and "left" was echoing through his brains.

I looked at Kennison and was like I could hear him thinking. I guess that's how I was when I was that young, too. Not like I played football or anything. I probably could have played football because I have the size, but I was always too involved with my extra-curricular activities to do any extra-curricular activities.

Kennison was just standing there like he was waiting to get tackled. I seen this big-ass kid, same like Kennison's height but maybe three or four times his weight, coming in for a hit like a sledge hammer coming in for a sledge.

I don't know what had come over me but it was like all my parental instincts just kicked in real hard for my nephew. It was like I got the big ESP message from my sister/cousin Dori to "Save my boy! No let my boy get hurt!" I wasn't going to stand there and watch him get runned over by a junior varsity player the size of two NFL linemans. My only thought in my head was "Save Dori's boy! Save Dori's boy!"

So I went in full steam to save Dori's boy.

The monster was two inches away from Kennison when I plowed in from the other direction.

OK, so maybe I just a little bit rusty for sports after spending all that time in prison, but I did lift some weights in the rec yard sometimes when the body builder bulls would let me take a turn for five minutes. I mean, I didn't think I was that much out of shape.

Kennison ended up like the tuna in a tuna sandwich between two slices of bread getting pressed together really hard. Me hitting him on one side, the big kid on the other. Kennison was squeezing out from all over.

When I opened my eyes, I was looking at the clouds.

I turned my head to the side.

Kennison was flat on the ground with his eyes spinning around his head. His cheering section was around him screaming his name to get up, get up, oh God he dead! Please get up! They were so thick and crazy the coaches couldn't hardly get in to check on Kennison's condition. They looked him over and said he was going be sore like a bastard, but he was OK. Tough kid. No broken bones. No need go hospital. Just take it easy for a few days. The girls was all crying and grateful. They wanted to hug him but was afraid to hurt his bruised body.

Kennison made out like a hero.

The big guy made out like a hero. He won a place on the starting defense.

The coaches made a complaint to the school and now I cannot go to my nephew's football practice anymore. Ever. And I not supposed to go to the games but I think they going have hard time keeping me from sneaking into the stadium if still get the hole in the fence on the up part by the bushes like there was when I was in high school. They never fix stuff like that. They never check IDs at the gate. So I think I'm in the clear.

Until Jorene told Dori that I showed up at school today, checked out the underage cheerleaders and almost got her brother Kennison killed during football practice.

So now I banned from showing up at the kids' school. Not like the way the school banned me from going to the football games, which is only a threat because they wouldn't know me if I showed up anyways. Doreen's ban is a for real ban, because if she catch me anywhere near her kids when she not around, she going kill me first and hurt me later. She going kick me off her sofa and bury me in the sand behind the building. She going broke my ass, make me pick 'em up and put 'em back together piece by piece so she can broke 'em again.

"You get the picture, Bobby?"

Yes. Oh yes I do.

Nighttime when Doreen was giving Liko his bath and Jorene was talking on the phone, Kennison was sitting at the kitchen table staring at his homework.

"Eh, boy," I told Kennison.

He looked up real slow and gave me the "Who, me?" look.

"Yeah, you. What other boy get sitting at the kitchen table I talking to?"

Kennison looked around to see if get anybody else but him. He don't see nobody, but he not sure. He gave me the I-don't-know shrug with his shoulders but they don't go up too far because of the extensive bruisings.

"You was tough in football practice today, man. I was so proud that you was my nephew."

He stared at me like I not talking English.

"Why, Uncle Bobby, you was there?"

"Of course I was there! You no remember when the big kid was going tackle you and I rushed in from the side and saved your skinny ass?"

Blink, blink. Trying to remember.

"No."

"For real, Kennison. You took a big hit in practice today but I was there and I jumped in and absorbed the impact of the hit from you."

"Not."

"Ay, Kennison, you get concussion or what?"

Green eyes rolling up to look at the ceiling. He thinking, he thinking . . . what was the question again?

"Kennison, you remember getting hit in practice today?"

"Yup."

"And you remember the guy that hit you?"

"Kind of."

"And you remember the guy who hit him from the other side and pushed him away from you?"

"Oh, yeah." Could tell he bullshitting me. He don't remember nothing. But I let him go on account of the story I telling.

"That was me!"

"Oh yeah."

"You remember now?"

"What was your number again?"

"Kennison, I don't play for your team."

"Oh. OK. Maui High? What position?"

"Kennison, I your Uncle Bobby."

He looked at me like I nuts.

"So why you playing for Maui High then?"

"Kennison, you stoned or you stupid?"

Kennison actually reacted to this question. He looked at me with little bit hurt, little bit anger in his eyes. He told me, "Fuck you. I just deep."

Ho! Good line! I gotta save that one in reserve.

Doreen walked in the room, Liko wrapped in a towel balanced on her one hip, mad hand sitting on her other.

"Why you bothering Kennison when he doing his homework? And why you get the TV on distracting Kennison when he get his homework? You know the rules, Bobby."

"Yup." I turned off the TV.

"What is the rules, Bobby?"

I hate it when she make pop quiz on the rules.

"The kids' homework comes first."

"And?"

"And I come second."

Doreen took the towel off Liko's back to zing my head with it. In one fast move, she zinged and had 'em wrapped around Liko again. He didn't even know it was missing. Didn't even feel a draft.

"You don't come second. You don't even come last. You not on the list at all. You just here sleeping on my sofa for a little, small, short little while until you get your ass in gear and your life on track and then you are out the door never to return to my house again, you got it? Hurry up and get your shet together and get out of my house!"

Liko gave me the big eyes like "Dude, you hanging on by a thread."

Kennison went back to staring at his homework.

Jorene came in after her phone call was pau and switched on the TV. She could see me opening my mouth to tell her she not supposed to but before any sound could come out, she shot me the finger plus the stink eye. That's a double shut-up-Uncle-Bobby right there.

I took my smokes and went out on the balcony. I was out there for the whole rest of the pack. I counted 57 black trucks with monster tires and custom paint jobs go by. Some people in Wailuku are living large, I tell you that.

After everybody went to sleep, I went back in and lay down on the sofa. I was lying there couple minutes in the dark before I realized Kennison was still sitting at the kitchen table staring at his book. Same page and everything. In the dark. I think he was sleeping with his eyes open. I could hear him breathing and it was the sleep breathing, deep and slow.

I was worried Kennison got one concussion. I started getting nervous. I thought maybe he got hurt bad and something was wrong with his brain. But with Kennison, hard to tell.

"Boy," I yell-whispered to him.

Nothing.

"Boy! Kennison!"

He open his eyes and look around.

"You OK or what, Kennison?"

He rubbed his face with his hand. The bruises were getting dark purple already.

"Yup."

"You was sleeping at the table."

Kennison looked around him.

"Yeah, and?"

"Not kind of weird you was sleeping at the table?"

He looked at me like I nuts. "No, I do that all the time."

He stood up and I watched him walk to make sure he not stumbling or weaving. He was actually walking pretty good.

"Go sleep now, Kennison. You had a tough day."

"No shet. I feel like shet."

"Yeah, you got hit pretty hard in practice today."

Kennison turned and I swear to God he tried for hook his hand on his hip like the mother and the sister but his arm was sore and his hip was sore and the thing just slid off his body.

"'Cause of you that's why. Who told you show up at my football practice and tackle me when I busy getting tackled? That is no class, Uncle Bobby. You made me shame in front all my friends and all my chicks. Fucking loser."

He turned and shuffled off to bed.

Wow, he is Dori's boy. Deep down inside him, when he tired and buss up and half asleep, he get that little bit of Doreen that come out.

That boy going be all right in this world. He handsome, he tall, and in his heart of hearts, he get his mother's pissed off style even if most of the time he's too beaten down to fight back. If he use that on the football field he going be a star. Deep, my ass. He is stupid. But he get Dori's mad streak. That's pretty much all he needs.

CHAPTER 4

DOREEN WAS ON MY ASS TO GO SEE MY MOTHER.

Was different, but. She didn't yell at me. She made all sneaky-nice. Not super-nice, because I would have noticed and got wise. Doreen had warm me up slow, like frozen stew meat in a pot. I didn't see it coming.

We was sitting on her balcony eating dried squid and drinking soda, talking story like when we was kids. Like when we was kids and she wasn't beating the shet out of me. Then all of a sudden she busted out the "Bobby, you know, you should go see your madda" action.

Ho, that made me choke on one big squid piece.

Back when we was kids, I used to rip off bags and bags of dried squid from the store near Iao School. The label said was "hot ika" and yeah that ika was fucking hot. I stashed the hot ika underneath the Iao School windbreaker jacket that I got from somebody's open locker. After a while that jacket came all stink with sweat from running around Wells Park playing chase master and all the hot ika I stashed in the polyester lining. Hot ika gets super stink when get hot. I was going throw the jacket away but then I thought nah, put 'em back where I found 'em. I broke into that kid's locker—I think it was the same locker, close to, at least—and shoved that stinking shredded jacket in there. Mahalo for letting me use your stuff, Kevin S, whoever you is. He got his jacket back before the end of the year so that should have made him happy even though the inside smelled like dead squid.

I used to bring home the squid and catch hell from my grandma for stealing stuff from the store and then catch more hell from her for not stealing something useful like cigarettes or beer since I was going steal something anyway. Then me and Doreen used to sit down with my grandma out on the porch and eat squid, peel paint and talk about stuff other people said they seen on TV. Back then, that was good times. And then we got a new used TV from the second hand store and we didn't have to make conversations while we was eating. We could just watch "Bonanza" and peel the paint in the living room.

Now Dori was digging in the bag for the big piece of squid all tangled together. I had my eye on that one for me, but I made like I was cleaning under my fingernail and let her take the best one. Ladies first, especially when it comes to squid. That's the kind of brother/cousin I am.

I watched her sucking on her big squid and her face almost look happy. Then shet, she caught me looking, me smiling at her smiling, and she showed me the finger, told me to fuck off, and moved her ass so her back was facing me, like I was invading her squid sucking privacy.

"Ono, yeah?" I tell her.

"Fuck you, squid-stealing bastard," she said.

That kind of hurt because I actually bought this package. First time in my life. But I didn't say nothing in my own defense because she was having a good time and I didn't want to ruin the moment.

I think Doreen likes having me around to fight with. Me, I know not to push too far. She like this kind of stuff, the back-and-forth, I say something, she come back at me—like how Sonny and Cher back in the day. Love/hate. But I always gotta let her win. Which is not too hard because she fast with the mouth and fast with the brain to cut me down. It did cross my mind that she's as much of a bastard as me, but I didn't want to point that out because these days, only guys are called bastards, not chicks, and it doesn't really mean the same thing as it used to. It just means the same thing as fucking jerk. She says it with her mean voice but when I hear it, it's like she's saying, "My beloved sweet brother cousin."

"Fuck you, Bobby, you sack of shet," and I hear, "You my closest relative and that's why I can talk to you like this."

"Get your fat sweaty ass off Kenji's pillows! Poor dog, now he gotta sleep where all stink!" and I know she's saying "I am so glad you are a part of my family and a member of this household."

I love my sister Doreen. She treats me worse than any woman ever did. That's satisfying. A man don't feel like a man unless a strong-willed woman is pissed off at him. That's when you feel your manness all proud and glowing. If you just one loser, a woman like that don't pay you no attention. But if you pissing off one wahine like Dori, that means she sees enough promise in you to want to whoop your ass and make you better.

My mother knew how to treat a man bad, but not like Doreen. My mother treated you bad in a way like she didn't love you. She wasn't watching out for you. She was trying to get in your way. That's the thing about Doreen, she don't get in your way unless you getting in her way. Nah, but my mother, if she wasn't getting in your way she would die of boredom from nothing better to do. I wonder who she hassling these days.

I made the mistake of wondering that out loud.

"So go see her. Grandma said," Doreen grabbed the plastic bag and was licking the small squid crumbs out of the corners.

"Gramma said? Gramma's dead."

I didn't duck my head fast enough. She hit my skull so hard I thought my whole hair was gonna slide off my head.

"No say that. Don't you ever say that."

Doreen's eyes were getting teary and I knew I had about 15 seconds before she was psycho at me for making her sad.

"I sorry, Doreen. I promise. I promise promise. I love Gramma too, you know."

Big sigh. She patted my arm with her squid-and-spit hand.

"I know. And Grandma love you. But she love me more. That's why she talk to me."

I was able to keep my mouth shut this time, but I tried to make my eyes big like, "Really? Wow! Tell me more!"

"She come to me in my dreams. Or when I driving by Kahului Harbor, that smell always reminds me of her. Or when I taking a shower, if I stick my head underneath the water too long I hear her tell me, 'Doreen! Pau da water already before da water man come turn 'em off!' She guides me and stuff."

Sometimes I hear our grandmother yell at me too, but that's only the echoes of all the yelling she did when we was small. That stuff lasted in my head till now.

"I had this dream last night. She was wearing that orange flower shorty-muu she used to wear to do yard work and she was calling and calling out to your mother and when your mother didn't answer, she told me to tell you you gotta go find her."

Doreen had a look on her face like I was supposed to say something big, like "mahalo" or "oh wow" or something. Me, I was scrambling for words and the right ones were slipping away like . . . like squids.

"I don't remember one orange flower shorty-muu."

"Bobby—"

"Don't slap my head! I remember! I remember!"

Wa-pack!

"Owwee!"

"Never mind the muu, stupid, I telling you Grandma said you gotta go find your mother. You know what you supposed to say now?"

"Thank you?"

"No, stupid, you supposed to say, 'But where could my mother be?' and when I tell you, then you can thank me. You get plenty to thank me for."

"I bought you squid."

Wa-pack.

"Dori, you got older but you got stronger."

Wa-pack, wa-pack.

"I thought you like dried squid."

Pack-a-pack-a-doosh!

"Eh, I like that right hand double slap, left hook combination, Dori. That's mean!"

Doreen was proud. "Mahalo. I learned 'em from my second to last ex."

Which one was that, I was thinking? Wally the car thief or Dennis the coke head with the lisp? Don't ask about the guy, I told myself. You no like know.

"So you like know where your mother stay?"

I no like know about that, either, but Doreen was on this like a dog smelling cat. Like cat smelling squid. Like squid smelling whatevers. Maybe squids no can smell.

"Women's prison, drug treatment or crazy house?"

Wa-wa-wa-pack!

She had to swing three times before she caught a part of my body, and even then she only caught part of my leg.

"She live in one HOUSE."

"What?"

"In Wailea."

"WHAT?!"

"And when she not getting her nails done, she learning golf."

My jaw dropped so far the thing scraped the sand and kiawe beans two floors down. My mother learning golf is about as believable as a monkey learning how for cook. Sure, the monkey can throw around some bananas and shet, but in the end nobody wants to eat it and it's not even all that funny to watch.

Doreen dug her cell phone out of her shorts pocket. And I mean dug because the shorts was so tight the pocket didn't even have chance to be a pocket. It was more like a slot. More like a slit.

"I get her phone number right here. My mother said this one is current. Here, go call her."

Doreen held the cell phone out to me. She saw the look of shock on my face. She rattled the cell phone with all the sparklies and danglies and pictures of her kids hanging off.

"You can use my phone."

A cold chill went up my nuts. I knew right there Doreen was setting me up. Was one thing for her to sit on the lanai, eat hot ika and shoot the shet with me. Was another thing to offer to let me use her cell phone. That would be like saying I could drink milk at breakfast. That would be like saying I could sleep on Kennison's bed and he can take the couch with the dog. That would be like saying I could use her truck to drive out to Wailea to see my good-for-nothing mother. Fuckin' spooky.

"And when you like go visit her, you can use my truck."

I just about pissed my pants with the fear and the horror. Her finger with the homemade fake plastic nail tip super-glued on the end like a big Chiclet was beep-boop-beep pressing all kind of buttons. She shoved the sparkly, shiny phone at me and I heard ringing. I dropped my cigarette in my soda can and put the phone up to my ear.

"Hello, Mommy? Dis Bobby. Your son. Your child. The oldest. No, I not the manslaughter one, I the possession with intent to distribute one. Yeah, long time no see. Like since I was elementary school. So how you doing?"

Sheesh, life must be good because Mommy sound like she splashing in the Jacuzzi with a mango colada in one hand and a guava martini in the other. Happy happy Mommy. Laughing, saying nice stuff, telling me she'd love to see me. Life is great. Bubble, splash, bubble.

This I gotta see.

I let Doreen drop me off in Wailea. I was too scared to borrow her truck. I didn't drive nothing in over three years and I never did have a legal license anyway. Too many ways I could screw it up. Plus, I was nervous going to see my very own sweet mama in her new rich hood. According to Doreen's mother, my mother had hooked up with one guy from the Mainland who was loaded, clueless, and had a thing for "island ladies" with faded tattoos and missing teeth. I had the directions written on a piece of paper and a bunch of spray painted carnations I ripped off from the Saint Anthony graveyard. Doreen dropped me off by the big subdivision sign and took the kids swimming down Kamaole beach. I figure Mama can get her butler to drive me back to Doreen's. If I go back to Doreen's. Mama's sofa might be better.

I get to the address and there's no house there. There's part of a house, like the foundation and some beams, but no house. There's some construction stuff and a stack of lumber. Must be the wrong house.

Then I see a portable trailer off to the side in the dry bushes and all of a sudden the door opens and who do you think is standing there looking like one of the prison mahus who don't have mirror or razor?

"Eh, Bobby! You get smokes?"

Turns out Doreen's mother got a few details wrong. Turns out my mother got a druggie friend on the construction crew let her squat in the trailer for a few weeks while the builder was waiting on a late permit from the county. Turns out the trailer doesn't even have a bathroom but my mother didn't let that stop her from making her own lua in the corner. She squatting in the squat house. She flopping in the flop house.

Turns out the number Doreen had is from a cell phone Mama ripped off from someone's car at the beach. Turns out my mother is worse than a crack whore. She's a crystal meth whore. Turns out the only reason Doreen's mother knew how to find my mother is because my mother been calling her every day hitting her up for cash. Turns out my mother is more fucked up than I could have ever dreamed in my worst nightmare. Turns out that motherfucking Doreen was trying to fuck with my head by dumping me on my fucking mother. Couldn't be, right? Doreen didn't know. She wouldn't set me up like that, right?

Fuck!

So now my mother is asking me for smokes, asking me to buy her beer, asking me if I know how to cook up nail polish remover into her favorite hit. I gave her the spray painted carnations. She tried to eat the stems. I said I gotta go.

I hitched a ride back to Kahului and walked all the way up to Lower Main.

Doreen was sitting on the sofa with Kenji watching the news.

"So?"

"You no like know," I told her.

"I LIKE know!"

"My mother is homeless, hopeless, toothless, shoeless, shet-faced, and totally fucked up."

"But she was happy to see you, right?"

If I had the guts I would have smacked her. Lucky thing for me I don't have the guts.

"I had to tell her who I was, like, five times."

"She's getting older."

"Doreen, my mother is like 45."

Dori's face was like Iao Valley when the clouds roll in. I could see her eyes get dark and cold.

"So what?"

"So what what?"

"You not moving in with her?"

"She don't live in one nice Wailea house, she homeless in one stink Wailea construction trailer!"

"So? She's your mama!"

"She get rats and ukus!"

"So maybe it's your turn to take care of her, you ever thought about that? You so selfish, Bobby."

"She like me cook her drugs. I no like enable. I learned that in my Al-Anon group."

Wa-PACK!

That one was off the charts hard and caught me totally unaware.

"OW! FUCK! WHAT?!!"

"Goddamn it, that's all."

"You thought she lived in one nice place so that I could go live with her and get off your couch, right?"

Doreen shook her head. Her at-home highlights glowed orange in the television light.

"No, I figured she was fucked up."

"So you thought I would feel sorry and go help her and get off your couch?"

She sadly peeled at her fake nail tip.

"No, I knew you would bust out that lazy ass Twelve Step detachment shet."

Eh, no talk about my Twelve Step detachment shet. That shet gets me through the day. I was thinking that but I didn't say it. Detach from my detachment. Serenity now.

"So you really had the gramma dream or what?"

Doreen got up from the couch and pulled her jeans shorts out of her ass crack. I took the opportunity and lay down on the couch. The part where she had been sitting was warm and toasty. Mmmmm, ass cozy is the coziest cozy.

"No be stupid. Grandma is dead."

"So what, Doreen? You was hoping my mother was crazy high and would shoot me dead on the spot?"

She stretched and yawned. So tired from work. So tired from the kids. So tired from life. Poor sister/cousin Dori.

"Shoot you, stab you, chop you with one fish knife."

I laughed. Doreen didn't laugh back. Fuck, she wasn't joking.

Big sigh.

"Whatevers. So long it gets you off my damn sofa."

She yawned again and turned off the TV and went down the hall to bed. I lay down in the ass warmth and closed my eyes. All of a sudden—

Wa-PACK! In the dark. Doreen had one left that she couldn't save for the morning.

"You so piss me off, Bobby."

I fell asleep with my head bleeding on the dog's pillows and I dreamed of my gramma and that ugly orange flower shorty-muu.

CHAPTER 5

DOREEN'S KIDS DON'T KNOW HOW LUCKY THEY ARE. They growing up with a mother that love them so much she kicked out their daddies so they wouldn't be no negative influences on their lives. If was just her, she would put up with a man's bad action until he drive her into the ground, but for her kids, she wanted better. She wanted best. Doreen love them so much she kick their ass if they screw up so they learn not to make mistake next time. She love them so much she make herself the good example and she do the right thing, no matter what, no matter if hard.

Doreen turned out pretty good considering how her mother was. Doreen's mother went prison three times for trying to kill my mother. The two sisters always went for the same guy. They had three kids from the same three guys. Same three guys, each of them had one kid. Total of six kids, two moms, three daddies. Hard to explain, but me and Dori get half-brothers and sisters that is cousins to each other but not to us. Our family trees is all tangled with vines.

My earliest memory isn't very early because I think I screamed through my first year and slept through the next two. At least that's what my gramma used to tell me. When you're screaming and sleeping, you don't have much time to take notice of stuff around you and make a mental note for bringing up later in prison creative writing class or when you lying around on a sofa trying to figure out your life.

But my earliest memory is when my mom and Dori's mom were best friends for a day. I remember going to visit my mother and her sister at the Hui Opio Ikaika job training and life readiness program. The Opios was finished their first six weeks of court-ordered life skills classes and were having a picnic party to celebrate up at Kepaniwai. All the girls in the class brought their babies to show off to the other girls. My mother was kind of out in the cold because I was getting old already, almost four, I guess, and I wasn't as cute as the ones that had just popped out. Everything changes when kids get teeth. That's when they stop looking innocent and start looking dangerous. My mother already had two other kids but they was in foster care Lahaina side and their foster mother didn't have no car to bring them around the pali for no picnic party.

Doreen was same age as me but she was still cute. Girl that's why. You can put ribbons on the fountain-style hair-do, ruffle panties, and shoes that squeak and they look baby-cute until they ready to drive.

So was just me, my mother Trinette, my sister/cousin Doreen, and her mother, my Aunty Lizette, and all the other high school dropout young mothers and their cute babies with the pierced ears, both girls and boys.

What I remember was all the babies getting passed around from Opio to Opio and everybody saying "Ooh da cute!" "Ooh da precious!" "Ay, so cuuuuuute da baby!" and me, standing by the barbeque grill holding on to one red Miko Meat hot dog that fell in the dirt and watching everybody telling everybody how cute everybody's kid was except for me. And some of those babies were dog-ass ugly. Even Doreen was getting her share of "Ay, da cuuuuuuute" action.

And then this one fat chick, either she was pregnant with twins or she was humongous for a 16 year old, she told my mother, "Eh, Trinette, you kid's upepe nose went stretch out your chocho when was coming out or what? Sheeet! Dat bugga must a hurt!"

Say what you like about my mother, call her every name in the book, but no say nothing bad about her chocho. That is crossing the line, her one line that she get.

All of a sudden, my mother and the big tita was throwing blows and throwing cake and somebody had some nunchakus and pretty soon it was a full-on bloodfest and nobody got to graduate to the "second step preparedness" that day. My mother was so mad that the tita called her chocho stretched-out. She said it was as tight as her ass, which if you saw my mother at the time, wasn't all that tight. And then she said that Doreen get the same nose and Lizette's chocho was fine. Just ask Tino Camaro, who was one of the other girl's boyfriend at the time. Aunty Lizette jumped in, "Yeah, ask Tino about Trinette's chocho, too."

Tino's chick and all her backers jumped in and was the two sisters against all the rest of the girls and Trinette and Lizette was unbeatable. They both lost couple teeth, but the other girls was no match. Everybody knew don't fuck around with the sisters. They would try kill each other later over Tino, but in that moment, they were united as one. I remember watching the two sisters grabbing chicks by the hair and flying them left and right in the small pavilion, the social workers screaming, the babies crying, the teriyaki beef falling onto the cement floor.

Then somebody called the police from the hanging-from-wires pay phone and all the Opio girls got arrested.

And then I was crying by the stink koi water lily pond, watching my mother go inside the police car in handcuffs screaming about her small snatch. When she went to sit inside the police car, her pareau came up and her Dove shorts went to the side and everyone could see she was lying her ass off. She was lying her chocho off. That thing wasn't small at all. There it was, flapping in the breeze like the doorway of a pup tent.

My sister/cousin Doreen came up to me to give me a cone sushi she took from underneath the plastic wrap on the table reserved for the social workers and job trainers. I didn't like the sweet/sour rice taste of cone sushi so I whacked her hand away and the whole chunk of rice went into the water. Doreen got mad and shoved me inside the limu water with the cone sushi. Had plenty toads in that water. I remember the feeling of the toad tadpoles trying to swim inside my nose.

And not like I making one "poor thing" story about my childhood or whatever. That's just what I remember. That is my earliest memory— my mother's friend from juvy job training class asking if I busted up her chocho coming into this world with my big fat nose and me headfirst in the stink water with tadpoles trying to swim inside my head.

The third time Doreen's mother tried to kill my mother, my mother got arrested for "mutual affray" because she was trying to kill Dori's mother at the same time. The two sisters did time together and they ended up bonding in a Women's Christian Ministry class. They were cool after that. Mostly. When they beefed, they wasn't trying to kill each other no more. They was only going for maiming. Was nice.

Me and Doreen kind of get that same love/hate going on like our mothers. I love Doreen, she hate me. Well, she no really hate me. She love me deep down. I am her closest blood relative in the world next to her mom and her kids and our dad. Even closer because she related to all them only one side but with me, we have double blood. She would do anything for family, and me, I'm family. She would do anything for me.

Which is why it's cool that I lift couple bucks from her wallet every so often. And sometimes Kennison's wallet. And Liko's piggy bank, which is really a turtle or some kind dinosaur animal but he still call it a piggy bank. He not so good with his animals yet.

But not Jorene's wallet. Oh no. That girl is smart like the mother but she not tired like the mother. Still young that's why. Get more chance she count her money at the end of the day and going notice when stuff is missing. Plus, Jorene don't have the love for her Uncle Bobby yet. She still see me like one parasite and one loser. I gotta prove to her how I really am inside.

Which is why I gotta take her mother's money. Just for now. Just while I still yet getting on my feet. To help me get on my feet. Takes money to make money, right?

As soon as I'm pulling in a good salary, I going pay Doreen back. And Kennison. And Liko. And maybe buy one nice present that Jorene would like, like one glitter bowling ball so she can go Aloha Lanes. Maybe she can go college on a bowling scholarship. You never know. Worlds can open for you if you take a chance. Me, I am all about taking that chance.

But until my chances open my worlds and bring me some cash, they just helping me out the way family help family out. The way I would help them out if I had the bucks and they was all trying to start their lives over again.

And I'm thinking all these big thoughts of how I going pay for Doreen's kid go college and buy her one nice house and yeah, even one big new sofa and wow, I got myself all tired from all my big plans. Better lie down and rest my head from all that thinking and planning. Better take something to help me sleep. My life is on an upward climb, that's for sure. I better rest while I can.

CHAPTER 6

I LASTED TWO HOURS AT MINIT STOP.

I figured the job would be perfect for me since I had some industrial kitchen experience from school time. The cafeteria manager lady used to tell me I could wash pots and hose down trays better than any other fifth grade boy. At least that's what I think she said. Was hard to hear with all the pots banging and water spraying and kids yelling because they was getting steam burns from the hot water.

Warren my parole officer turned out to be pretty fucking useless in the getting-me-a-job department. His big advice was "Get yourself a job." That's it. Seriously. Not how, not where, not even a little hint like "Hey, I know this guy . . ." No connections, nothing. You're on your own. That's the parole system, I guess. If it is to be, it's up to me. I seen that somewhere in my drug treatment reading materials. Sounds good until you start to think about it realistically and go, yeah right, if I like one job, somebody ELSE gotta hire me! That ain't up to me! That's up to Da Man.

Da Man at Minit Stop was one lady named Velma. Velma didn't want to hear about my job skills and my job readiness. She didn't really care I had a prison record. She didn't want me to get a TB test or piss in a cup. All she wanted to know was if I could lift 60 pounds. Shoot, I tell her. One hand. She tell me no, not supposed to. You gotta lift with your legs.

Lift with your legs? What the hell does that mean? Pretty much lifting involves some arm action, no?

My job was to carry the frozen potato wedges from the freezer in the back into the store and empty the boxes into the fryer. That's my main job. Got other jobs, too, like clean the toilet, empty the fryer oil into the storm drain at the end of the night when nobody looking and make big body when the teenage kids come in drunk looking to hassle the cashier and steal Twinkies.

But most important is supply those wedges. Those things run out, everything comes to a screeching halt. People can get gas plenty other places on this island. Other places sell sushi, manapua, and slush. But only Minit Stop get those monster big-ass 5-pound slabs of potato dipped in batter and then deep fried to a fat, long, dick-looking rod. That's gold, baby. Those wedges are the love drug of the whole town.

I started eating them frozen. I didn't eat before I got to work because I figured I could make do with, what, couple burned ones? The one that fell on the floor? The one left over from last Thursday? I not picky.

But not enough fell on the floor and you gotta leave them in the oil super long, like half an hour, to get them too burned to serve. That batter that they get on top them is like some heavy duty insulation. The thing get brown, more brown, golden brown, but never burns black and the potato part inside always stays all potatoey and fluffy. So fucking ono, that fucking fluffy potato.

I tried to make friends with Theresa, the lady working the cash register during my shift. I told her hey, Teri, I can call you Teri? You get anything broken you need fixed, you let me know, because I get skills. She tell me as a mutter o flack—that's how she talked, mutter o flack instead of matter of fact, because she just had gum surgery and had fifty pieces of cotton gauze in her mouth, poor thing but it sounded so cute coming from her serious face—she tell me yesh, as a mutter o flack, if I ged a chanz fleas can I flix da toasser.

"Toaster? What for you need one toaster? Nobody going come inside one convenience store for make toast!"

Come to find out they sell Pop-Tart single servings and they let customers heat 'em up if they no like eat 'em raw.

I tell you, the world got so fancy while I was locked up.

I thought I could pull the same toaster trick on Theresa that I pulled on Kennison, but Kennison is either stoned or stupid and Theresa is a checker. She checks stuff. I say I cleaned the bathroom, she go check to make sure I cleaned the bathroom. I say I swept up around the filling islands, she go outside go check I actually swept around the filling islands. I go outside on my smoke break, I see the surveillance camera turning to watch me. Theresa checking that I not smoking by the gas tanks. Theresa checking I didn't throw the match. Theresa checking I not eating potato wedges from the warmer. I no watch out, she going call Velma.

Well, since she was always looking, I had to clip some of the frozen ones from the freezer.

I tried to make like I was making experiment. I told her I was trying to fix the toaster and I was testing to see if it worked on the potato wedges and eww, it didn't! Still broken! Still frozen! Yuck! Yuck, yucky, barfy, yuck.

She didn't buy it.

Velma got called.

I guess didn't help that she could see the hot ika packages poking out of my pants pockets. I should have never given that fucking maroon Iao School windbreaker back. That thing was the best. So roomy. So discreet.

There's Theresa, ten yards of cotton gauze stuffed in her mouth, woozy from the nitrous oxide, face swollen like she got whacked with a cricket bat but still busting on my ass. I love you, Theresa, but I already get one sister/cousin. I don't need non-relatives jumping in to bust my balls.

She can barely talk after oral surgery but she managed to get it out loud and clear that I was eating the merchandise. That's some miraculous recovery, Oh Saint Theresa of the Bloody Root Canal.

Theresa called boss Velma while I was still trying to fast talk my way into an explanation she would believe. She's not a believer, this Theresa, even though she wears a gold cross on a gold chain around her neck. She believe in God and goodness of man but she don't believe in Bobby. She don't believe one goddamn word I trying to wave in front of her face. Plus, she tell me she get the surveillance video for proof.

So that was strike one with Warren. I lost count how many strikes I already had with Doreen, but her, she has more like a sliding scale of infractions. She use discretion in her punishment. Maybe I gotta sleep in the hallway and give the dog the sofa this time. Maybe she not going kick me out, just kick my ass.

But Warren was disappointed.

"You may be charged with theft."

"Oh, no, no, no. It was just a misunderstanding. Nobody pressing charges. We all friends."

Yeah, me and Theresa got to be good buddies when I promised her I wouldn't say nothing about the pack Marlboros she sold to an underage kid because he told her was for his poor old Gramps waiting outside the parking lot in the hot rod Acura. She don't fall for nothing from nobody except someone with a poor old Gramps story. That is her blind spot.

Maybe I know about a little bit surveillance video too, Theresa my love. And Gramps in the Acura look like he's about 14 years old.

So me and Theresa parted as friends.

Warren said I need to look for another job. I tell him help a brother out. He tell me the county is looking for guys to weed whack on the side of the road. I tell him thanks, thanks a lot. I allergic to most of the weeds that get whacked. Not like I need to break out in hives any time soon, but thanks for the suggestion. Good one. What else hard manual labor ideas you get for me, Warren my man?

Warren go, "How are things going with your cousin?"

I was going to launch the whole sister/cousin explanation thing but Warren had that "I ate a big lunch" look on his face so I cut him some slack on the complicated family story.

"It's great. Doreen is great. Her kids is great. It's really, really, really, really great."

"I'll need to come by for a home visit."

Ho! Not! I cannot believe I walked into that one! Doreen would shet the shet of ten well-fed people plus two elephants if I told her I was bringing my parole officer home to her place to meet her and her kids.

Better make sure he come by when Dori is busy working and the kids is all in school.

"Let me know when your cousin and her children will all be there. I'll need to speak with everyone in the household."

Shet, even the dog get dirt on me.

I decided to take a couple of days to think about how to make that one happen. Maybe Doreen would meet a guy and move in with him in the next couple of weeks. Maybe I would find a big diamond ring in the sand, go Kamaaina Metals and bring home a fist full of money for my sister/cousin and that would make her all happy and grateful that I was crashing on her sofa. Maybe she would get conked on the head with a big piece of luggage when she was driving the rental car agency's convenient airport shuttle and she would forget how much she hates me and how much of a burden I am to her and her kids and when she finally wake up from the coma, she would love me like only a sister/cousin could love a brother/cousin.

I better get me a job.

I checked out the newspaper. *The Maui News* had not too much of anything going on. Sales job at a whale art gallery in Lahaina. Sales job at a whale art gallery in Wailea. Sales job at a gecko art gallery in Makawao. Fire knife dancer for Kaanapali luau.

Crap, of all the job skills training I had in prison, nobody ever did bother to teach me no fire knife dancing. Not even any non-fire knife dancing. I didn't get no dancing instruction at all. Fucking useless waste of my time, I tell you.

Wait, there's one.

Tour leaders and drivers wanted for Maui downhill bicycle company. Shet, how hard could that be? Ride bike down Haleakala? No need pedal. No need make any turn-offs. Just follow the road and make sure the brakes work and pretty much you just coasting the whole time. Cruise job. That's funny, right? OK, not one of my best but I still have some humor even when I stressing to find employment. That is one of my strengths.

Gotta always remind yourself of my strengths or else you get bummed and pathetic.

Then I was thinking that maybe they have drug testing before they let you ride on the bikes and take tourists down the mountain. Probably. I wouldn't want to pay money to follow down the mountain behind no crack head junkie on a bike. You never know if he's going to lead you into the bushes and jack your fanny pack or whatevers.

Not like I cannot pass a drug test. No money, no party. But I been through all of Doreen's expired cough medicine, her Midol, her liquid smoke (which was not what you would think it is) and her oregano so I'm clean though I can tell I have that monster waiting to jump on my back as soon as I get my money rolling in.

I would say that I'm lucky. My monster isn't a big monster. Just a persistent monster. I tell 'em go away, he go. But he always come back after a while. He tell me, "Hey, Bobby! You know you would sleep so much better if you had a little hit. Hey, Bobby! You know you would think so much faster if you had a little hit. Hey, Bobby! You so fricken hilarious when you have a little hit. Have a hit, Bobby. It'll make you more wonderful."

Ah, that monster of mine. He piss me off but he know me so well.

But other than drinking a bottle of old Nyquil and smoking a jar of moldy oregano, I hadn't gotten into any of my old monsterish habits and I wasn't going to get into trouble until after I got paid. I could worry about that then. Get the job first, get paid, and then worry about the rest of the parole-ordered drug testing later.

They said I look like I have strong legs so I got the job. Mostly they want somebody to reassure the tourists that everything is safe, safe, safe, and carry the bikes out of the trailer at the top and into the trailer at the bottom. I can do that. I can certainly do that.

I just gotta learn how to ride bike first.

I begged Kennison to let me use his old Mongoose bike to practice. He said he don't have a bike.

I go, "What the hell was that I saw you riding between your legs the other day down the road?"

He looked at me totally straight. "Charmaine Rodrigues."

How can a block of government cheese like my nephew Kennison be getting more chicks than me? I gotta borrow his football jersey or something because I know it ain't his brains, his lope-y body, or his personality because he don't have nothing of nothing. Green eyes. Football jersey. That's his magic.

I told Kennison I would give him half my first paycheck plus the first joint from the first bag if he let me use his bike for practice for my new job. He told me his friend borrowing his bike. I said then I like borrow 'em back. He told me he borrowing 'em from this other guy. I said, "Then let me triple borrow and I give 'em right back." He said, "Borrow only go up to two in Wailuku. After that is steal."

I was about to crack his head and tell him no try make up complicated lies because his little brain cannot even keep the small ones straight, but Kennison got this look on his face like he's telling the God's Honest Truth that somebody bullshitted him about long time ago and he believed all this time.

Poor kid. So hard being trusting and stupid. Green eyes and football jersey don't protect you from that.

I told him, "Look, I not stealing. I going pay whoevers. Like rent. Rent-a-bike. Hey, it's like you and your friends starting a business. You rent me the bike and split the money with your friends. Maybe buy something nice for your chick. Maybe buy something nice for your mother. Your mother would like that. That's you being . . ." I was going to say "industrious" but I didn't want to fry his small little brain, ". . . that's you being smart. Rent the bike, Kennison. I pay you back."

"OK, but don't let Mama Dori find out."

"Why?" I tell him, "Renting a bike is you being so smart."

"Me being smart is no tell Mama Dori."

Ho, I love it when the kid's three brain cells connect together for a brief and shiny moment! Hooray for Kennison! He get the trick-the-woman moves in him! He growing up to be a real man someday!

I said no worry, I good at keeping secrets from Mama Dori. He goes, "Yeah, right, but if she catch you riding my bike I gonna say you stole it."

All that bargaining and pleading and dealing for the practice bike and I ended up crashing it into a dumpster the first 15 minutes. More worse, was the dumpster behind Minit Stop, and Theresa seen me on the surveillance cameras. She sent the new potato wedge worker outside to tell me they had it on videotape.

Theresa not my friend no more.

One of these days I gonna send Liko in with cash to buy my smokes and when she sell him the cigs I gonna call the cops and testify and testify and testify until she get her Minit Stop Employee Badge revoked.

The bike was so smashed the front tire didn't even roll anymore. Didn't have a kick stand but the thing could stand up all by itself because was so bent. I practiced pedaling but not going noplace like a fat lady trying to work off a brownie. I got the pedal part down good. Right foot, left foot, right foot, left foot. Kind of like walking except your ass part is sitting down and your feet just going in small circles. What was I worried about? This is easy! Now all I gotta do is figure out the balancing part. Plenty of time riding down the mountain to work on that.

First time I ever went up Haleakala in my whole life. I seen the thing in the distance from the football stadium high school time, but going up there is a different story. Ho, that fucking mountain is big like one fucking mountain! I felt like one guy on the nature shows, like I was going conquer the mountain and come back down one hero. I closed my eyes and imagined myself skinny and stink with a beard and bandana and a funny accent. I can do that.

I never did get to ride the bike down the mountain. I got all carsick riding in the back of the van all the way up to Haleakala with all those coconut oil-smelling tourists yakkety fricken yakking about breakfast buffets and sunset cruises and hula shows. I tried to think about conquering mountains, but cannot be brave when you fighting a battle of wills with a raw Pop-Tart that wants to come back up and say howzit. Marty the group leader told me to sleep it off, clean the barf off the bumper, and drive the van back down to the office in Kahului in an hour or so.

You sleep so good when it's cold. And Haleakala is fricken freezing, but with the engine running and the heater going, it's very cozy. Very cozy.

But it uses up kind of plenty gas when you sleep with the engine running like that for five hours. The bikes didn't get picked up at the bottom of the mountain. The picnic lunches didn't get delivered to the picnic area. The van didn't get back to the office for the second run of the day, and I got carsick on the ride going down with the manager who had to drive up with the gas can.

So I didn't pass my probation with the company. I never even got to piss in the cup. I not sure if the oregano would show up, but that Nyquil can't be legal.

I need me a job.

CHAPTER 7

I JUST FINISHED MY MORNING CRAP and was getting ready for my after-crap nap when I heard Doreen's keys in the door.

Shet. I jumped on the couch and braced for impact. My eyes scanned the room for evidence. Shiny Pop-Tart wrapper left over from what I ate from the kids' stash. Milk carton I not supposed to drink from and not supposed to leave out of the icebox. Television I not supposed to watch all day still on and hot from being on all day. Underwear I not supposed to use like as if was shorts. Cigarettes I not supposed to ever, ever, fucking ever smoke in her house.

I am dead. I am dead. The only way she not going kill me is if she can think of a way to keep me alive and hurt me bad.

I caught a look at her face when the door swing open. Hard to see against the sun glare off the Sand Hills hill of sand behind the apartment building. She just looked like a big black shadow with a chopstick coming out of the top of her head. I don't know why she don't use clip to make her hair stay up. Chopstick don't hold and she always gotta take her hair down, wind 'em up, poke the chopstick in, again and again. Take 'em down, wind 'em back up, poke that chopstick back in. I told her one time, Dor, if you going use one chopstick inside your hair, maybe go ahead and stick the other side in too so in case you buy box lunch and you don't have fork, you at least get the chopsticks from your head to eat your chow fun. Probably should wash first, but. That one look kinda crusty.

Doreen had tell me shut my mouth about beauty tips. She don't buy no box lunch. She take sandwich from home or she go without. That's the kind of mother she is—she go without lunch or she eat Spam sandwich from home to save money so her kids can have the educational advantages she never had. Plus, she hate chow fun.

She closed the door with her ass because she was carrying something kinda big in her arms. I was going help her close the door all the way but she got 'em already before I could even adjust my ass to stand up from the sofa. She didn't even yell at me for being useless and unhelpful.

Ho, shet, something must be really wrong.

She put the package down on the sofa and I looked and wasn't a package, was Liko, but he was wearing paper clothes like the kind the prison doctor wear when he gotta examine a patient that might be spewing something filthy contagious. Liko was sleeping, and Doreen put his head all gentle on the dog pillow. His paper clothes made crinkle noises when he shifted to get comfortable.

I took notice Doreen look like she was crying.

I put my hand on her back to make nice and I was bracing for when she gonna swing with the combination whack-my-hand and slap-my-face for make me stop touching her. But she never do that. Instead, she kind of made this sigh/sob noise thing and she buried her face in my chest and held on.

Holy crap.

"Doreen? Dori? The small boy OK, right?"

Big sigh.

"Yeah. Oh yeah. Liko is fine. I just running out of options is what."

So she told me the whole story.

We sat down at the kitchen table and I poured her a glass of warm milk from the carton I left out and she never even notice. This was Doreen like I never seen her before. This was Mama Dori hurtin' for certain. This was Lady D without a man and without a plan.

So what had happen was the nursery school Liko goes to from 7:30 in the morning until 5:30 at night had an outbreak of mean shets disease. Three of the kids got it plus two of the ladies who watch the kids. Liko probably didn't get it because he don't eat nothing at school except for pencil erasers. He don't like the teri chicken/teri burger/shoyu hot dog menu rotation.

But the ones who got sick got 'em bad. Bloody diarrhea and what-not. I started to make a joke to make Dori laugh but then I thought, wow, what can you say about shetting blood? Where's the humor there? That just is what it fucking is.

The victims of the mean shets disease had to go hospital and get fluids and go through tests. Blood tests, ass tests, head to toe tests. Everybody going be OK, but the school got closed until they figure out what the hell happened. They scrubbing stuff, bleaching stuff, throwing stuff away. Liko couldn't even wear the clothes he was wearing because some of the shet blood and blood shet might have gotten on him.

Daaaaaaaaaamn.

I never did hear of a nursery school on lockdown before. I looked at small Liko snoring on the sofa wrapped in white paper like a steak. Poor kid. He get it rough. At least he has a good mama, though.

But Mama Dori looked like her tank was pretty damn empty.

"So what now?"

Doreen wiped some of the black makeup tear streaks that went from her eyes down to her chin.

"What you mean what now? No more what now. What happens now is I'm fucked. "

More crying. Shoulders shaking. Head on the table. Black tear drops splashing on the tile floor.

If Liko not in school, Dori cannot go work. If Dori cannot go work, she cannot afford this apartment, not with her loser exes all refusing to kick in some child support for how many years already she lost track. "And, no offense," she told me, because in the moment she using me for venting purposes and not venting ABOUT me, so no offense, "but not like you kicking in anything for the rent to help keep the family going, know what I mean? Not like you contribute, you know, anything."

Oh wow. Now I felt really bad. Hurt more when she says no offense and means no offense because then, it's just the straight truth, no angry insult with big exaggeration. This was for reals.

Gee, I guess I could maybe help out a little more.

Doreen blew her nose into the same Kleenex she had gripped in her hand for 20 minutes of crying and venting, crying and venting. The Kleenex was all soaked and shredded but my sister/cousin is thrifty and she won't allow more than one tissue per cry. Her hands was slippery with snotabata and tears and her shirt had stains where she used it to wipe the flood of makeup, but no matter what, she never going allow herself the wasteful luxury of grabbing a second Kleenex out of the box that has to last through all the crying for the rest of the year.

"So how come Liko cannot go one different nursery school?"

Doreen paused from her crying like she cannot believe I don't know that answer, like maybe I splashed down from a planet covered in nursery schools all bright and cheerful where everybody can just come-on-down.

Speaking of, I was missing my "Price Is Right" sitting there playing Mr. Everything Gonna Be All Right to my puffy eyes snot hands sister/cousin. But I told myself maybe right that moment I not going bring that up. I got some survival instinct still intact yet.

"Bobby, nursery school is like life. Get plenty choices for the rich people. They get the half-day school, the full-day school, the school that teaches kids fancy shet like language arts and French and ukulele. People like us, we don't get choice. Liko's school teaches him to sit on a square of carpet that isn't even soft enough for Kenji and watch videos on their buss-up TV because they don't have a DVD player. They don't go on field trips. They cannot afford construction paper. They don't give the kids glue because half of them learned to sniff already from their older brothers and sisters. This is the free nursery school for people like us. You think I can get him into another nursery school? Not in this fucking lifetime."

I was trying to listen to all what she was saying but I was still thinking of "The Price Is Right" showcase showdown. First time I seen a guy bid one dollar. They usually do that in the beginning part, when the item is a washer/dryer or a can of peas. I hate it when a guy make like he is so fucking sure that all the other guys guessed way over the price so he just says all sassy, "One dollar." I know that's part of the gamble, but I love it when somebody go "one dollar" and then there's the ding-ding-ding because somebody else got the price exactly right. The One Dollar Guy gets all shame right there. Good for him, fucking know-it-all. I love it when know-it-alls gotta admit they don't know shet. But today, first time I seen a guy bid a dollar for the showcase showdown at the end, but kind of no make sense because if you guess close, you win both showcases and you not going get anywhere close if you only bid one dollar because those things are in the $15,000 range at least.

But now Doreen was venting and I as her brother/cousin was nodding and nodding and doing my duty so I will never know how it turned out for the One Dollar Guy.

"Ah, you don't know, Bobby. You don't know what it's like to try to do your best and the world just keeps knocking you down no matter what. Better to be like you, yeah? Just don't try, then you never get hurt."

Wait, what? What you just said? Ho, I was picturing myself in that brand new aqua spa in the showcase package. Twenty-four soothing jets to wash away the tensions of the day. That's a lot of fucking jets, I tell you, and though Doreen don't give me no credit, I got my goddamn tensions as much or more than the next guy. As much or more.

Doreen wiped her whole face on her shirt and started to get up from the table. Liko moved in his sleep and his butcher paper suit rustled. The sound made me hungry for a nice T-bone. Hey, maybe I could get a job working Takamiya market. They get nice steak. Nah, the old dude who run the butcher shop pretty strict. I not sure he would dig my action.

And then it came to me. I need a job. Liko need a babysitter. Perfect!

Doreen must have been really, really, totally, very desperate because she didn't tell me to shut the fuck up. In fact, she was asking questions. So how will this work? What activities will you do with him? What learning opportunities will you provide? What will I feed him for snack, lunch, and second snack?

Gee, Doreen, you asked Aunty Shetsquirts Preschool all these questions?

So we worked it out. I going watch Liko while Dori is working and she goin' give me little bit cash—just a little, not too much because she says I would just go out and buy smokes and booze and coke and fuck everything up, which is so unfair and not true because I scored a couple cases of smokes and boxes of Stoli from the stockroom at Minit Stop during the two hours I was working there so my essential needs is already taken care of and hidden underneath the plaid cushions of my sofa friend.

My end of the deal is I gotta do educational stuff with the small boy, not just put him in front the TV all day, which is fine with me because pretty much from 11:30 until 3 p.m., there's nothing to watch except for reruns of "Law & Order," which I don't like because they make prison look totally unrealistic with their fancy talk-story rooms where you can sit down with your lawyer and the cops and drink coffee, smoke cigarettes, rat out your cell mates, and make demands. Yeah, right.

She like me do educational stuff, like take him on field trips and whatnot. I told her yeah, yeah, I love field trips. We can go anywhere he like. I started naming places. Every place is too far, too expensive, or too dangerous.

Wailuku pool!

No.

Ocean Center!

No.

Kepaniwai Park!

Hell no.

Well, what about—

"No, Bobby, you not showing my small son the prison."

Crap, I thought that would be a good one, like the "Don't do what Uncle Bobby did" field trip. I was running out of suggestions.

Library?

Oooh, Dori liked that one. OK then, me and Liko will go on up to the library every single day of the week. We going hang out, look magazines, watch videos, eat lunch from the county building snack bar across the street.

Wait, what??? Doreen was about to scold me, I could tell.

No lunch from the county building? No? Really?

"No videos, Bobby. If you going library, you gotta read books. That is what a goddamn library is for, Bobby."

Oh yeah, yeah, yeah, yeah. Right, right, right, right. Books. Got it.

My first day of being Liko's babysitter got off to a bad start. We went down Minit Stop to buy the small milk for his breakfast. When we came home, he was half into his Oatie-O's when he busted me eating slush float. I carried it all the way back from the store behind my back and he didn't notice, but he busted me slurping in the hallway. Then he wanted slush float for breakfast, too. Kind of hard to tell a three-year-old kid "no" when they get the magic piercing scream to use as a weapon. That thing is deadly, I tell you right now. I thought I could outlast his lungs but 20 seconds after he started screaming, my ears was bleeding and he didn't even take a breath yet.

OK, OK, OK, fine. Uncle Bobby going share with you his slush float.

Piercing scream again. He no like share. He like his own.

OK, OK, OK, fine. We go back to the store and Uncle Bobby get you your own slush float.

Big piercing scream, bigger and worser than all the other piercing screams. He tired walk already. He like me go get 'em for him.

OK, OK, O fucking K already. Uncle Bobby go get you one slush float. Just wait right here in the apartment and I come right back. No touch nothing. No do nothing. No open the door if somebody knock.

Theresa was yelling into the microphone at a guy at Pump #4 who didn't know how to pull the hose out of the little hose cradle. He didn't know she could see him on the video camera and didn't realize "Mitha numma foa" meant him. "Poo da leva! Poo da leva, Mitha numma foa!"

Trying so hard.

I walked right in and made a nice big slush float. In fact, I was thinking, I should make two. I can keep one in the icebox until tomorrow. Save me time making my breakfast.

So I made two slush float. One part vanilla ice cream from the soft serve machine, three parts strawberry slushy from the slushy machine. Dairy Queen used to make 'em better but get something kind of satisfying about making your own.

Come to think of it, they get one six-pack cardboard drink holder, so I figured I might as well take care of my breakfast for the rest of the week. That's thinking ahead, Bobby. That's thinking like a responsible can-do kinda guy. This is me getting my shet together, I told myself as I swirled the soft serve into the cups and filled the rest up with slush. By the fourth cup, the strawberry slush maker was making gassy fut-fut sounds like was running out of juice so I made the rest with the green lemon-lime slushy. Maybe he don't go so well with the vanilla ice cream, but what the hell. I already set up the 6-cup cup holder and sometimes you gotta be adventurous.

This is me being adventurous, I told myself. Theresa was busy yelling at Pump #4 and the line of customers was backing up down the chip aisle already. Poor Theresa. I didn't even get to tell her bye. I walked out of the store balancing my 6-cup cup holder that didn't do such a great job holding 6 cups. This is me improvising, coming up with solutions on the fly, being flexible. No more strawberry slushy? No problem! I can handle the green lemon-lime.

Cup holder don't really have the nuts to hold six cups? No problem! Watch me hold them in two hands, lean 'em against my gut and glide-walk all the way back to Dori's place and not spill one drop. This is me utilizing my skills and talents.

I small kind left a trail of green and red slush float from the scene of my crime all the way back to Doreen's apartment building, but that's OK. I was wearing most of what I spilled and I can just suck my shirt later. This is me not wasting what I've worked for, I told myself. When I got up to Dori's place, still had at least three-quarters full in every cup. I call that a success.

This is me being kind to myself. This is me seeing myself in a positive light and giving myself credit for good effort.

I got up to the door of Dori's apartment all ready to open up and give the kid the best breakfast of his little life and, crap, the thing was dead bolted from the inside.

This is Doreen's damn brat kid screwing with his Uncle Bobby.

I knocked on the door with my head because my hands were full carrying the 10 pounds of leaking slush float.

Nothing.

I leaned my ear on the door and I could hear the television on and little footsteps on the tile floor.

"Liko! Open up! It's Uncle Bobby!"

Nothing. Damn kid.

"LIKO! Open up the door! You gotta slide the bolt from the inside!"

Smart-ass gave the answer I pretty much knew he was going to give: "My Uncle Bobby told me don't open the door for NOBODY."

Jorene must be coaching him on smart-assedness. He sounded like a little boy version of her. He probably had his hand on his hip and everything.

"But I'm your Uncle Bobby. I need you to open the door for me."

"Uncle Bobby said don't open the door for NOBODY. He didn't say don't open the door for NOBODY EXCEPT UNCLE BOBBY."

Him and the sister, the two of them going be lawyers, I tell you. Smart, smart, smart-ass and out to get you. That's them.

I had beg, plead, try my reverse, double reverse, triple reverse psychology on him but nothing. Goddamn and the morning was turning to midday already and the sun was reflecting off the sand on the Sand Hills and my beautiful two-color rainbow of slush floats was melting into sad pools of colored sugar water and the flies was starting to notice.

"Mommy said you have to listen to me, right? So open the door!"

Pause.

"I cannot open the door! I don't know how!"

And then it was big crying. Wailing. Howling. Shet, he scared.

I was thinking damn it, Liko, I don't want to break down your Mama's door. That will pretty much take away all my Hero Babysitter Uncle points. Plus the wood look really thick and I not working out pumping iron, doing lat squats and whatnot like I used to.

So I put down my six-pack of slush floats and went downstairs to assess the climb.

I no like climb. I no like fall. I no like nobody see me half-climbing, half-falling, landing on the kiawe-bean-covered sand underneath the apartment building, ripping my only shorts and conking my only head. That would be so shame.

Fuck it. No choice. I told myself this is me doing what needs to be done.

I hiked up my shorts, took off my buss-up jailhouse slippers and started climbing. Hey, Mr. Building Builder, a fucking fire escape would be nice.

Between the thorns on the kiawe trees, the rusted metal railings, the cracked jalousie windows, the old ladies screaming—OK, only one old lady and she wasn't screaming at me, but she was screaming pretty loud at her cats—and the yellow jackets buzzing around my head, took me about twenty minutes to scale that dangerous vertical distance all the way up from the concrete slab foundation to Doreen's second-floor lanai.

I hooked my foot over the lanai railing and hoisted my fat ass over the side to safety.

Breathe, breathe, puff, puff, cough, choke, spit, breathe.

I looked inside the sliding glass door and I no could believe what my eyes was telling me they see.

Puke and barf everywhere. Green on the floor, red on the sofa, red and green on the walls. Splatter spots everywhere like someone was target shooting the plastic cups. The dog was covered in slush float. Liko was covered in slush float. The two of those little bastards must have opened the door and had at it while I was climbing up the side of the building. Don't know how to open the door, my ass. Damn kid. I wanted for string him up when I got my hands on him. Show him the meaning of respeck.

I went to open the sliding glass door to go inside and—oh—locked. Which is very strange since I just had come outside this morning to have my morning smokes and I know I didn't lock it when I came back in because I never do. I always scared one of the kids gonna slide the door closed when my back is turned dropping a cigarette butt off the lanai and they going sneak out, go school, and leave me stranded out there all day.

Oh that stinking kid, he fucking locked me out twice.

And he was all full up and all barfed out sleeping with a blob of red and green spit hanging off his chin and a big smile on his face, his head resting on the dog's ass, the dog's ass resting on my sofa.

See, the boy is happy and contented. I am a great babysitter! Part of me knew that Doreen wouldn't see it like that, but.

I thought about climbing down, but then what? I probably still locked out of the apartment door and at least up there I could keep an eye on him. If he looked like he was getting in big trouble, I could buss the glass and go in and save him. But if I climbed down, it would be like I left him alone with nobody watching and Doreen would kill me for that.

So I pretty much spent the whole day on the lanai chewing on old cigarette butts and watching the body and fender shop across the street while Liko slept off his sugar rush and barf fest. I tried calling to people walking past to help me out but not like Lower Main get much in the way of pedestrian traffics and the people who do walk around down there are pretty much not the kind of people you want helping you get down from a balcony and breaking into your sister/cousin's apartment.

I fell asleep on the crooked lawn chair until I heard Kennison open the sliding glass door.

"Eh?"

Kennison has a way with ehs. He can make "eh" sound like just about anything he wanted it to. This time, his "eh" was like, "So, Uncle

Bobby, wanna get in the house and clean up all this shet before Mommy come home or what?"

And I was like, "Eh!" which I meant like, "Thanks for waking me up. Now you can do me a real favor and grab some towels because this shet is everywhere."

Kennison gave me a blank look like he didn't understand my "eh" but he did take his small brother into the bedroom to go look at muscle magazines.

I had to hands-and-knees panic clean. Hardest work I ever did my whole life.

When Doreen came home, everything was back just the way she left it in the morning. I even scrubbed most of the red and green stains off Liko and Liko's clothes. I am the domestic god. Amazing what Ajax can take off, even on skin.

Doreen started in with the "So tell me everything you did today" action like the mamas on TV always do to their kids. The only thing my mother ever did ask me was, "Bobby, you get smokes?"

"So how was the library?"

"Fine."

"What did you do at the library?"

"Read."

"What books did you read?"

"Uh, something about a bunny."

Ho, good answer! Good answer! Kids' books always have shet about bunnies and shet! I never did read a kids' book or have a kids' book read to me my whole life and I came up with that one out of thin air. I am so good I should have my own show.

"What did Liko eat today?"

"Uh, he had milk for breakfast and, uh, fruit. Fruit for lunch. And milk and fruit for snack, pretty much."

Liko came into the room with a shet-eating grin on his face. A slush-eating grin. A slush-barfing grin. He looked like his little brain was trying to compute who would get in more trouble if he told, me or him.

Weighing his options. As soon as he consult with sister Jorene, I'm a goner. I know already.

And then, unbelievable. The only stroke of luck I ever had in my whole life. The phone had ring right at that moment and Doreen got distracted from her line of interrogations.

And was the lady from the preschool. And they passed inspection. Somebody who didn't wash hands after changing pull-up pants had serve the lunch, and that filthy dirty preschool aunty was to blame for the mean shets disease and she got herself so fired. Who would have thought would be something small like that to start one fricken epidemic, no? Anyways, nobody gonna be getting the mean shets from them no more. They are clean and clear. Liko can go back to his school.

Doreen's face unwrinkled like somebody blowing up an air mattress and she looked younger and almost happy. A little. She was so relieved that Liko can go back to school because he was doing well in that program even though it's a cut-rate low income school with crappy teachers and terrible classrooms. That's Liko. He know how to work the system and get around his surroundings.

Yes, I said. Yes he do.

I saw a splash of slush barf on the floor by the kitchen counter under the phone. Doreen was going spot that spot any second and the brief evening of family peace will be ruined forever.

I tried make mind-meld with the dog.

Kenji. Kenjiiiiiiiiiiiii! Go lick up the barf! GO-LICK-UP-THE-BARF, Kenji.

His little doggy brain must be tuned to mine from all the nights we spent ass to ass on the sofa. That fucking dog stood up, went to the floor by the counter and scooped up the red barf with one big sweep of his tongue.

"Ew, Kenji, what you eating?" Doreen gave him the one-eyebrow-up.

Kenji made like "What? What? Just licking the floor, why?"

I mind-melded him, "Good dog! Very, very good dog!"

He mind-melded me back, "Yeah, you owe me one, asshole."

CHAPTER 8

SOMETIMES IN THE MIDDLE OF THE NIGHT when I lying on the sofa and cannot sleep because the broken spring is kadoinging in my back, I listen to the toilet singing to me.

Once on a moonlit night when the street lights were gold and the kiawe trees shone silver against the hollow tile building, the toilet sang me lullabies and I cried real tears into my dog-stink pillow.

Last week I woke up from a dream about swimming in strawberry slush float because the toilet was singing show tunes. Something about Annie or Oliver or one of those ragamuffin Haole kids.

Mostly the toilet just hums long, sad notes. I think it has the G7 tuning but I not sure. Maybe. Gotta check my woodshop ukulele.

I know it's probably air in the lines and if Doreen takes notice or one of the kids complain then I gotta make like MacGyver and figure out how to rework the plumbing so it stops with the Best of Broadway Review at 2 in the morning.

But for now, before anybody take notice, before anybody lodge a formal complaint to Mama D, I'm digging on the tunes. It is my own private radio station. KTOI. That song is the shet!

Holy crap but I crack myself up.

Oh shet, I said crap! I am too fucking funny. I no get a grip on this snorty snorty laugh wheeze laugh right now I going wake up the kids and Doreen is going to come out here with a baseball bat and erase my face.

OK, OK, OK, OK, think of something else. Something not funny. Something dreamy and sweet and relaxing.

Like surfing. Yeah, that's it. I can just lie here on the sofa and dream about surfing. Riding the waves. Shooting the tubes. Bobby would go and all that.

Except I no surf. How you gonna learn to surf when you no more car to go beach and the beach is far? How you gonna learn to surf when you don't have a surfboard? How you gonna learn to surf when your family's version of swimming lessons is some uncle getting drunk and throwing you in the fish pond at Kepaniwai?

Thinking of that stink brown water was not relaxing and soothing. Just like I could still feel the cold scrape of those ugly fish against my face. I tried not to scream so that none of the fish parts or limu water would go inside my mouth.

Remembering that time and trying not to think of it but reliving the horror was making me all nuts. I have to lie on this lumpy-ass fucked up sofa all still and quiet when all I really wanted to do was kick off the dog blanket and go out for a couple six drinks. This is worse than prison. This is torture. I gotta get out of Doreen's house before I go crazy. I don't know karate, but I know ca-ray-zay.

"Bobby . . ." the toilet called out to me.

"Yes?"

"Let it go."

Would be a toilet to tell me that, yeah? I started snort-giggling again.

"Bobby!"

This shitter is fucking persistent.

"What you like?"

"Relax!"

The toilet started to hum a sweet little tune and then did something so thoughtful I felt all loved and special: it started to run. Oh! I love the sound of the water filling and filling and filling that tank that would never fill up! Was like falling asleep on the beach. Was like listening to the rain on the roof. Was so peaceful and calming and healing I went to sleep so good on that sofa, one hand hanging off the edge, the other one happily cupping my nuts.

Jorene woke me up with a knee to my head.

"Get up, Uncle Loser. Somebody here to see you."

I rolled off the couch and tried to stand up in one smooth motion but it didn't work because my foot was asleep from hanging off the sofa arm all night and it wouldn't hold up my weight. Ka-doosh on the floor. My ass landed in Kenji's water dish. Good fucking morning.

The only thought in my head was my visitor gotta be Warren my probation officer and fuck me, did I forget sweaty shetty Warren was showing up today? I gotta get me one of them day planners so I can keep up with all of my important appointments.

Or maybe was my crazy mother come here to bum a smoke and see if get anything she can steal and sell.

My mind was going through both possibilities trying to come up with the best "take care of my business" plan depending on how the thing turn out.

But coming through the door just as I lifted my ass out of the dog water dish was not doo doo Warren or meth mouth Mama but the sweetest piece of ass Lower Main street ever seen: Corina Molina, my old girlfriend from eighth grade time. I stood up as fast as I could even though my asleep foot slipped little bit in the dog water that had spilled on the floor. My nuts was sticking out of my shorts little bit on that last move when I tried to stand up from the floor. I think Corina saw. She smiled little bit. I think she liked seeing what she saw.

Yeah, Corina baby. You just look and look and keep on looking because I looking at you and I like what I see and pretty soon you going get more of me to look at, if you catch my drift.

Man she was hot.

Tight, tight jeans, probably the same ones she wore eighth grade time. She must have gained 30 pounds and grew five inches since then and these jeans were begging and pleading to let go already.

Tank top with rhinestone letters across the tits spelling out something so shiny and rhiny my tear-filled eyes couldn't make it out to read it right. Bitch, snatch, chooch—I think I could make out a "ch" shining over by her left armpit. The rest was a dazzling blur. It could have said "church" spelled out right across her chichis because she was holy fucking cow.

Hair long, long, long past her double-D ass and short, short, frosty blonde short around her face and the top of her head. The fanciest girl mullet Chieko's Barber Shop ever created.

Rings on her fingers, rings on her toes, rings all up the side of one ear and OH! She get one pierced tongue when she talk! You know what that means!

Oh wait, no. That's not one tongue earring, she just eating Tic Tacs. Or maybe her tooth is loose.

I saw her mouth working, the black eyeliner around her lips stretching and moving, but I couldn't make out the words. My head was all spinning with thoughts of our hot and heavy eighth grade love. Sharing the same hard ice cup after school, our tongues running across the same frozen sour juice. Giving her hickeys with my hands because I got tired sucking on her thick skin. Making sure she got the chair with the hole in the seat in Mrs. Hamada's homeroom class so I could sit right next and reach my hand underneath and touch her panties with my middle finger. That was sweet heaven, a stinky stink better than the dried squid. You are the hot ika, girl.

Oh Corina my love, why did we have to break up? Didn't I love you enough? Didn't I treat you right? Didn't I give you everything a man could give?

Or was it because you caught me trying to steal your scrip at the Saint Anthony School Carnival? I told you I was sorry. I was just hungry and the Pronto Pup cost like six tickets.

Jorene was rolling her eyes.

"You not listening, Uncle Bobby. Are you stoned or something? I thought you not supposed to get stoned or nothing because you're on PROBATION after just being released from PRISON."

"Shut up, Jorene, you gonna blow my cool." I tried to say 'em low, like a whisper under my breath, but Jorene was not working with me at the moment.

"Blow your cool? As if you get cool to blow! All you get is a rap sheet as long as your arm full of every lame-ass petty and unimpressive crime a jackass can commit, the bad habits of sleeping past noon and smoking cigarettes in the dark and a pair of jailhouse BVDs so buss up that even your broke ass dick trying to run away from you."

I reached down to check. Damn it, Jorene. She always gotta be right.

"Stop dreaming and listen to the lady or else she going call the cops."

Maybe that wouldn't be so bad. Prison beds not as fucked up like this sofa. Sometimes I miss my cot in the MCCC. Toward the end had my shape all pressed into it and was kinda homey.

Amazing what you can get used to.

But oh, Corina, I could get used to you, you big bad girl you. Come to me, my Miss Lower Main first runner-up. Let me teach you all the things you once taught me. I've been practicing. Practicing alone the last couple years, but still yet, I've put in my hours.

That black-outlined mouth was moving and I was nodding yes, yes, whatever you want, yes.

"So what you waiting for?"

I wanted it to be like a sweet invitation. I tried to hear it like that. But it was a scream, an order, a demand for action.

"Nothing, nothing, what? I not waiting. So, Corina, what you like me do?"

She was about to start screaming again but then she stopped short.

"Fucka, how you know my name? I never did see your face before. Let me see that dick again."

Jorene rolled her eyes and walked down the hall. Probably preparing her detailed monitor's report for Sergeant Mama. Fucking great.

I pulled open the puka of my underwear to give Corina a little peak.

"Bobby?!"

I promise, I could hear violins and pianos and all that fancy shet music all swelling up in my ears and my head and everywhere else. It was the most romantic moment of my whole life.

"So how you been, Corina?"

I tried to sound all smooth and caring.

"Yeah, we can catch up later and whatnot, maybe we can poke for old times sake, but right now, your toilet is leaking into my apartment so you better shut off the water valve or else my whole house going be under water."

Shet.

"Nanny nanny boo boo," the toilet sang.

Fucking traitor. I going get you.

I spent two hours trying to make like I knew what I was doing cranking on water pipes, tightening up intake valves, assessing the pooling pattern on the floor, matching up the dripping pattern on Corina's ceiling. After all that, I told her well, I did what I could do but maybe we should still call the building super.

"Super what?"

"Intendent," I told her. I don't understand the black eyeliner around the lips. Does that make her face like a coloring book so she don't get the lipstick stuff outside the edges? Trippy.

"This not the kind of building that has a Super Intendent. We no more even a Regular Intendent. This not public housing. This is low-income."

She said that all proud, like hell yeah I pay for this hot, stink apartment with my upstairs neighbor's toilet pouring down through my ceiling. I pay for it all by myself with no handouts from the government! Whoo-hoo!

"So you telling me there's no building manager or maintenance man or building owner to call when this kind stuff happen?"

She gave me a lost little look, like if this was going to take more than yelling at somebody, she had no idea how to handle. I just wanted to kiss the lips inside the big outline and make her feel better.

"The guy who owns the building is pretty old. He cannot fix toilet or nothing."

Sad little face under all that glorious, mulletous hair. I love you Corina, even if you did give me that little nick on my tip with your crooked front tooth.

Oh yeah, THAT'S why we broke up. I still get the scar. Took months for scab over. Only after I healed I realized I actually like a girl who bites. But by then, she was long gone, chomping on somebody else's pupu pup.

"Well, I did what I could do. I think so I fixed the problem. See, not dripping so much anymore." I did my confidence voice.

"But it's still dripping." Doubtful droop in the black outline.

"That's just the residual drip." Bobby busting out a big word he heard on Dr. Phil. I don't care that man is bald and loud and ugly, you can always learn something from that bastard. "That's the water that came out before I fixed the leak. Still dripping because it came out already. But the water that came out after I fixed the leak not going drip out because I got 'em in time. You understand?"

Corina nodded her short hair part of her head. The long hair in the back followed a few seconds later.

"So I going be OK?"

"You going be fine." I smiled my "you going be fine" smile.

"Cool. You like poke?"

I fast changed my smile to my fake "I'm interested but I'm not that easy" eyes. I still remember how to play Da Game.

"Nah, Corina, I gotta go back upstairs, make sure the kids are OK, start dinner before Doreen come home, you know, family stuff."

"Can be just a fast poke. We'll be pau before your wife come home," Corina was running her hands through the long part of her hair to look sexy. Her fingers got stuck in a massive tangle.

"Doreen's not my wife. She's my sister and my cousin."

Corina stopped yanking at her bird's nest hair. "The poking your cousin part, that is OK but I think so the poking your sister part is illegal."

Sometimes it takes too long to explain. Sometimes, you should just let people think what they're thinking even if what they're thinking is wrong. And with Corina, I could tell that she was going to forget what she was thinking, anyway. She probably already forgot my name.

"So Tony, you wanna poke? I wait till you pau clean the toilet water."

That's the most romantic thing anyone has ever said to me.

Corina followed me upstairs to Doreen's apartment and sat on the couch with Kenji while I made like I was going to clean up all the water in the bathroom. There was a lot of water in the bathroom. The hole I drilled in the floor to drain all the overflow into Corina's apartment wasn't at the center of the pool. I poked another hole in the floor closer to the deepest part. I only used a small screwdriver, but I guess so everything was soft already from the water and it caved in to a bigger hole. Not too big, though. Only about six inches across. Liko cannot fall through or anything. The small boy is safe. I put one magazine over the hole in the floor to make sure nobody got hurt. The water poured all into Corina's apartment along with dirt and some pieces of toilet paper that had missed the bowl. So now the bathroom looked pretty clean. I am so good.

"Yes, you are."

No more singing outta' you, Mr. Crapper.

"Come, Billy, come sit on me."

"Goddamn it already, you fucking toilet, shut your mouth and close your lid!"

Oh wait, that last part came from Corina.

I turned around and Corina had tears in her eyes and her eyelinered lips were pouty.

"You no gotta talk to me like that, Stanley. I just trying to be nice."

How did she get those tight-ass jeans off her big-ass body so fast? Amazing. So amazing I forgot the pain of that long ago bite. All I could think of was the love. I joined her on the sofa and I JOINED her on the sofa. She suddenly remembered my name was Bobby. The spring kadoinged. Her chi-chis kadoinged. The spring got into it, like boing-a-boing-a-boing-a-boing. I got into it, boing-a-boing-a-boing-a-boing. She got into it, calling me Bobby, Bobby, my long lost love Bobby, I sorry for that time I . . .

Oh, don't say it! Don't say it! Never speak those words!

"I so sorry for that time I munched your dick."

FUCK! Thinking of the pain now. Owwee.

"You was just so tasty that's why. I couldn't help it."

OK, OK, OK, OK. Back on track. Tell me I'm tasty again.

"You tasty, Bobby. You so tasty. You so tasty like one hot pancake sandwich from Tasty Crust Restaurant by the old Wailuku Sugar Mill."

"Ooh, I like that kind. With the pork and beans inside?"

"No, with the corn beef and cabbage."

"What? Ewww." Shet, losing it, losing it.

"With the pork and beans, Bobby. The two pancakes, one on top, one on the bottom, all covered with syrup and smash together, hot, buttery, soft and smooshy, and in between . . ."

"Yeah?"

"And in between those pancakes . . ."

"Yeah? Yeah?"

"In between those pancakes are the sweetest, hottest, stickiest pork and beans I ever did taste."

"Oh yeah! Yeah, Corina! Oh! Oh! Oh! Shet!"

"The biggest, fattest, nastiest pancake sandwich stuffed full with pork and beans and syrup so good I just like take a big big BITE!"

"AAAAAAAAAAAAAH!"

Everything happened at once. Hot and cold, go and stop, happy and sad.

All that, plus Doreen came home. Right then. Right that very second.

When I think back to that moment, I wonder if it was the hole in the bathroom floor that made my sister/cousin kick me out of the house.

She didn't give me time to explain how I had actually saved her whole apartment by making the hole in the floor.

Sometimes I think it was all the wet toilet water towels I had piled up in the hallway. If Corina hadn't come in to rape me, I would have had time to throw the towels in the washing machine at the laundromat down the street. Or at least put them in a big garbage bag so she wouldn't notice. But the way things happened with Corina, I didn't have too much time to clean up. I was busy.

When I went through everything that happened up to that moment, I can see now that I was probably not the easiest guy in the world to live with. If only Doreen gave me a chance to explain that I was working on getting a job but I was waiting to hear back from a couple of places but was hard because when I went to apply, I couldn't remember her phone number all the way. 242-873 something. If only Doreen gave me a chance to explain that my first check would definitely be going to help pay rent, buy Pop-Tarts, replace the Nyquil and Midol and oh yeah, the bottle of mouth wash I found because after I took care of my few basic essential needs, the rest of my money was all for her and the kids. If only Doreen was in the mood to hear about my plans to fix up her apartment with all the skills I learned in prison shop class. If only she gave me the chance to push Corina off me, put on my pants and explain.

But when Doreen walked in the door, she wasn't in the talking mood. She didn't even need a minute to look around the place and see what happened. It was like she saw everything before her key even hit the lock. Maybe Jorene tipped her off because she didn't take a moment to assess. She just flew open the door and before I could say anything, me, Corina, and the stink sofa were flying out the sliding glass door off the balcony, down, down, down onto the dirty-soda-can-and-kiawe-bean sand below.

The force of the landing made Corina's mouth clamp down on my shoulder. Now I going have one scar there, too.

A second later, my pants, my slippers, my Fujinaka shirt and a couple of dog pillows came flying down, too.

"Dori! What you doing?"

"Go before I pour battery acid on your head!"

"I think I drank that."

"I have a secret stash."

She was looking around for more stuff to throw out the window. My jailhouse toothbrush came flying. My ukulele. Half the slush float I ripped off then forgot I had. Ew, don't throw that! Splat. Damn. Kenji was watching from the window and I swear that fucking dog was laughing.

"What about your sofa?"

"Kenji no like sleep there no more. The thing stinks like you!"

I looked and Kenji was nodding, like yeah, brah, keep yourself a little cleaner, would you? Lick your balls every once in a while or something.

Hate that dog.

My pack of smokes came flying out the window. A book of matches. Corina's tulip-leg Chic jeans.

"Dori, wait! I'm your brother/cousin! You cannot just throw me out!"

Shhhhhhhhhk-POOM! Doreen closed the sliding glass door to the balcony. I looked up and she was giving me the finger. Jorene was in the bedroom behind the frosted jalousie windows giving me the finger. Kennison was behind her teaching Liko how to give me the finger. The fucking dog gave me the paw finger.

Corina started the long process of yanking on those tight-ass jeans on her big-ass body. She hardly noticed we got thrown out the second story window. She thought it was part of my ride.

"So what, Marvin, what you like eat for dinner?"

CHAPTER 9

I ASKED CORINA TO MARRY ME.

I figured might as well since we were going to be living together. Fresh start, make 'em legal, all that crap.

Then I found out she already married.

Then I found out her husband is a guy I knew on the inside. Paco Ichida was a bad dude. Not too smart, but really strong. Not too big, but really dangerous. You get a guy like that mad and he's a killer. Otherwise, he's just your basic compulsive gambler turned collections expert. On the inside, he ran the spread sheets for the high school football games. I won dollar-fifty on a Lunas game one time. That was choice.

I felt so bad that I poked my friend's wife. Him doing time, me doing her. That's totally bad style. I'm gonna owe him one, maybe let him have a turn at my future wife someday. Let him use my truck. Buy him a case of beer. Something.

"No worry," Corina told me, "I already cheating on him with Chala. I cheating on Chala with you."

Goddamn, I only knew one Chala in Wailuku and if that's the Wailuku Chala I thinking of, my ass going be more dead than if Dori find out I had some of her cash shoved inside the sofa cushions.

Corina said Chala got arrested three days ago at a chicken fight in Waihee, so no worry, he didn't even have his bail set yet. We had plenty time to explore our relationship together before Chala can call his bail bondsman, so relax and be free.

My Corina is so romantic.

Plus she not too sure about her marital status because when her and Paco got married, he was still married to a chick from Honolulu and they never did get that all cleared up.

So yeah, go get married. Why the fuck not?

Chicks love my sweet talk.

Corina helped me carry Doreen's sofa into her and Chala's apartment. The thing was way heavier that you would expect. I mean, it hardly had any sofa stuffings inside to make it comfortable. How the hell did Doreen launch this big thing with me, Corina, and Corina's big ass on it? That's what I like know. That fucking sneaky dog must have helped. Woof woof, asshole. I ate your Milkbones for snack, motherfucker.

Corina's apartment was starting to get that wet towel smell from all the water that poured down from my ex-friend the toilet. I tried to figure out a way I could poke holes in the floor to drain the rest of the puddles out, but that trick don't work so good when you on the ground floor of one cement slab building.

I took a look around and assessed my new place of residence. The hole in Corina's bathroom ceiling from Doreen's bathroom floor was pretty much the smallest hole in the whole place, not counting Corina.

Ah, I shouldn't say bad stuff about the love of my life. Even if she is a total slut, she's my total slut. At least for now. Until her boyfriend get out of the police cell block or her husband get out of prison or she bite my love rod too hard and make me come to my senses about her wicked ways.

But damn, her place was punched to shet. Had more pukas in the walls than a beach park bathroom. Than a beach park bathroom in a local part of the island, that is. I bet you the tourist beaches get nice stalls. With locks even. Imagine that.

Corina didn't have no lock on her door. She didn't have no door on her door. Even the hinges look like they surrendered in a fight. They were just limp metal lumps hanging by the side of the doorjamb.

The windows was broken, the screens all hanging like loose skin, the glass part around every light was broken and jagged, like somebody was playing piñata and ran out of stuffed donkey.

Hate to say it but Doreen's sofa was by far the nicest thing in the place. Lumpy, ugly, orange plaid sofa sleeper with the pullout sleeper part long ago pulled out and pulled off. Ass dents on both cushions from hundreds of hours of ass time. Stains from the dog, the kids, the family who owned it before Doreen found it at Goodwill, the families who owned it before that family owned it, and most recently me and Corina and our special love stains. Little bit blood from my shoulder bite.

Poor puka plaid sofa had gone many miles, but was still the bright spot in here. It had taken the weight of so many assess and just kept on taking. Only Corina could understand that kind of pressure.

Ah, I shouldn't talk bad about my sweetie.

There I was making building inspector around her apartment and there she was in the kitchen making me canned corn beef and cabbage for dinner. What a kind and loving woman. The cabbage was black and brown from many months of wilderness survival in the bottom of Corina's ice box. The canned corn beef had a picture of a cow on the front like they're telling you yes, no matter what you think you tasting, this really is beef. Promise.

Me and Corina ate dinner by candlelight because most of the light bulbs was busted, too. It wasn't really a candle, just a piece of broken kitchen cabinet I set on fire with my lighter. It cast a smoky glow on Corina's glassy eyes and gave the short hair in her mullet a glowing halo.

It would have been a romantic dinner except for the major ass gas. I wouldn't say Corina was a bad cook, but I was glad I was spending the night in a house with a working toilet.

In between my cramps, I snuggled with her on the sofa and we laid out the ground rules for our relationship, which pretty much came down to I gotta split as soon as one of her men came home and she cannot chomp me anywhere below the waist. Nibble, OK, but no drawing blood.

We decided on church wedding. Something small, like that place Britney Spears went in Vegas. Corina never did go to Vegas and I never did leave the island, but she says her cousin went one time and the food is so cheap you save plenty money by eating all day because it keeps you away from the gambling.

My sweetheart is so practical.

We talked about our future house. Something small and cute in Kahului, a fixer-upper since I was so good with my hands.

We talked about our future children and she told me all the names picked out: Chalene, Chalaine, and Chalette for the girls; Chala Junior, Chalson, and Chalbert for the boys.

My name is Bobby.

She glanced down at my dick.

"Oh right. Bobby."

She tried to do the conjugations: Boblene, Boblaine, Boblette, Bobby Junior, Bobson . . . like counting sheep, so drowsy . . . and then her big mullet was fast asleep on my pins-and-needles shoulder and she was drooling on my chest.

I finally fell asleep when the street lights went off. The sun shining in the broken windows was less bright than the street lights shining on the sofa all night. I slept through the day so good under the soft and fuzzy blanket of Corina's long part of her hair.

It was evening time when I woke up sticky and stink, crampy and crooked, listening to a man call out my name.

"Bob? Bobby? You there?"

Cannot be either one of Corina's men because they wouldn't be using that "office" sounding voice. They would pretty much be killing first and screaming second.

If that stinking toilet followed me down here I'm gonna be so pissed.

Hee! That is really funny and when I get time I'm going to think about it and figure out why, but I kind of busy right now.

So who the hell is calling my name? Not nice, like a friend, but businessy, like maybe it's my turn in line and I not paying attention. If I had a boss, I would think maybe it was my boss looking for me to get me to do something I don't want to do but I don't have no boss since I don't have no job. All I get is . . .

Shet! Warren!

I fucking forgot that my sad sack of shet parole officer was supposed to come check out my living situation tonight!

Think, Bobby, think!

And he was supposed to have dinner and meet the family.

Think, Bobby! You no like go back jail! Not now! Jail had its perks but nothing as perky as Corina Molina's sweet fat ass.

I stuck my hand deep into the puka of the sofa cushion and felt around for my stash of cash. Corina thought I was trying something and her head instantly dropped to my shoulder and started gnawing. I going have to borrow some of Kenji's Milkbones for this chick if our romance go on much longer. I running out of virgin skin.

I found my roll of bills and peeled off two twenties. I pushed Corina off the couch, helped her find her panties and gave her the money and instructions.

"Baby, you can go grab us dinner? Get something family-ish. Something you can feed kids."

"We get kids?"

"No, Corina, my sister/cousin get kids."

"I think so the sister part is illegal . . ."

"I just meant get something that a kid would eat. Get chicken. No get vodka or pakalolo or meth for dinner, OK?"

"You sure?"

"Just get chicken, OK?"

"OK!" She headed toward the door without a shirt on. I had to grab her arm and tell her to finish getting dressed.

"What you going get for dinner?"

I was learning that with this girl, you gotta do plenty pop quizzes.

"Chicken!"

"Very good. Where you going get the chicken?"

"My uncle's house. He get chickens."

I pictured her bringing in one wounded fighting cock and getting blood and chicken feathers all over the nice ugly plaid sofa.

"Just go Minit Stop, OK? Go Minit Stop and get some chicken."

"Okey doke." And she was off with a toss of her mulleted head. Off to hunt and gather, off to find food to feed her man. So happy. So busy. So glad to be of service.

Shet, who knows what the fuck she's gonna bring back?

I heard footsteps on the concrete stairs heading up to Doreen's place. I was out the door in a flash, one hand pulling up my shorts, the other hand trying to button my Fujinaka.

"Warren! Warren! Warren, my main man! Warren!"

Oh, just the stink old drunk who lives in the corner. Never mind.

I body checked him into the broken stair railing as I ran past him to get to Doreen's place. I looked back fast kind just to make sure I didn't fling him off the railing to the cement and sand below. Nah, Old Stank Grampa caught his grip with his cane on the broken railing and got himself right back up on his feet. He's fine. Fine enough to show me the finger, crooked and old but still working for flipping people off. That old dude is tough.

I got to Doreen's place just as good old Dori is about to spill all the stinking little beans on me, and that girl get plenty beans when it comes to her cousin/brother. And there she was, just about to spill every last bean of it. And maybe some extra beans too.

"Warren! So nice of you to drop by! Welcome to the lovely little place me and my ohana like to call home. My fiancé is out arranging a lovely dinner for us. We do hope you'll join us. In the mean time, please come in and make yourself comfortable. Can I get you a cold beverage? We get water. We even get ice water if you like make fancy. Would you prefer a Barney cup or would a Teletubbies be more your type? Please let me introduce this lovely young woman here who is my sister and also is my cousin. This is Doreen, her lovely daughter Jorene, and her sons Kennison and Liko. Cute, yeah? And such good kids. Lovely, even."

Doreen looked me dead in the eye to make sure I knew what was going to happen before it happened. It hurts more that way.

And then she blew. She spewed. She ratted. A couple of times I thought she was trumping up some charges, you know, embellishing and shet. And then I thought about it and it was like, "Oh crap, I guess I did do that, huh?"

Still, she made it all sound so BAD.

It really is all in how you look at these things, you know. Most of it was harmless, unintentional, or just misunderstood.

I hate it when somebody knows you better than you know yourself. Damn it, Dori. You really suck when you're right and you're always fucking right. Always.

Warren kicked into gear. Turns out he get two gears. Tired gear and "shet, now I gotta do something about you" gear. For government workers, that second one is high gear. Warren said I had one more option for placement. Not back to jail, because I did a pretty good job of not hanging with felons, not reoffending, and not pissing dirty on my tests since I was catching Liko's piss in a jar, so not enough reason to send my ass back to lockup. But clearly I was a "stress" to Doreen's home life and family situation and since she was already in the "at-risk" category, what with being a broke single mother from a disadvantaged background and having at least four racial minorities in her heritage. I had to cut my family some slack and take my action elsewhere.

The way Warren said it, not like I was getting kicked out. It was more like he was moving me to another department where my skills and attributes would be better utilized. He made it sound like I was getting promoted. Shucks, Warren. You make me feel proud to go group housing.

He said I could take the sofa. I made like it was the one thing holding me together. He goes, "You're invested in that sofa?" and I go, "Ho yeah. Big time." He don't even know how much.

"I love that sofa, Warren."

Big sigh. Shoulders drooping. "We'll work it out."

Doreen was nothing but happy I was going to live in a halfway house. I told her I would come by often and help her with stuff around the house. She said forget where she live or else she gonna move. I told her I could stick around to help fix up the hole in the bathroom and drag the sofa back upstairs. She said don't go near my bathroom and I never want to see that fucking sofa again as long as I live now that there's Bobby jizz on the upholstery fibers. I said I'll make sure to let her know how I'm doing. She said she don't need updates, she can see my whole future already and she not even psychic.

Doreen act mean to me sometimes. But then I tell myself that she talk that way to her kids too because she want them to do better. It's that reverse psychology thing. Doreen like me to do better, too. She love me like she love her kids, in a protective Mama slap-your-head-to-make-you-shape-up kind of way.

I love you too, Doreen.

I thought she was wiping a tear from her eye with her finger but then I caught on that it was her middle finger and she was trying to flip me off in front of Warren my parole officer without him catching on that she was being rude.

That's her. Always classy.

Warren helped me load the sofa onto the top of his car and secure it on with some surf ropes he kept in the trunk. I guess so back in his day Brother Doo Doo Man used to surf but nowadays he pretty much just go work, go home, take a crap, eat dinner, crap again, go lie down. He tired from being tired already. Too tired to talk me out of bringing the sofa.

I grabbed my stuff from Corina's place and took one final look around at what once was but will now never be. Made me little bit sad. Me and Corina could have had a good thing together. She had a good heart, that girl. And a big ol' ass. I hope whoever put all those holes in the wall don't come back into her life and punch more holes. I hope Corina does better, better than me, even, though I must say I would have been an improvement in her romantic life. I don't punch holes in walls. Only in bathroom floors and only when I gotta troubleshoot in a crisis situation.

I left with a sad heart until I considered that maybe all the holes in the walls was from her chewing like a rat when she lonely. Run Bobby run. I like the biting but not the bleeding.

I met Warren in his car and made sure the sofa was tied on the roof good and tight. I looked up to Doreen's place to see if her or any of the kids were waving me goodbye. They must be all busy talking about how they gonna cope without me. I gonna miss them, too.

Warren took off in his little putt-putt social worker mobile. Why do guys like him always buy tan-colored cars with the engines of a fucking moped? I don't get it. State job, right? Buy some wheels, dude!

"So where is this place?"

Warren sighed and looked at his watch, the international male symbol for "long drive and I really gotta pass a load."

"Upcountry," he said, and we headed up the hill.

As we left Wailuku, we passed by Corina holding a box of chicken in one hand and a case of beer in the other, chewing gum like there was no tomorrow, walking fast in the dirt on the side of the road, her platform rubber slippers kicking up dust as she hurried home with dinner for her man.

CHAPTER 10

SO THE HALFWAY HOUSE WAS MORE LIKE a quarter-way house because it ain't halfway between jail and home and it ain't halfway between rehab and sober living. It is still mostly jail, mostly rehab, all-the-way low income. Locks on the outside door, no locks on the bathroom door. Lots of sign-in sheets. Lots of reminder signs on the walls like please turn off when not in use, phone calls limited to only 10 minutes, no mouthwash or other toiletry items containing alcohol allowed on the premises.

The place was mostly empty because they just had a fire. They had to throw away furniture and throw out the guy who started the fire and some of the other "clients" who got freaked out that Firebug Freddy kept lighting up the sofa and the beds.

So they were pretty happy to see me and my plaid buddy show up. Glad I brought my own furniture.

Warren said he was gonna work it out where my disability check was going to cover my room and board and I was thinking, "Disability check? When did I get disabled?" The only big injuries I could come up with were Corina's love bites. Disabled? Did my Corina take him aside and tell him about the last few times when things didn't go her way? NO FAIR, Corina, you wore me out, girl!

I was thinking I should probably set him straight about the disability check but then I thought, nah, let him find out on his own. Let him work it out. I need a little R&R, a little Bed and Breakfast, even though this place was kind of Bring Your Own Bed and Make Your Own Breakfast. I could hang out here little bit, couple-three months, while Doreen works through her anger issues and Warren works through his "Hey, this guy Bobby don't have no disability checks" issues. Fine with me. One big vacation.

The place was like a barracks in the boonies of Pukalani. Must have been an old dairy or something because had lots of mystery drains on the floor. They musta had leaky cows in here.

The main room had a TV behind a protective plexiglass. When you looked at the protective plexiglass, you could see why the TV need plexiglass protection. Had all kinds of dents, gouges, dried food, smudges, splatters, sprays, chunks, whatever that people had hurled at the TV. Must get pretty crazy in here during "Wheel of Fortune." Must get some real hotheads trying to buy vowels.

Big sign above the television: Please do not throw bodily fluids in this room.

Oh, so it's that kind of party.

Had five bedrooms with two guys each sharing a room. I got the room in the back that used to belong to the firebug. Warren helped me drag my sofa into the black corner where Uncle Hibachi used to sleep. And then Warren was off. Off like a bird with a running start. Off like a kid hanging out the classroom door when the recess bell rings. Off like a fat man on doughnut day. Off to work stuff out.

Took me a while to realize that the halfway in this halfway house was not halfway between jail and the outside or halfway between rehab and the real world. It was halfway between crazy and full-out fucked in the head.

The straps on the beds clued me in. No wonder they don't have no locks in the door. If somebody gets nuts, they just shoot 'em with a tranquilizer gun and tie brother to the bed. Nice.

Fuck!

Although if things got hairy, maybe I would act up too just to get me one of those happy needles in my ass and score a sweet night's sleep. The bed shackles are a little bit too freaky-deaky, though.

I looked around and I noticed other stuff, too. No curtains on any of the windows. No mirrors in the bathroom. No curtain rods over the shower stalls. No poles in the closets. Only plastic stuff in the kitchen.

I noticed even the trash cans don't have no trash bags inside. What the hell kind of damage can you do with a trash bag? I gonna have to research that one.

Dinner time everybody lined up in the kitchen and got a paper bowl of chili and rice and a paper cup of pills. My paper cup was empty. I tried tell the house manager lady, Sonya.

"I don't care," she told me.

"But I don't have any pills," I told her.

"Your intake chart doesn't have any notation for medication."

"That's what I saying, I don't take no medication."

"Talk to your case worker about that."

"No, what I saying is, can I use the cup for juice or soda or something? Or maybe you want your empty cup back for somebody else?"

I was just trying to be helpful. Sonya gave me the look that said she don't want no help from a client.

Client. How did I ever end up being a client? Client used to mean a guy with money who wanted what you selling. These days, 'client' is short for fucked-in-the-head. Client means crazy.

I'd rather be a con than a client. Shet, at least a con sound cool. Client sound like you get problems. Don't get me wrong, I know I ain't perfect, but my problems ain't like CLIENT problems.

Sonya didn't want her cup back. She didn't want me drinking out of it neither. It ain't for water or juice or soda or nothing. It's for meds. It's a meds cup. Everybody got a meds cup at every meal. And since I don't get no meds, all I got is the cup.

After dinner everybody sat around the living room to stare at the plexiglass around the TV. The thing was so scratched and cloudy and dirty and warped that cannot see nothing from the TV screen except some blurs of colors and some flashes of light when the scene change to another scene. Ricky, this dude with a crazy mohawk that goes not front-to-back but side-to-side, hid his eyes from the TV flashes because he said that's how they rob your brain. Too late for you, Ricky. Your head got fucking cleaned out.

I was thinking if they turn up the sound, maybe at least we could listen to see what the show is about. But the sound was from behind the plexiglass too and was already cranked up full blast. Full blast didn't get too full blast in that place. They made sure of that.

After about 40 minutes of watching the flashing lights, the whole room was snoring in their chairs. Me, I could have keep on watching those lights until late in the morning because I was coming up with my own little story in my mind about being wasted at the Maui County Fair and trying to steal rides on the Tilt-a-Whirl. But after a while, the chair not so comfortable and I had my friend the sofa waiting for me in the black back room. The back black room. Whatever.

Had a bed in there for somebody else but nobody in it. Cool. Private room. I was hoping whichever Nutty Professor is my bunkmate keep his crazy self in the living room for the rest of the night. I wanted my alone time. Calgon, take me away.

I went sleep and I dreamed of my gramma again. I woke up and she was sitting by my feet on the sofa smoking a cigarette. Crap, is crazy contagious? I'd rather have the mean shets disease.

"Eh, Bobby!" she told me.

"Go away, Gramma."

"Bobby! Listen to me!"

"I no like come crazy so no talk to me, Gram."

"Bobby, you listen to me!" Gramma was pulling my ear with her ear-pulling Gramma hand. Owwee. Gramma's fingers was strong from rolling her own cigarettes for over 60 years.

"You listen, Bobby and you listen good!"

"OK, OK, OK, all right, OK already. Sheesh. Just letta go my ear. You keep pulling 'em, my ear going stretch and hang down to my shoulder already. You no like your grandson with one side hanging ear, right?"

"Not like you get good looks that going waste."

"Ho, Gramma! You dead but you fast! Zinga! Good one."

"Zinga nothing. I here to give you a message."

"Oh good! My back is sore from carrying in that big fucking sofa. The thing hardly get stuffing but still yet so heavy."

"Not a massage, you fucking idiot. A message."

Yeah, OK, so I was messing with her on that one and she knew it. She tried to slap my head for that but her hand just passed right through and all I felt was the wind from the whoosh.

"Wow, Gram, trippy! Do it again!"

"Fuck you, Bobby. I no do tricks like one dog."

My gramma was a cranky-ass ghost. I was hoping the afterlife would be good to her after all the sufferings she did in this world, but she still had that ratty-ass orange flower muumuu and the hair that needed washing and the buss-up old lady brown weave sandals. Jesus didn't give her much of an upgrade. That sucks ass.

"You look good, Gramma," I told her. Me trying to be nice.

Whoosh! She tried to slap my head again. Passed right through. I love that.

"No lie to me. I look worser than the day they planted me in the county cemetery."

Poor Gramma. She was right. But that whoosh was awesome.

"I like tell you something, Bobby. I like give you guidance. I like say something important to you because you my grandson and you my descendant and I love you, sort of, as much as anybody could love somebody like you. I like give you this message, Bobby."

"Shoots." I swung my feet off the sofa and onto the floor and sat up to hear my big message from the great beyond. "Give it to me, Grams."

Her eyes got all big and scary and the tip of her home-rolled cigarette glowed red and then it started shooting flames and sparks like a big magic wand. What the hell was Gramma smoking anyway? I always had this sneaky thought it wasn't straight tobacco. Gramma floated up from the sofa in a cloud of smoke and her hair stood on end, which it usually did because Gramma had some crazy hair, especially when it was crazy dirty like now, but this standing on end action was extra super spooky.

I braced myself for what she was about to say. She took a deep breath and said all scary with the gravelly voice—

And I'm going to myself, "Bobby, don't shet your pants. You only dreaming. Bobby, don't shet your pants. You only dreaming and you no like ruin this nice uncomfortable sofa."

And my gramma said: "BOBBY!"

All echo-y and loud.

And I was like, "Yeah?" And I tighted up my ass just in case. All worried and nervous.

And she said, "STOP FUCKING UP!"

Except she made it sound real Scooby Doo spooky, like "Stooooooop fuuuuuuuuuuuucking uuuuuuuuuuuuup!"

And I was all, "Wow, that's it? That's all you got? My shet was secure inside my ass the whole time because that was not even little bit scary."

Then my gramma made a television remote control appear in her hand and she changed the channel in my brain to a classic TV cable channel. The video was old and faded and fuzzy, like something from the 1980s, and there was this fat kid running around barefoot outside on a dirt road. Poor kid, hard time run when you that fat. Look him, all the kakios on his legs from mosquito bites and road rash. Head shaved down to nubs so the ukus can't make house. Feet hanging out of slippers so small that the middle part bust through the rubber puka already. That's somebody's sorry-ass looking housing baby right here.

And then welfare baby turned around and oh, check that face. Big brown eyes, chubby cheeks, hair all wild and knotty, huge-ass nose that stretch from one side of his face to the other. So sad for the boy, he poor plus he ugly.

And then it was like, oh nah! That's me! So cuuuuuuuuute!

Then Gramma made me watch video of some of my greatest hits.

The time my gramma's friend brought over lilikoi chiffon pie that none of us kids were supposed to touch until after dinner. I touched. I just wanted part of the whip cream part but somehow that ended up to scooping out a big chunk of the sweet-sour inside of the pie. Then I figured I might as well eat it all and say it got lost rather than just eat some and leave the rest there and get totally busted. I ate the whole thing, didn't even try to clean up the evidence. And me, lilikoi chiffon all over my face going, "I don't know what had happen. Maybe somebody came in and stole 'em. Not me, but. I didn't see nothing."

The time I fell asleep with gum in my mouth and when I woke up, I had Hubba Bubba all stuck inside my hair and I went to cut 'em out with a scissors and I cut too much so I kept cutting to try to even it out and pretty soon I ended up so rat-eat and bald I just took my uncle's razor and shaved everything off to start over. I told everyone I was going army and that hell yeah they taking fourth graders now. I tough, that's why.

The time in sixth grade when I went to use the teacher's bathroom in the school library during detention and I accidentally missed the toilet and ended up pissing on the floor. I was so tripping out on the fact that I pissed on the floor of the nice teachers' bathroom that I kept pissing on the floor while I was thinking about how I had just pissed on the floor. When I looked around to see if anybody could see me pissing on the floor I accidentally started pissing on the walls and on the crepe paper flowers on the top of the toilet tank and on the door and then it was pretty much ceiling-to-floor piss in that small bathroom.

Eh, Gramma, how you got video of me using bathroom in the sixth grade? That's kinda weird.

Gramma's cigarette was smoked down to the nub and her ghost was fading fast. It was like as soon as her cigarette go out, she going disappear too. What the hell was she smoking?

"I trying to make da point that you gotta stop fucking up."

"Yeah, OK, you said that before the home movies."

"You, Bobby, when you fuck up, it's like rolling down a hill. You just keep fucking up. You just keep on rolling, down and down and down some more, picking up more dirt and leaves and rubbish and shet as you go."

"Like Sand Hills?"

"Like shet hills. Stop fucking up. You fucked up already. Pau. It's over. Stop rolling down the damn bloody hill."

I think my gramma had some more pointers for me, but just then, her cigarette went out and she disappeared like when you turn off the TV late at night but you can still see the outlines of the people on the show you were watching. I could see her outline for a few seconds before my eyes adjusted.

All righty right. Stop rolling down the damn bloody hill. I can do that.

I looked over and saw that I had a roommate after all. Brother wasn't strapped down. Guess he not too crazy. He was sleeping like a big lump on his bed. He looked kind of like Kenji at the foot of the sofa, all round and curled and gassy.

I didn't miss that dog at all. Swear to God.

I lay down on my sofa and stretched out my legs all the way. First time in a long time I could stretch out my legs all the way to the sofa arm without that fucking dog getting in the way with his warm fuzzy breathings and drooly snugglings.

Ah shet. I missed the dog.

I missed everybody.

I miss Doreen and all her "do nots" and the way she always looked at me like she wanted cut my branch off her family tree. I miss the way she used to save the burned part of dinner for me because she know I like stuff well done. I miss how she used to yell at me to take a shower because I stinking up the place and then yell at me when I do take shower because I taking too long and using up all the hot water.

I miss Jorene with all her sassy ways and her telling me how this guy was in love with her and that guy was in love with her and when I ask about some guy she said was in love with her, she tell, "Mind your own business, fuckwad!" That girl is going places.

I miss Kennison and his stories of football glory. "So what you did in practice today, Kennison?" I would ask him all the time.

And he would go, "Got hit."

And I would go, "Right on, braddah! Take it like a man! And did you hit back? Make a few tackles? Make a few plays?"

And he'd be like, "Nope. Just got hit."

Oh that boy. So young but he's ready for the real world.

I miss Liko, that little guy going between being a baby and a big boy minute by minute. Wants to drive car and raise hell but wants to watch Barney and hear stories, too. When I was leaving, he the only one told me bye. I mean, he showed me middle finger, but he wiggled it a little like "bye-bye" so I know secret-secret that he love his Uncle Bobby.

My eyes were getting all leaky on the sofa pillow now. I miss my family. I never did miss nobody when I was inside, but that was before I knew what real love truly is.

Real love is a family who take you in on their sofa no matter how tough their lives are, how hand-to-mouth they gotta live, and no matter how much Froot Loops you eat, hot water you waste, and ass space you take up in their apartment.

That is love. Shet.

And then there's Corina. The best worst sex I ever had in my whole life. Where was my sweet girl tonight? Was she lying in bed thinking of me, whispering my name into the moonlit night: "Freddy? Jimmy? Henry?"

Was she dreaming of me and the romantic night we shared among the stink wet towels and the wads of floating toilet paper on her floor?

Was she gnawing on the wall of her apartment, scratching that special itch that she should be scratching on me?

And by the way, did she eat the chicken all by herself? Shet, that was my forty dollars.

Then, for just a couple of seconds, my gramma's voice was right there in my ear, not quite whispering because you don't have no whisper left from smoking roll-your-own whatevers for 60 years. Plus, she dead so she not exactly at her best. But there was Gramma rasping and wheezing in my ear kind of soft-like so she wouldn't wake up my roommate the lump.

"You gotta go back, Bobby. Doreen and the kids need . . ."

Yeah, I was thinking, they do need me. They do.

"They need the money you stashed in the sofa, asshole."

Shet, this all-seeing dead Gramma is even way more harsh than the all-seeing alive Gramma used to be.

Gramma picked up a Bible that was sitting on the banged-up cheap pressboard dresser by the door. She swung it at me and I was already laughing anticipating the whoosh and then—

Poom!

Connect! Ooooooouch!

Gramma laughed her mean-ass Gramma laugh and then she disappeared.

CHAPTER 11

SO I DIDN'T FIGURE OUT MY ROOMMATE/MAIN MAN/BEST BUDDY was Corina's boyfriend until he walked out of the shower bare-ass naked and I saw the bite marks on his dick.

He told me his name was Chuck, but that dick attached to him belonged to a man that belonged to Corina. Chala? What the hell happened?

Come to find out Chala woke up one day in jail and started talking like a Haole and that's how they knew he had mental problems. Not like talking like one Haole means you get mental problems. Plenty people work really hard to talk like one Haole and most of the time it means you got something going on. But to be Chala from Wailuku, one man with limited vocabulary and limited teeth, one guy who never in his life did ever speak the "r" on the end of a word like "super" or "summer" or "brother" to all of a sudden wake up one morning and get the gift of Haole gab, well, that means that either he was possessed by one good-talking ghost, he was sneaking college courses on the side the way some cons sneak crank—or else he got a brain tumor the size of one mango.

They sent him hospital and sure enough, there was the mango in his head. And was a big Hayden mango, too. And wouldn't you know it, was in a place where they couldn't do surgery but the lucky thing was he not going die too soon. Pretty much.

So they sent him psych ward for a while, but other than the new trippy way he can talk like Bob Barker or Alex Trebek one of them other smart Haole dudes, he was pretty much normal and mellow. I mean, compared to halfway house standards, he was normal and mellow. Outside, you would see him and go wow, that guy must have a tumor the size of a mango in his head because he acting weird.

He was still strong but. He looked strong as a bull. I better remember not to let him spock my dick bites. If he found out I poked his old lady he probably wouldn't bother with the fancy well-pronounced words to describe how fucked up he's gonna make me.

The second night after I moved in, Chuck/Chala came inside our room with a bottle of pineapple swipe.

"It's from the pineapples that were grown around here."

For all I cared, bradda could have made 'em with his own piss and wouldn't have mattered to me. This was nectar of the gods. Smelled rotten, tasted like dirt, went down like gasoline on fire but oh, the buzz was fanfuckingtastic. I almost felt like I had a mango the size of a tumor in my head, too.

Wait, I said that wrong. I mean a head the size of a tumor in my mango.

Ho, I am funnier than usual on this shet!

So while my mango was busy growing buzzy heads, me and Chuck/Chala did the big male bonding thing.

"So Robert, tell me about yourself."

Robert? He get the same problem with names like Corina get. No tell me she growing her own head mango, too.

Well, I sure as hell ain't showing him my dick as ID.

"Oh, uh, well, first of all, my name is Bobby."

"Isn't that what I called you?"

"You called me Robert."

"Isn't Bobby short for Robert?"

"Usually Bobby is short for 'you motherfucking loser taking up space on the sofa.'"

Chuck/Chala thought that was hilarious. I really have to admit how fucking funny I am, even when I not even trying.

"So you're not Robert?"

"I not too sure who this Robert dude is, but me, I'm pretty sure I'm Bobby."

"That's your given name?"

Well, actually, the story is a little bit complicated. See, my mommy was really thinking I was going to be a girl and Doreen was going to be a boy since my mama's sister's pregnant stomach was pointed like a boy was inside and my mama's stomach was round. Round like a, come to think of it, mango, since we on that theme at the moment.

Mango body parts, pineapple liquor. It's a fucking fruit stand in this house full of fucking fruitcakes! Ha!

Chuck/Chala stopped in between drinks of the swipe.

"You swear a lot."

Oh excuse me Mr. Speech and Language. Sheesh.

"I just trying to make my point." I told him. "I don't have all the fancy kind words you get in your mango these days. I gotta stick to your basic fuck and shet."

Chala/Chuck tipped his paper pill cup at me like making a toast and let me go along on my profanity-filled life story. I tried to watch my fucks and shets and stuff, though. No need get excessive when you just trying to be colorful and emphatic.

Emphatic? Where the heck I picked up that word from?

This booze was like higher education.

So anyways, I told him, my mother was so sure she was going to have a girl that she didn't have no boy names ready. Lucky thing I came out with a dick or I would spend my whole life with a messed up name like Trinetta or Trinilyn or Absadie, the classic low class classy name which is supposed to be spelled like Abcde but my mommy didn't know how to spell the alphabet.

"My sister has a daughter named Abcde."

Chuck/Chala looked like he was offended.

"Oh, sorry."

"I'm just kidding. I don't even a have a sister!"

He busted out laughing and all I could think of was wow, he could talk perfect Haole and he could even make Haole-style jokes. This guy was so touched by the hand of God. I was kind of jealous.

OK, so back to the baby Bobby story.

When came time to name her newborn son, my mother didn't have any names ready. She tried Trinold, Trinford, Trinson, all the usual, but sounded junk.

The nurses tried to help. What's the baby's father's name?

All us girls call him Mr. I Promise I Going Pull Out.

Maybe you can name him after your own father?

What, call my kid "Unknown"? I don't think so.

Maybe you can name him after your favorite teacher.

Name my kid Gilbert Nomura? No thanks.

Then how about some place special to you?

Name my kid D-building Girl's Bathroom? Fuck no.

She finally decided to name me Bobby because her water broke when she was in the hospital lobby. Made sense to her at the time—broke plus Lobby equals Bobby. But you have to understand, she was pretty loaded on painkillers on account I was a big kid and I broke her chocho coming out.

Chuck/Chala was cracking up. Nice to have an appreciative audience after the stone faces I always got around Doreen's place.

Not that a broken chocho is all that funny. In terms of human tragedies, a broken chocho is right up there with the mean shets disease. I no make jokes about that kind stuff. That's uncalled for. Now, a broken ass is funny, and I would make jokes about somebody's broken ass all day long. But I guess so if the ass got broke because of the mean shets disease, I would have to lay off. But then again, it's one of them case-by-case basis things so if and when it comes up, I'll figure it out. Why, you know anybody who ever got his ass broke with the mean shets?

"Yeah," Chuck/Chala told me. "And was fucking funny!"

He was rolling laughing. Me, my eyes got all big.

"Whatchoo said?"

"I said you, braddah, you sucking hilarious!"

Oh my God, I cured his mango! It's a miracle!

By the time it took me to get Chuck/Chala to stop laughing and to listen to the words that had come out of his mouth, the regular words had all dry up and the nice-sounding Haole words was back.

"I promise, braddah, you was normal there for a minute."

"I suppose that might happen from time to time with a condition like mine."

"How weird is that?"

"It's pretty weird, I must admit."

We was quiet little while drinking the stink swipe and thinking whatever thoughts we still had that could swim around the cotton rolls in our heads. Was nice to have a drinking buddy again. Not like I ever had a drinking buddy before, unless you count my mother and her sister. I like keep Chala as my friend forever. I like grow one head mango of my own and make a club. I like him and me and Corina live all together happily ever after. The booze made all things seem possible.

"So you, Chala? How come your mother named you Chala, Chala?"

"Well, I was named after my grandfather, Charles, but when the kids around Wailuku pronounced my name, it came out the other way, like, you know."

He couldn't even say Chala anymore. Sad.

"Go try," I told him.

"Charla. Chulla. Chollah. I can't do it."

OK, that was one of the most fucked up things I have ever heard in my pathetic fucked up life. One grown man who cannot pronounce his own name. I wanted to cry. Wait, I was crying. I was fucking sobbing. Ho, that pineapple booze! Got me so in touch with my inner feelings at the moment. And then I thinking, wait, I talking right now or I just thinking real loud? Chucka, you can hear me?

"I hear something. Is that you?"

"So wait now, Chala, Chucka, what the fucka . . . you going by Chuck now because you can pronounce that one, right?"

"It's my last name."

"Who's your last name? It's? I seen that one on TV one time, about these guys playing baseball and that was super funny. I don't remember the It's part."

"No, Chock is my last name."

At this point I was so pickled it took about 20 seconds for anything to land on the surface of my brain and then another 30 seconds or so for it to waft down into the part where I can think about it.

Waft? Waft? Where the fuck I got waft from? This is the most beautiful night of my life. If only Corina was here then I could use all these fancy words on her. For a second, I had it all figured out. I would love her and she would bite Chuck Chock's ding dong and mines would stay safe. We would all have our designated places. This could work out so perfect.

Chuck/Chala Chock was dancing around the room now. For all I know, he could have been sitting dead still, he could be dead, maybe he was never there in the first place, but in my happy head, he was doing a goddamn booty grooving jig. But when I looked at his face, it was a frown, a big, droopy frown, getting bigger and bigger. He no cheer up soon his whole mouth going sag down to the floor like a water hose.

"What, what, Chucka, what? No be sad! You was just laughing a minute ago. You was dancing the electric slide."

"Bob, we're out of liquor."

Ho man, I felt that one in my gut. It was like he told me the saddest thing in the world and my heart just bust like a balloon right there.

"Noooooooooo!"

Took a long time for that word to come out, and even after I shut my mouth, I was still saying 'em. I was quiet and I listened to my "no" being yelled in the room by me. I sound so sad.

"Yeeeeeeeeeeeeessss!"

Chala's yes lasted about five minutes.

I have never been so fucking plastered. Must have more. Must.

"Sssso we go get sssomemore," I told Chala.

"Letsssss go!" he told me and he made this jaunty little move with his pointer finger, like "tally ho!" or some shet like that and one more time I was impressed with the depth of his new talent. Brotherman could even gesture in Haole. That is fucking amazing.

"So where's your friend?" I asked him. I was getting up and looking around the room for my jacket when I remembered I don't own a jacket. I miss the Iao School windbreaker. I promised myself right then and there that I was going to go to the campus one night and bust down lockers until I find one my size and steal it back. For old times' sake.

"You're my friend." Chala get some hangdog eyes when he's plastered. A guy could fall in love. I thought about giving him a little bite. I not like that but right now, I dunno. Maybe.

"Not me, your other friend."

"You're my only friend."

He said 'em so sad the two of us bust out crying right there.

Oh Corina, your boyfriend is such a dear, sweet man. Don't you ever let him go, not even for a good-looking rascal like me.

"No, for real but, Chala. Your friend who gave you the swipe."

"Oh, no one gave me this."

"So how you got 'em?"

I could see this one coming a mile away.

"I stole it."

"You mean you . . . swiped it!"

I got ready for the big crack up but Chala was still kind of quiet and hurting from his big confessional that I was his only friend, me the guy who just poked his chick the other day. Thank goodness he don't know that part of my story because I think that would bust the mango in his head and I don't know what it's like for a man to have mango jam in his brains and I really don't want to see.

Chala/Chuck got all serious. So important for him to tell the story right. So hard to make any words, Haole or otherwise, come out of his mouth right now.

"Somebody made pineapple swipe from the pineapple fields here in Pukalani. I found his stash. Shhhhhh!" His beefy finger was over his lips but he couldn't hold it for the whole shushing so he anchored the tip inside his nose to keep his hand steady.

"I didn't know they had pineapples growing around here."

"They don't."

"So where the pineapples came from?"

"Around here."

"You mean before time."

"It's been a few years."

"So how old is this booze?"

Chuck/Chala almost fell asleep coming up with the answer. I almost fell asleep waiting for him to talk.

"Ten, twenty, fifty years maybe."

"Ho da old!"

"That's how you know it's ready."

We nodded at each other in agreement. Oh yeah, the liquor was ready. We were ready. Ready to go out and get us more aged pineapple piss.

The halfway house had locks on the doors but those were easy enough to pop with a knife, which I improvised from one of the bars of the fold-out sofa sleeper. Damn thing never did fold out but at least it won't be poking my ass all night anymore. There was a tall fence around the property. Didn't look too high-tech or nothing. More like a cattle fence than prison perimeter. This place is so low-income.

My head was too slush float to figure out how to disarm the alarm or de-electrify the electric fence, so we just climbed up and jumped over. Lucky thing it wasn't plugged in. If anything started ringing or my nuts got zapped on the wire, I wouldn't have noticed anyway. So happy. Oh so fucking happy.

So we go running through the vacant land next to the halfway house, land that used to be pineapple, used to be dairy, used to be farm, and will one day be some rich guy's deluxe estate as soon as they can kick the house full of spooky losers out of the hood.

Chala was running ahead of me and he looked so cute with this little Oompa Loompa waddle. I don't know how he can run like that because he one tall guy with long legs, but somehow his feet went to the side on each step like he was wearing clown shoes and his knees stayed stiff so he went weeble wobbling full steam ahead to steal the bootleg liquor.

Chala was the best friend I ever had.

We gathered up as many bottles as we could carry and then put an old piece of plywood down over the hole where the rest of the stash was still stashed. Yeah, nobody will EVER find this stuff! So secret! Shhhhhhhh!

My chin got all spitty when I do that. My lips were numb and not holding the shape right. Even when I swore it didn't sound right. Came out like "fugg." I was losing my grip. As if I ever had any fuggin' grip.

We sneaked back to the halfway house. The outside lights was on. I thought I heard an alarm but I wasn't too sure. We went in the door and went laughing, snorting, cackling back to our room. We were so hilarious. We put the bottles underneath Chacka's bed. Shhhhhhhh! No tell! My shirt was wet with spit already from all the secret shushing.

We decided to go sleep already. Just little bit. Take a tiny nap so we can start drinking again refreshed. OK? OK? Chala, you still there? OK?

Chala was passed out on the floor, his hand still underneath the bed where he was trying to hide the last bottle of booze. We carried out as many bottles as we could carry, maybe 20 each. Oh no, wait. Cannot be 20 each. Those are big bottles. Maybe 10 each. We had couple casualties on the way home, so total what we brought in the door was maybe five each. Or maybe was five total. I cannot remember. All I know is that I was so happy I did this brave, exciting adventure with my best friend and we conquered the elements, faced the obstacles, and outsmarted the doubters. I felt so Boy Scout. I felt so Man Scout.

I was just going lie down on the sofa little while. Just rest my eyes. My eyes was little bit tired from all the laughing, crying, laughing, crying we did. Just a small nap. Just a little snooze. Would have been better if they turned off all the outside lights outside. The place was all lit up like the sun.

Or maybe that was the sun and we were out all night until morning time and nobody caught us when we came home because they on their weekly outing to Longs. You know how mental people love their weekly outing to Longs.

Or maybe they were worried about us and turned on all the lights so that we could find our way home safely. Aw, that's so sweet.

Or maybe we were out longer than we thought and nobody was here when we came back because everybody moved. Or everybody was cured.

Or maybe we turned on the lights before we left. That could have happened. Maybe. We were so busy when we left. Hard to keep track.

Or maybe the light was from a big fire and Ignacio Inferno is back in the dorm.

Was I sleeping and dreaming all this action or was I still awake with my head going a mile a minute? Honest to God, I couldn't tell the difference. That was some good bad shet.

When I woke up, I was in the hospital and my head felt like I had the whole fucking mango tree growing inside, roots and fruits and all.

I asked the nurse about Chuck Chock and she told me sorry, he's gone.

Oh no! My best friend ever in the whole world died and I lived? That ain't freakin fair at all.

"Mr. Chock didn't die. He got better. He went home to his wife."

"Wow, I thought if he wasn't in the nut ward he had to be in jail. How'd he score the pass to go home?"

"Well, he's dying."

"You told me he was OK!"

"I said he didn't die. But he is dying."

How's this nurse, eh? She was wiping my ass and pulling my leg at the same time. And no ask me about my dick bite, lady, because that there is personal.

But after a few days of chitchat and ass wiping, me and Nurse Wanita got to be friends. Not good good friends like me and Chala/Chuck was, and not special friends like me and Corina was, but just friends like she looked out for me, laughed at my jokes, and told me, "You'll be OK."

I figured out Wanita loves me.

She told me I'm lucky I not blind or stupid after all the poison I drank. Come to find out my best buddy Chucky Chocky didn't find pineapple swipe, he found pineapple field poison. Lucky was weed poison instead of rat poison or whatevers because that stuff don't only work on rats. And lucky was in a hole next to a leaky irrigation ditch because the stuff was mostly watered down after all those years of rusty bottle caps. And lucky we passed out before we could drink some more or else we would have probably passed out forever. Wait, what?

Wow, I was lucky.

Lucky to be nursed back to health by you, Wanita.

"You sound like you're getting better."

"Lucky I not blind because then I couldn't see how beautiful you are, Wanita."

She yanked out my dick tube right then and there and I had to go bathroom by myself after that which was fucking sore, sore, pissing pebbles shetting bricks sore, to tell you the truth. No more little ass wipes from Wanita any more. And I loved those Wanita wipes. I should have kept my damn mouth shut.

CHAPTER 12

AFTER THE HOSPITAL, THEY TOOK ME BACK to the halfway house. I thought maybe was gonna turn out that I had to go jail or mental ward or something, but I guess if you funny enough they never think you're full-on crazy and drinking couple gallons pesticide you mistook for pineapple swipe ain't criminal enough to score one of the few available beds in prison. It's almost like a competition to get in. So, what you did? Sneak out and try get drunk? Ah, that's nothing. I got a guy here who did armed robbery at the old folks nursing home during broad daylight afternoon bingo. Sorry, brah, you not bad enough. You only Bad Lite.

When I got back to my sofa, I was pretty much Da Man around the guys in the house. They all wanted to hear my war stories.

"So how did you get out?"

"Uh, pop the lock on the door."

"Oh yeah. But how did you get over the gate?"

"Uh, climbed it."

"Wow! How did you do that?"

"I dunno. Hand, hand, foot, foot, get to the top and swing my ass over. Pretty standard."

The dude with the sideways mohawk, Ricky, was angling to be my new amigo. He was getting me juice and giving me cigarettes like he was auditioning for the job. Couple times I caught him running his hands over my hair like maybe he wanted to make us look like twins and I told him back off, asshole, no even think of mowing my hawk.

House manager Sonya was keeping a special eye on me. I could tell she thought I was good looking and was checking me out to make sure I wasn't really mental. I don't think she would ordinarily give any of her full-on crazy clients a chance, but me, my only crazy was crazy in love, Sonya baby. Aw yeah.

But then I got pills in my paper cup.

Shet.

I told myself that's OK because it didn't mean I had a diagnosis or nothing. They just didn't want me running out in the middle of the night drinking things I find in the bushes. I could understand that.

The pills made me so sleepy I couldn't sleep. They made me so calm that it pissed me off. All I could do was lie on the sofa exhausted and agitated and too futless to do anything about it. I could sleep all day but I couldn't go sleep. I wanted to punch somebody's head but I couldn't lift my arms. I felt like I might as well give up and die but that would take too much effort.

Couple-three weeks of this Night of the Living Dead, Day of the Deaded Live, and Miss Sonya decided what I needed was a job.

And I was thinking, job? JOB? I thought this was a halfway house. Job isn't halfway. Job is all the way.

She told me I get to keep the money I make. I was like, shoot! Maybe I can buy some real pills that will let me sleep through all their crap pills.

She gave me a list of options. Companies nice enough to hire mental people. Most of them I already applied when I was living at Doreen's place, but maybe if I mention the mental designation, I might have a foot in the door and a mental leg up. Plus, if they catch me slacking off, I can always pull the "Oh, sorry, eh? Hard time cuz I mental!" excuse. Even though I not mental. Because I not mental. I think. But I was so confused and futless I wasn't even sure.

I looked down the list: food service, food service, food service. Oh here's one: food service. I pictured myself in the puffy white chef hat like my main can man Boyardee pouring wine and sweet talking rich tourists.

Couple of months flipping mahi burgers and I could open up my own restaurant, House of Bobby, where my speciality of the house would be Bobby Burgers made just the way my gramma used to make 'em with more breading inside the patty than in the bun and a squirt of watered down ketchup to drown the taste.

Sonya popped my chef balloon. She said food service for us clients pretty much means washing baking pans and carrying sacks of potatoes from the back freezer. Been there, done that, didn't work out.

Then I seen this other one. Looked like they been searching around long time for the perfect guy because the listing was from last year. High energy personality needed for public relations position. I was thinking, that is so me! I get great public relations! Whenever I go out someplace, I'm always "Hi! How you? How you folks doing?" to all the people I meet. Everybody loves me! I'm a people person.

I told that to Sonya. I told her, "Me, I'm a people person. I cannot be in the back chopping onions and shet. This the job I want!"

She said they don't let the clients chop onions because of the knives.

Well, good, because I not cut out for chopping onions. Get it? Cut out? I was too drugged out to even laugh at that one.

OK, Sonya told me. Tomorrow I go down Kahului on the Handi-Van with the rest of the lolos and when they go Longs, I go job interview at this nice restaurant called El Chocho or something that don't mind hiring crazy people so long they don't piss in the beer or whatnot.

After that big song and dance for Sonya, I had to go back to my sofa and sleep for couple hours. I was so tired putting on like I excited to go work. How I going work when I'm so tired? I figure I gotta cheek my meds tonight or I never going impress the boss.

Sonya caught me holding the pill in my mouth. I thought she was going torture me or come after me with a tranquilizer shot and a big-ass needle, but no. All she did was say super-mean, "Swallow that pill!" and before I could stop myself, boop! The thing was down my throat and I was getting comfy on the dog-stink pillows and settling in for an 11-hour night of watching the ceiling.

Next morning, I got dressed up in my friendly friend Fujinaka, which, I took notice, was so tight only the top two buttons could reach to their pukas. I gotta make me more pukas.

I went to comb my hair in the mirror and fuck me, I forgot no more mirror. So I tried to just comb 'em by feel and I don't feel nothing. My bangs was gone, my bushy part in the back was gone, I was feeling breezes on my scalp that I never did feel before. I started slapping around my head and shetty shet shet. That fucker Ricky mowed me while I was sleeping. I had one big strip of fuzz going straight across my head from one ear to the other like one hairy Miss Maui tiara. One of my ears was bleeding where he nicked me with the . . . fuck, I cannot think what he used to shave my head. Not supposed to have razors in the halfway house.

Potato peeler. That sneaky bastard balla-headed my head with a potato peeler.

I was going kill him, but when Ricky seen me come outside into the parlor, he looked so proud and happy just like he was going cry a happy cry. Killed my fight right there to see him look at me with those adoring bufo eyes.

I figured what the hell, he mental. Let him have his fun. Maybe I could borrow the potato peeler later on to take the rest off. Go bowling ball. Start fresh. But first, I had a job interview.

I got on the Handi-Van with the rest of the guys in the house. Took for-fricken-ever to get loaded into the van because, not to sound too mean or anything but those bastards walked like the spooky guys in the Thriller video. Step-drag-step-drag. Hurry it up, Michael Jackson. I can scare you more than any ghost would ever dare to try.

So it turned out this El Chocho ain't no fancy white tablecloth joint. It's the kind of place where tourists are supposed to drink so fucking much they don't realize they paying $35 for two Taco Bell specials. Turned out the interview was like "You're here. Great. Get in the back and change clothes."

And wow, turned out public relations isn't saying howzit to people at the door and telling them to come in and have a seat. It ain't even sitting in the back office making plans about how to get more customers. Public relations was wearing the big taco suit and dancing around like a fucking fool on the side of the road waving at cars.

If I wasn't so doped up I would feel insulted. But with all the pills Sonya was giving me, I was just mostly numb with a tiny bit of pissed off that didn't really matter because I was too fucked to do anything about it.

Took me about 40 minutes to put on the taco suit. I didn't know where my head was supposed to stick out or even if WAS supposed to stick out. Does tacos have heads? Best guess, Bobby, best guess. I put my head through something and zipped. I went outside and Marie the sassy waitress laughed all sassy and told me it was upside down.

Upside down? What the fuck?

"So like my head is where my ass supposed to be? Then why is there a hole there?! Not like I going be wearing the big taco on the crapper if I gotta take a dump."

Sassy Marie just laughed and laughed.

I went in the back and tried again. When I zipped up my taco this time, I had one leg, one arm in the same hole both sides. Looked something like a army camouflage spider with my lettuce hanging out.

Sassy Marie told me look, stupid, you not supposed to wear the taco vertical. This one horizontal taco. And I was like how the fuck should I know. I don't eat French food.

When I finally got my taco on right, I was so worn out I was ready to pau hana, clock out, and go home. Shet, but, my waving shift had only just begun. I was able to stall through about an hour of it on the front end, but the rest of the day was gonna fucking drag like a mahu in a muu.

OK, that one was pretty funny, but probably only to me, and I couldn't laugh because that would take too much effort. Ha. Ah, no work. I was so loaded.

So I went out on the sidewalk next to the street and started waving at cars.

"Hi, howzit. How you? Oh, you folks hungry? Well, then eat me. Come eat over here. Hey! Hey you! Yeah, you. Come eat over here. Good the food. Not like they let me sample or nothing, but they told me it's the best in town and I believe. And look at me, I not the type to believe stuff that ain't true. Just because I'm a grown man standing here in a taco suit doesn't mean that I don't know what is what."

"Hui! Come! Come over here, goddamn it. Try a taco! Come on, just try! Try a taco! Eh, lady, no act like you cannot hear me while you trying to roll up your power windows faster than the electric power switch can roll. Come here and eat me! Look my lettuce. So leafy, yeah? And my salsa. Make you like chacha dance, right? Come on, bitch, come over here and taste my fucking carne asada!"

Every 15 minutes the restaurant manager came out to tell me to jazz it up a little bit, act more animated. I was like hey, a cup of coffee wouldn't hurt. He made like the place had a policy about that. I was like yeah, I get one policy, too. I don't do no fucking River Dance in a taco suit without a little caffeinations in my veins, dig?

He made like he no comprende and I was like no act, Mr. Lester Shibata, born and raised Wailuku Heights. I heard you speak English already.

Lunchtime, Sonya brought me a sandwich and more meds.

I was like, wow, Sonya, I can barely stay awake on what you gave me already. I no like fall down on the job.

And Sonya, no compassion, eyes rolling, heard it all. She said, "This was ordered per your charts."

And I was about to argue back when she gave me the "Bobby, swallow your pill" and like a pansy dog, boop, I did just like she told me.

I was so plowed with those pills, I think that's why I ended up holding onto the windshield wipers of the Dodge Dart for a couple of miles before the car finally came to a stop. If I was totally straight, I would have let go after the first intersection.

Middle of the afternoon, my high was so high, my low was so low, I was staggering around the sprinklers and windblown hibiscus in the median strip yelling at cars about how carne asada is just a fancy word for hamburger. People were honking at me and telling me to get off the road and I was yelling back, "Not me, YOU! Why you driving on my median strip? That's MY median strip!" and they was driving so close they drove off all the hibiscus bushes and only had asphalt and lines. Sad for my little median strip oasis.

My taco suit was so fucking hot and my sweat stains was making me look like a very greasy lunch. Parts of my shredded cheese was blowing off into the traffic and my sour cream was so fucking sour and brown.

I didn't see the lady coming because I was leaning over trying to pick up one of my tomato chunks and thinking, "Wow, this not even real! This tomato is just terry cloth material! Holy shet, somebody turned some old towels into a big taco and now they trying to feed that to the people. Soylent green is tacos! Soylent green is tacos!"

The lady didn't see me because the sun was in her eyes, because I was leaning over yelling at the terry cloth tomato and because she about 105 years old and because she had all kind ailments and medications that she shouldn't be driving already, although she never did admit that in the police report, from what I heard. People on certain medications not supposed to be driving. You would think somebody that old woulda known that one already.

And to think she tried blame me for her "accident." Hey lady, I get news for you! When somebody hit somebody with a car, the guy who got hit is the victim, OK? Sheesh, just mow me down, keep driving and then tell your lawyer that I the one caused you pain and suffering! How's that for DA NERVE, lady!

The whole time I was hanging on to the Dart windshield wipers, the old lady was screaming at me, "Get off my car! Get off my car!" She even turned on the windshield wipers trying to scrape me off like maybe I was a half-dead grasshopper stuck to her window and I was grossing her out.

She took me on a long ride all through Kahului, up Beach Road side, to Wailuku and back again. She finally stopped at the police station where she honked the horn until somebody came out to tell her to stop. Then plenty cops came out to have a look. Then they discussed if they should go ahead and call the ambulance since the hospital is just right up the road or should they make the lady keep driving to the emergency room. But then if she did, who would park her car? Or should we just drive her? Maui cops. So fucking thorough.

So finally one cop said listen, we'll just call the hospital, describe the situation and ask them what they like us do and about 20 minutes later, an ambulance came ambling down the hill, no lights, no sirens, no hurry.

The ambulance guys got out and they seen what had happen and boom, they started to get excited. They rushed over with the gurney and the serious faces. And what!? They checked the old lady! "Are you all right, ma'am? Can you wiggle your toes? Do you remember what day this is?"

And I was like, what the fuck, you guys! Me the one who got runned over here! Me the one bleeding all over the taco suit! Me the one with traumatic injury traumas! Hello!

After they took the old lady to the hospital, they waited around a while, had a snack, took a smoke break, and then sent the B-team to come peel me off the Dodge.

They had to cut me out of the taco suit. The good thing was that it was a puffy taco suit so my injuries could have been a lot worse without all that fake terry cloth lettuce padding. The other good thing was that all the blood-looking stuff everywhere was mostly the fake taco sauce and my sweat.

When I got hospital, the nurses was asking me if I needed anything for the pain. I was thinking that's a trick question. Why, what pain? Did something happen? That's when they started on the "Are you on any medications, prescribed or otherwise?" action and I was so proud that for the first time in my life, I could say, "Oh yes. But it's ordered per my chart." The nurse looked at me like yeah, right, and I told her, "I promise. I'm legal."

And then they peeled the rest of the taco off me and tried to cut off my Fujinaka. Save the shirt, fellas. That's my lucky shirt.

They had the nerve to laugh at that one and I wasn't even being funny.

CHAPTER 13

WHEN I WOKE UP IN THE HOSPITAL after surgery, I had a fat angel watching over me.

She was patting my hand and telling me everything was going to be OK.

Wasn't Wanita, because Wanita asked to be taken off my case the last time. Something about me being too friendly with her. I figured she had some feelings for me that were getting in the way of her professional duties. I felt sorry for her. Hard to be in love with your patient if you a nurse. I would have worked it out with her, but. We could have waited until I was cured and then taken our relationship to the next level. Just sponge baths and heavy petting while I'm in the hospital, but later when I'm healthy, more, Wanita, so much more. But Wanita chose to go her own way, to sacrifice her love for me for her career. Sad. I must have broke her heart. I should send her some flowers. I should steal her some flowers.

So there was this fat chick sitting next to my bed, head bowed down on the sheets, hand squeezing mine, crying and praying and Ay Jesusing.

Corina? No tell me you got fat and religious on me.

Oh, no, wasn't Corina. Was . . . wait, I knew this face. I knew that nose. Wide, double wide, triple E, stretching from one side ear to the other. I could see that nose through the fogs of my post-surgery anesthesia. The widest nose I ever seen, wider than even mines.

Sister Taysha!

She Ay Jesused a bunch of times and kissed her fingers.

"Bobby! You alive! Ay, I thought . . . I no like say what I thought . . . but I thought you was ready for kick already!"

Sister Taysha with her big nose and kind words.

Come to find out I got two broken legs, a broken arm, a ruptured spleen, and a cracked pelvis.

That last one had me worried. Cracked pelvis? Is that the same thing as broken dick?

Taysha told me no, the pelvis part is more ass-related and the dick part is on its own.

Hoooo. Sigh of relief right there.

She told me that I get pins and plates in my legs and now I might ring the metal alarm when I go courthouse and I tell her, well, they usually wand me down and make me go through the back door anyways but why, I gotta go courthouse for this? I wasn't driving.

She covered her mouth with her shiny maroon fingernails like she said something she didn't want to say.

"Ooopsie!"

Why, what?

Well, she never like say nothing and get me worried.

"Well, you already said something and I worried so you might as well say the whole something because that's pretty much the same effect."

"Well, the daughter of the lady came with their lawyer and they were making like you gave the old lady pain and suffering."

"Pain and suffering! I the one with the broke dick!"

"Pelvis. Cracked pelvis. It's different, I promise."

Took plenty coercions on my side and Ay Jesuses on Taysha's side, but she finally let out that the old lady's daughter said was my fault for jumping in front the car and they want damages for the old lady's medical bills and the big dent on the hood of the Dodge.

"Holy crap!"

"No say 'Holy Crap,' Bobby, that's taking the name of the Lord in veins."

"So how come you can say 'Ay Jesus' and I can't say 'Holy Crap'?"

"Because I lifting my troubles up to the Lord. You just making profanities."

"Can I say 'fricken crap'?"

Big sigh. I think she was either praying for an answer or praying for a new half-brother.

"Yes, you can."

"Mahalos."

"No thank me, thank the Lord."

"Mahalos, Lord."

"He the one with all the forgiveness and love and miracles. He the reason why you still here."

Mahalos Lord for making sure I was rip shet on tranqs when I got whacked by the old lady in the Dodge. You spared me that pain. Mahalos for letting it be an old Dodge and not a new BMW because even though I don't have bucks to pay for a piece of crap car, I sure as hell never in my life gonna have the dough to pay the bill on no BMW. Thank you for sparing me from that, Lord. Thank you for letting it be a sedan and not one of those big Maui trucks because the taco couldn't have protected me from that grill. Thank you and mahalo nui, Lord, for letting this happen while I was working for a restaurant chain under the care of a care home so that any liability that bounces to me will bounce right off and stick to those guys. They was supposed to be looking out for me, not sending me out to play shooting gallery in the street with me being the duck. Mahalos to you, Lord, for bringing my fat sweet half-sister Taysha to keep me company, cry on my hospital gown, and preach my goddamn ear off. I could have been resting here all by myself, dopey and peaceful and maybe, just maybe a little bit lonely but no, you sent good old Taysha my way and now my days and nights are filled with her attentive sisterhood. Who needs a big ohana when you have a born-again sister?

See, to tell the truth, this new fat Taysha chick wasn't nothing like the Taysha me and Doreen went to school with and avoided. We didn't grow up together because me and Doreen was mostly at our mothers' mother's house and Taysha, she hung with her own mother. Our mothers wanted to beef with her mother because of the fact that she screwed around with our father around the same time as they did up Kepaniwai. It was all, who dat bitch think she is, anyway? It was like she cut in line, even though it was a long, long line and all the girls got their turn.

And not like our daddy had any family reunions on his side. That would have been a fucking brawl. So we didn't see sister Taysha for family stuff.

Me and Dori used to see Taysha in school and we would fast run the other way. Taysha was trouble. Not fun trouble. Pest trouble. Always trying to bum cigarettes, always trying to get in on the latest jack, always trying to catch ride on the handlebars of somebody's stolen bicycle. She was skinny back then. Skinny and not too bad looking, but not pretty like Doreen because of the big-ass nose.

Now she had a big-ass everything and the weirdest thing is even her nose put on weight. Looked all bloated and puffy. Lucky thing the puka part was huge otherwise she would have hard time breathe.

The Jesus thing was new. She picked that up when her husband left her. She went through a rough time, she told me, but now her life was back together thanks to the Lord.

The Lord, plus Tony, this guy she met at the salad bar at Wendy's.

And I'm all, yeah right, you telling me you go the salad bar at Wendy's and she's like, shet yeah, they get all you can eat chili and rice and they keep the pudding vat full, too. I put on 20 pounds at that salad bar.

And I was smiling up inside because I made her say shet, so I knew she still had hope yet. Not like the old Taysha was all that great because, to tell the truth, she was needy and annoying. But this new Taysha was a pain in the ass, know-it-all, holier-than-everybody.

And then she told me about Tony. Tony is so this and Tony is so that. Tony is the moon and the stars and everything else, ay Jesus. And she told me all about how they going Vegas together this summer and maybe can I watch their house while they gone. They probably going get married up there but they still talking about it, and Tony is the love of her life sent to her by Jesus, ay Jesus.

And I was all, try wait. What you said about your house?

Oh yeah. She told me her and Tony have this house. Tony built the house by himself. He can do anything. He cook for her, drive her around, do her laundry. He is the sun and the rain and couple sparkly rainbows all rolled into one, ay Jesus.

But wait, back up about the me watching the house part?

Oh yeah, she said, well, they're going to Vegas and she was thinking that I could watch the place for them. There's a handicap toilet in the garage from when Tony's mother used to live there but there isn't any furniture because they had to bomb it for fleas after she died.

I was getting a picture of this Tony bastard living with his flea-bitten mama and now my fat-bitten sister and already I don't like this guy.

"So how you found out I was in the hospital? Had newspaper stories about my traumatic accident and miraculous survival or what?"

"Oh yeah," Taysha told me, "but nothing about you. Was only about the poor old lady and how scared she was to have this big taco flapping on the hood of her car like a marlin. Ay Jesus."

Ay Jesus was right. Me the big victim, me the big survivor, and all they get about me in the paper is me the big taco.

"So how you knew was me?"

I imagined my orange shorty muu gramma calling her. Maybe she saw I was hurt and she went to Doreen to tell her but Doreen didn't answer her psychic phone cuz she was at work and don't nobody call her at work, even on no psychic phone, and so Gramma had to go outside the family to my other sister. Taysha was the kind of chick who would answer the psychic phone no matter whose ghost gramma was calling. And she would stay on the line so long the ghost would get tired and hang up.

And as I was going through this scene of my mind with my gramma trying to get off the ghost phone with Taysha and Taysha trying to tell her about Jesus and my gramma arguing back, "Jesus?! You don't even know the guy. Me and him went out drinking the other night and he is fucking hilarious." I took notice that Taysha was wearing the same kind faded blue print pajamas that I had on.

"Whoa, Taysha, you got runned over by a Dodge Dart too?"

Fuck! I would hate to see the damage on that vehicle.

No, no, she told me. She was in the hospital because they had to remove another toe.

"Another toe? How many you had removed before?"

Two, she told me. So now, three total. Seven more to go, Ay Jesus.

She held up her foot high as she could, which for her was only a couple inches with all that leg fat holding her thigh in the wheelchair. The bandage on her foot was as big as a coconut.

"I caught diabetes," she told me. "It's genetic. Runs in my mother's family. Nothing I can do about it."

She shrugged her huge shoulders, two ham shanks sitting on the sides of her head, like "Oh well."

And I was thinking, yeah, nothing you can do about it except eat a fucking carrot every once in a while and kind of lay off the pudding vat at Wendy's, whatchoo think?

Taysha was going on about how hard it is to have a chronic disease that you can't do nothing to cure and how wonderful Tony has been taking care of her, driving her to appointments, cooking for her, giving her sponge baths.

And all I could think is shet, that must be a big fucking sponge. Like the size of a mattress.

When Taysha wasn't talking about Jesus, she was talking about Tony and after a while I had hard time telling the two of them apart. They was both so perfect according to Taysha. Lucky thing I was on heavy medication so I could sleep through most of her visits.

I was in the hospital couple days until they was sure I was done with all the internal bleedings, which pretty much meant I had to shet in a little plastic hat so the nurses could look to see if any blood was coming out of my ass.

I hated that little hat. Ay Jesus I don't ever want to get the mean shets disease. Shetting in a hat so they can look for blood was close enough.

Taysha and seven of her toes went home before I did, but she still made Tony drive her back to the hospital every fucking day so she could sit by my bedside and yak yak fucking yak. Mr. Mystery Man didn't come up to say hi, but. Jesus is always with you but Tony got stuff to do.

Taysha sent Tony over to the halfway house to get my stuff. He picked up my clothes, my jail toothbrush, part of my broken woodshop ukulele, and a bunch of socks that don't belong to me. Oh, and get this. I asked and he actually got my sofa, too. Reunited. Mahalo Tony. I don't know if you perfect but you picked up points with the repo action on my behalf.

Taysha took home my bloody Fujinaka shirt and Tony got most of the stains out. He mended it and ironed it, too. She brought my lucky Fujinaka back to the hospital so I didn't have to wear the hospital pajamas to go home.

I knew that shirt was lucky because I was alive and I had a sweet sister willing to let me live in her house on our mean sister's old sofa.

My last day in the hospital, I was sitting on my bed eating a small slush float I made with Jell-O, crushed ice, and coffee creamer, and this little old lady shuffles into the room holding on to one of them walkers with the tennis balls on the bottom. She walked with only the bottom part of her legs, with these tiny marching steps from her knees to her feet. I was thinking was going take her five hours to come inside the room and that's a show I didn't wanna watch.

I finished my slush float and told her, "Howzit."

She was staring at the floor but when I told her "Howzit" her head came up super slow like one of those big turtles.

"You looking for somebody? You looking for your room? What?"

No good start a conversation with an old lady in a hospital. Next thing I knew I was getting the whole 20-minute list of everything that was wrong with her. She kept repeating some of her favorites over and over again. I think I heard "perforated bladder" about five times. Maybe that's the old lady version of broke dick.

I tried to jump in with questions to get her back on track.

"So, you getting better, right?"

"Oh no, every day, little bit worse. Of course, it's been this way for years."

Thanks lady. I really needed somebody like you to come in here and tell me that life is fucked and then you die.

"But you going home soon, right?"

"Oh no," she told me, "I'm just waiting for a space in the home."

Ho, bummers. I know what that's like, Aunty. All I going tell you is when you go sleep at night, protect your head. I pointed to my sideways mohawk.

But Old Aunty wasn't too interested in my struggles or my hairstyle. Or else she forgot her hearing aid in her room because she was going on and on like she was giving a speech.

Blah, blah, fucking blah. You name it, she had it and she wanted to talk about it. I was tuning out and wondering if I would be able to catch lunch at the hospital before Taysha and Tony came to pick me up. The hamburger steak was pretty tasty, though some salt would fucking help. And I was thinking about the mixed vegetables and fruit cocktail when something Old Aunty said caught my ear.

"Of course, since the accident when I hit the man, they won't let me drive anymore."

"Whoa, Aunty, what accident?"

"I hit a man in a burrito suit."

"Wow, what a coincidence. They should outlaw guys dressing as food and waving on the streets, no? Not safe. Me, I was in a taco suit when I got hit. Kind of the same thing, but not really."

She just looked at me, nodding like yeah, sure, Mister, I don't know what the hell you saying but it's my turn to talk again so shut up already.

And then I was thinking, wait, taco, burrito, maybe this was my car-bang old lady. Maybe I her food-costume victim.

"My daughter says the burrito was at fault, but I tell her no, no, it's me. I was the one driving the car and he was the one who got hurt. I got hurt too, but not as bad. And I tell my daughter, poor thing that man. I hear he's homeless and indigent. I should help pay for his medical care. I have the money."

What?! What am I hearing?! Jackpot! I could just check into this spa for the next couple months! TV mounted to the wall, laundry service, hamburger steak. I am home!

Then she said, "But my daughter says no, just leave him alone. He's not dead. You don't owe that guy nothing. He put himself in harm's way."

She nodded her head like she agreed with the bitch daughter. Shet, I was so sad from getting ripped off from the money that I couldn't feel happy that I wasn't going get sued.

A nurse stuck her head in the room and spotted the old lady. Could tell Aunty Old was a wanderer and they thought she was missing by the look of relief on the nurse's face. "There you are! Come back to your room now. That's enough visiting for today."

The old lady shuffled to the door and was almost out before she turned around and pointed a crooked finger at me. I thought I was going to get the "it was nice talking to you, young man" action but she told me, "My late husband used to have a shirt like that. He . . ."

But before she could finish, the nurse told her, "Let's go, Mrs. Fujinaka," and she shuffled away down the hall.

Chapter 14

TONY WAS THE WEIRDEST LOOKING DUDE I EVER SEEN in my whole life, and I seen some weird-ass weirdos, that's for damn sure.

Not to say that he ugly, because he not. In fact, he good looking in his own alien way and sometimes I caught myself thinking, eh, he's pretty sexy for a short dude.

Because let me just say that Tony is short. I don't mean 5'6" short. I mean big midget short. Like 4'10". Brown skin, blond Afro, one green eye, one brown. Try explain that one to me. Handsome but tiny. Him next to Taysha is like a peanut next to one elephant.

Heart of gold, though. Taysha was right. He the man. He made me wanna Ay Jesus every other sentence too. Ay Jesus, please let Tony have a sister and let her be mine.

Tony was a pastor of his own church. So cool. He got his own little worship group and he didn't even spend no time in prison or rehab. He was a straight-up good guy, not a reformed bad guy acting like he a good guy. I didn't know those kind guys existed.

I tried him out. Tried mention some of the names of the guys I knew inside who got out and did the "open my own church" scam to make money for their bad habits. Nothing. None of the names rang a bell.

He didn't even come to Jesus after a bad drunken driving accident or a mean divorce. Tony found Jesus after he got cured of nut cancer. How righteous is that? Jesus took away his cancer and took away his fears, he tells people. Amen. Jesus took away his left nut, too, but he don't mention that in casual conversations. But me and Tony, we had some deep conversations already and he opened up to me about his faith and his nut cancer and how Jesus changed his life.

I could picture that he used to be a player, little bit. Not like a major pimp daddy action, but like he had his share of chicks and maybe he had two one time, four one time, stuff like that. Not talking threesomes or fivesomes or shet like that. But two-timing couple girls at once. Leading them on. He had the sincere brown eye and the naughty green eye. Tell me, what chick can resist that?!

He didn't tell me none of that kind stuff but I could guess. Anybody that good looking had to have his pick of ass at the ass harvest. Guarantee.

But after the nut cancer and the sack surgery, his fuck around days was kind of over, from what I can tell. He had to take it easy. No spread himself too thin. Concentrate on a real relationship.

Of course, his most important relationship is with Jesus. He never let you forget that. Jesus made him the happy man he is today and he was there to spread the good news.

And I didn't mind hearing some good news now and then. Not like I had too much good news in my life. I liked hearing his preachings. Go down easy like a beer chaser after a pakalolo bong.

Tony had a full-on nice house in Waiehu. The place was always cool because that fast breeze come up from the ocean. The salt in the wind was little bit rusting the nails on the support beams. And the rain gutters. And all the door hinges and door knobs and screens and stuff. But other than that, the place was a fucking palace.

"Jesus has a real palace waiting and it's for you and for me."

"Amen, Brother Tony. But your house is still fucking amazing."

So get this—he had TWO bathrooms, one in the house and one in the garage! How nuts is that?!

Oh, sorry, Brother T. Didn't mean to take the word "nuts" in vain again.

How fucking sweet is that?!

He had three bedrooms in the house and a kitchen big enough to fit a kitchen table. He had one backyard with grass in it! Grass! Ca-razy!

Tony took care of his mother until she died. The fleas was from her dogs but they died, too. The dogs, not the fleas. But after the exterminator, the fleas, too. Tony had fixed up the garage for her with the pulley bed and put a high toilet in the garage bathroom. He said I could stay there until I was all healed up and even after that as long as I like. As long as I helped around the house and the church. Amen to that, Tony.

The cool thing was that his church didn't have no church. They met in the school cafeteria on Saturday afternoons after a hula halau had practice and the 4-H pau their meeting. He tried to book the cafeteria for Sunday but already had other churches making their services in there from morning to night.

So yeah, I told him I can help with the church. Like, what, pull out the big white Formica tables? Fold 'em back when pau? Shoot. I am there.

The Vegas trip they planning was for a Jesus conference. His church was very cool like that. Not like they going drink and gamble and fuck around up there. They just going go to the buffets and pray for sinners and maybe see a couple of shows and go shopping. That's what he told me, anyways. He didn't mention no nothing about them two getting married so I thinking that was just Taysha hoping to herself because, come on, if he was serious about getting married to my half-sister he would just do the wedding himself in the school cafeteria one Saturday afternoon, right? And who like really marry Taysha even if you half the man you used to be?

Tony helped me get settled into the garage where his mother used to live. He put Doreen's sofa in the corner by the little icebox even though he had the hospital bed with ropes in there. It gave me ideas of hoisting Corina up like a car on a hydraulic lift so I could check her engine. Heh, heh. Taysha said it's an old person's bed so you can lift up a leg or an arm for circulation or tie them down if they get nuts. I was like, eh, you don't have no neighbors who like to shave heads with potato peelers, right?

Taysha was all confused. She get that way when she don't eat enough because of the diabetes. She get that way when I joke around with her because I'm pretty fast. She not as fast as Doreen. Nobody as fast as Doreen.

I told her never mind, I just going sleep on my sofa. The tie-down stuff is too trippy.

Oh, and the bed could inflate, too. According to your fatness and where is the heaviest part of your body when you lie down. And I was like, gee, isn't the heaviest part of everybody's body when they lie down their ASS? And Taysha was like no, you would be surprised. You remember Genarra Franco in high school?

Oh yeah. The heaviest part of her body when she lies down would be her humungo chichis hanging off the sides by each armpit. I actually did witness that one time live and in person and it was something to see, I tell you that.

"You should try the bed instead of that old sofa," Taysha told me. "Might help heal the crack part of your cracked pelvis."

"Eh, you no mention my broken ass and I no mention Tony's busted nuts, OK?"

"His nuts not busted."

"Yeah, one was busted but they cut that one out."

"His nut is fine."

"Guys usually get two nuts. His one nut is fine but his overall nuts, they busted."

Taysha was getting all sad and upset already.

"I cannot believe you would talk about my Tony that way, after everything he did for you!"

I told her Tay, one thing I learning from Tony is that you have to live in the truth. That's why I no bullshit or exaggerate or tell big stories no more. Tony taught me that. So it's only right that if somebody say something I know isn't true I gotta correct 'em with what's right. And so in that spirit of the light I gotta say, and you know this, that Tony get some broken broke-ass nuts. Amen.

Taysha had to pray hard to forgive me but in her heart she knew I was right. Taysha was getting only half-love from her man. All of the loving, half of the load.

Still, the little broke-nut dude was the nicest guy in the world. He brought her flowers, took her to look at the ocean, and rubbed her feet after a hard day, taking his sweet time on all seven of her toes.

That's a man, I tell you. If I was a chick, I would be so in love with this blond fro little midget. Sometimes I wish I was gay. I would totally go for a guy like Tony. And Tony, if he was gay, he would totally go for a guy like . . .

AY JESUS! TONY IS MAKING ME GAY!

All that time in prison and I swear I never did think of no man like that and there I was with my broken ass and stash of meds dreaming of Tony when I'm falling asleep at night. The way he cut the crust off my sandwich. The way he fluff my pillow. The way his blond Afro glows like a halo in the bug light from the back porch.

That Jesus freak was making me a fucking fruit.

I was thinking gotta get my shet and hit the road or else I going fall under his green-eye spell. He only got one ball, but he had that green eye and that thing was dangerous. Sometimes I caught that sparkly, naughty eye looking at me and quick I had to focus on the safe, friendly brown one.

I told myself I going ask my gramma to come to me in a dream. Maybe give me some advice, tell me what to do in this situation.

Gramma showed up. "Fuck, Bobby. What now?"

I was like, "Wow, Gramma, how you got here so fast? I not even sleeping."

"You are sleeping. You just too stoned to know it."

"Oh."

"So you had a question or you just wasting my magic cigarette?"

"Yeah, so what should I do about this guy Tony?"

"This guy Tony what? He owe you money? Beef 'em."

"No, he super nice to me."

"Why, you owe him money? Beef 'em."

"No, anything he gave me he told me came from his heart."

"So what the fuck's your problem? My cig is burning and I tired listen to you talking bubbles."

"Something about him making me mahu."

"Yeah, and?"

My gramma didn't know how hard it is for a man to talk about this kind stuff with his mother figure person. But her, she never did cut nobody no slack.

"I—I—uh . . ."

"You killing me, Bobby."

"I thought you was already dead."

My gramma flicked her cigarette butt at me and it burned a hole in my holey shirt.

"OK, OK, all right already. I just going tell it to you straight. Ha!"

"What the hell that supposed to mean?"

"Oh, just one small joke. I don't know if you can catch that kind joke if you not alive and not loaded."

"Who says I not loaded?"

Oooh, Gramma! She always was my hero!

"So here it is. I falling in love with my sister's one-ball midget boyfriend."

"So?"

"So what should I do?"

"Fuck him."

"No, but the guy is super nice and treat me good and not like I get any other place to go right now."

"Yeah, so fuck him."

"Oh nah! What you saying, Gramma?! Fuck him like I should fuck him? Or fuck him like I shouldn't fuck him?"

"Like it matters. No tell me you never did fuck worse."

Gramma had a point there. She had more of those secret videos of me or what? Made me nervous.

But she didn't have the audio-visual part of her presentation this time and she was never one for giving no relationship advice. I had to sort out my man crush on my own.

"Laters," she told me. "Call me only if it's important. I busy." And she disappeared in her magic cigarette smoke. So fucking cool.

The next day, I was lying on the bed with the ropes trying to learn the ropes of the ropes, trying to get the hang of the hang, trying not to break my ass some more on all the pulleys and shet. Tony heard me banging around and swearing up in the garage so he came out to see if I needed help.

"Here," he told me, and he bent down by the side of the bed. "Let me turn this on for you."

SHET! SHET! SHET! SHET!

He was leaning over me so gentle and sure. Must be he knew how I felt. And me, with only my prison underwear on, the same one that started it all with Corina and the prick peek. Shet, guarantee he knew how I feel.

And then, VVVVVVVT! The bed started inflating and oh, oh, that made my cracked ass feel soooo much better.

"There you go. How does that feel?"

"Pretty . . . fucking . . . good . . . Tony."

I am so easy. He blew up my bed, I looked in his green eye, and I was gone. Take me, Tony. I am yours 4-ewa.

"You doing OK on the painkillers, Bob? Need some ice water?"

Oh Tony. Oh Tony. Ooooooh Tooooooony.

Fucking tease, he turned off the light and went in the house.

After that, I tried make friendly-friendly to Tony. I complimented his cooking when he brought me my dinner on a little tray. I said "Yes Jesus" whenever he said something that needs a "yes Jesus" at the end. I confessed to him bad stuff I did before time when I was younger and didn't have a cracked ass. I opened my whole heart to him.

I thought we had a nice little thing going on but damn it, I shouldn't have told him about the money I had in Doreen's sofa from Doreen.

"You have to give that back."

The brown eye was leading now, the serious one. I tried to look into the green one for the twinkle of "Nah, brah, finder's keepers! Whoo-hoo!" but the way he was looking at me, was only the brown one telling me, "You have to give that back."

"Yeah, right. If I do she gonna kill me."

"You have to do the right thing."

"Even if she kill me?!"

"You would rather live with the lie?"

"SHET YEAH!"

I told him fine, OK, whatevers, but at least let me wait until I can walk good because I gotta climb up those stairs to Dori's apartment so she can throw me out the window again.

Tony told me don't worry, he'd give her a call and tell her to come on by. Then we could all pray together.

I told Tony pass me my pain pills because my pain was coming back. He said he needed to go rub Taysha's seven toes so she could go sleep. That's not how I thought our night was going to end.

That fucking righteous motherfucker called Dori the very next morning first thing before she went to work. Right then, my pain pill-induced mahu crush on him just died. Fucking traitor.

Doreen came to the house straight after she clocked out from work, mad, mad, crazy mad. She figured was me the one who took her secret stash from the waterproof bag inside the toilet tank and she been wanting to find me, kick my ass, and get her money back all these months now.

What secret stash in a waterproof bag inside the toilet tank? I took this from your wallet.

I thought she was going to slap my face but she went straight for the electrical cord attached to the bed and yanked it out of the wall. The whole bed started deflating and owwee, was sore, sore, fucking sore.

"Where is my money, fuckhead!" she was screaming and screaming. Lucky thing it's so windy in Waiehu that none of the neighbors can hear her.

Oh wait, it's so windy in Waiehu that none of the neighbors can hear me. Shet.

I told her to go to the plaid sofa and dig around by the middle pillow, underneath by the springs part. She was digging and digging, up to her elbow in sofa and still couldn't find it and all I could think about was the bag of money she had stashed in the toilet. So who took that if wasn't me? Was it me? I get a little bit loopy sometimes. Maybe I did find it. Maybe I did take it. Maybe I spent it on all kinds of . . . essentials and I don't really remember doing it mostly because of the effects of all those essentials.

Doreen finally found the stash, which wasn't too much of a stash anymore because I had expenses and stuff. She was getting ready to kill me slowly when Pastor Tony came in offering to join us in a prayer of forgiveness. He gave Doreen the green eye of seduction, but in this case, Jesus seduction, but Doreen had immunity to that. She told him flat-out, "Fuck off, you little freak" and walked out the door with my money. Her money. Whatever. I was still alive.

Tony didn't save my soul, but he did save my ass. I loved him for that, just not in a mahu way. Fuck him. Asshole.

Late at night, I was lying on my sofa trying to comfort the cushions from the loss of the loot, and I heard something coming from the house. Boing-a-boing-a, ooh-ooh-baby.

Holy crap, Tony might be half a man but he's more than enough man for his woman and way too much man for me. Maybe his remaining nut ain't broken because he was totally curling Taysha's remaining toes.

And I could hear Taysha go, "Ay Jesus, ay Jesus, AY JEEEEESUS!"

Chapter 15

TONY WORKED A FULL-TIME JOB SELLING CELL PHONES in the mall so they could afford to go Vegas. Come to find out the church thing was only a part-time gig he did for the love of God. He didn't make money off the church, that's how perfect he was. He made his church service on Saturday and then he went work at the mall Sunday to Friday. If that's not God-like I don't know what the fuck is. But best of all, he could cook dinner like a motherfucker and he made me extra servings every night. I found my love for Tony again, even if he was a rat and I'm not mahu.

They for real was going Vegas to get married. They was going tack it on to the church trip so can write off the wedding like one expense. They was making their plans. Tony said he would do it himself in his cafeteria church, but Taysha had her heart set on one chapel wedding and all the cute chapels on Maui was all booked up with Japan Japanese weddings every single day of the year for the next three years. Taysha no like get married in a school cafeteria. I told her why not, maybe the school can make a buffet for the reception? Elementary school Tater Tots were the best.

Taysha tried to be holy but can tell I irritate her. Her middle finger is always twitching to flip me a "fuck off" but she resist, she resist.

Me, I didn't get to go to Vegas with them. Not like I was thinking they was going pick me to be best man, but I figured after all this time of living in their house, helping them with stuff, working through my disabilities to not be a burden on them, well, I thought maybe they would give me a little present like a plane ticket, a hotel room, and some gambling money.

Because to tell you the truth, things got pretty tight for me after Doreen took her money back.

Lucky thing I had my stash of painkillers because they pretty much took the place of my other essentials. Since I started back walking, I could crutch it down to the Mini Mart for my slush float. The hard thing was I had to eat it right there outside by the gas tanks leaning against the wall. No way I could do the crutch-swing-step dance up the road holding a slush float in my hands. I tried and it was ugly. My slush float didn't make it. My ass almost didn't make it. So I paid for my slush float every time and ate it right there. Not like I could slide past the register unseen. Hard with a cast from your ankle to your ass.

At least it wasn't Theresa's Minit Stop because if she was in between her oral surgeries, she would be busting on my ass even if I was straight up legit. The Mini Mart by Tony and Taysha's house didn't have potato wedges but they did have slush float and to them, I had a clean record. It was like I was moving forward in my life.

Warren came to visit me and see my new living situation. Tony brought us sandwich and juice on a little tray and told Warren all kind nice shet about me. Stuff about what a joy I was to be around, my warrior spirit, my undying faith, my struggle to heal. If I didn't know Tony better I would think he was majorly bullshitting because hey, I'm pretty cool but I ain't THAT great. But whatevers. Tony don't bullshit. He just don't.

Taysha was looking not-too-half-bad. Maybe was all that vigorous sexercise I heard every night with her and Old One Nut. Taysha said it was all water weight from the medications and pills and whatnot and she just pissed all that fat out.

Only chicks can piss fat out. Guys cannot. The fat would clog up our hose.

So anyways, Warren came by and he told me I was doing good. He asked if I was having trouble getting off the pain killers and I was like, nope, not a problem. Not a problem because I get like a two-year supply from working all the doctors, but I didn't tell Warren that part.

Warren told me the halfway house got closed down now and most of the guys who were staying there either had to go hospital mental ward or back home to their families. I was like yeah, I bet you was the mean shets disease because the way those fuckers would fly their spit and piss and shet around every night watching the TV behind the frosted plexiglass so dirty and old you cannot see nothing, well, was only a matter of time before some of that flying shet flew inside somebody's ham sandwich, I tell you true.

Warren told me no, they closed down because of me.

What the fuck?!

Hey, say what you like about old Bobby but I keep my shet to myself, pretty much.

Warren told me wasn't the mean shets that closed the place down. Come to find out, it was my accident. The Fujinakas suing the restaurant and the restaurant suing the halfway house. The halfway house was in trouble with the courts for putting me on the street in my condition. Me, I off the hook for-real-for-real. I might even be getting a settlement check for what I went through. Maybe two checks. Maybe three. Maybe the halfway house, maybe the restaurant, maybe Mrs. Fujinaka all gotta pay for my injuries.

I told Warren I would be happy to take the money, but not from Mrs. Fooj. Not like she not at fault here because that old bat fucking runned me over. Oh, she at fault all right, but I knew the husband and just like we family. I was willing to cut her some slack.

Warren told me her husband was a famous architect and they get tons of money.

I didn't believe because I seen that Dodge Dart.

He told me for real, they got one big house in Wailuku Heights. Old rich ladies always drive their same cars for, like, 40 years.

I was like, damn, I never did see up Wailuku Heights. Is it nice?

Warren got the look on his face like oh yeah, it's really fucking nice, nicer than one sad sack of working shet like me will ever see in my sorry-ass lifetime. His eyes were getting almost misty.

And so to make him feel better, I told Warren, "Well, OK, maybe I can take Fujinaka's money."

Warren popped out of his little daydream. He was probably imagining taking his three-times-a-day dumps in one nice bathroom with a view of Haleakala. Sorry, Warren, next time don't work in the judicial system. Get a real job.

"You should talk to your lawyer."

"What, No-Help Henry the Public Defender? I fired his ass during the trial."

"No, your civil attorney. Don't you have an attorney representing you in the accident settlement?"

Brother, in my world, you don't have a lawyer unless you got charges and I didn't have no charges as far as I knew about.

Warren said there could be a substantial sum of money coming to me and that I need to have a lawyer representing my interests immediately.

I was like, OK, send one down.

"We'll work on that," he said, which I knew meant, "You're on your own, asshole. I got stuff to do and craps to crap."

But Honest Steve Stevenson was happy to take my case.

I swear to God all I did was ask Tony if he could grab me the yellow pages phone book so I could look the pictures of all the lawyers and the next thing before I could even crack the book open to the "L" pages, Steve was knocking at the garage side door. Honest Steve could smell money on the wind like a shark smell palu in the water.

Steve said I get one very very strong case but it's very very good that I hired him because it's very very likely that the responsible parties will try to deny their responsibility to me for my very very significant claims and injuries.

I was thinking, yeah, sure. Try slow down, OK? You talk so very very fast the spit feels like it's raining.

Steve said I have to sign these certain-certain papers to make it legal that he's my legal representative and that I should read everything but it's OK if I sign now and read later because boy, yeah, there sure are a lot of long words in small print. Hardy har har.

Swear to God he laughed like that. Not "Ha ha ha" but "Hardy har har." Maybe they teach that in lawyer school so that you sound more polite than when you ripshit laughing out your nose, snorting and wheezing and whatnot like how most guys do, like "Bwa ha ha ha fuck snort hoo boy!" Like that. Hardy har har is more classy, I guess.

I told him gee, times is kinda tight for me right now with the accident and I cannot work and all. He can spot me now and I catch him with the payment later or what?

Steve told me don't worry. He will defer payment until the back end. Contingency, they call that. He won't get paid until I get paid.

That was the most beautiful thing I have ever heard. Steve was the best friend I ever had in my whole life.

Tony used to be the best friend I ever had in my whole life until he made me give back Doreen's money. He still cool and all that and I dig his cooking, but ever since the sofa money incident, he been catching me in my small harmless bullshits left and right. I cannot open my goddamn mouth without Mr. Pastor What's His Trip busting on my honesty.

I started telling him one good fun story about how when me and Taysha was small she used to always come with us Kepaniwai and we would swim in the cool mountain water together and catch opae and pick guavas.

"Taysha said you weren't raised together."

Fuck Taysha. I was telling a pretty story.

One time I was telling him about how my proudest day was when I graduated from high school.

He go, "Taysha showed me her class picture from that day and you weren't in it."

"Well, OK, so I took my GED, but I was pretty proud."

"Taysha said you still need to work on your GED."

"Yeah, well, I took the test."

"Taysha said you didn't pass."

Shet! Where was the compassion? Where was the understanding? Where was the love for a guy just trying to make conversation and bring a little hope into his own life? Fuck!

One time I tried tell Tony how when I was on the inside my father was the Man and because of that, I was the Junior Man and everybody treated me with respect. My father was the meanest criminal around with all his armed robberies, felonious assaults, breaking and enterings, and grand theft autos and whatnots.

Tony told me no, Taysha said our father lives in Lahaina and is a janitor at an old folks' home.

OK, now that was like blasphemy right there. Either Taysha is crazy or maybe we not related but everybody knows our father is Delbert Pacheco, the meanest mongoose on the planet.

Tony had to call Taysha to hobble into the garage and set things straight.

According to Taysha, there's two Delbert Pachecos. One is a bad-ass and one is a janitor at Hale Makule in Lahaina. The janitor one is our father.

"No fucking way."

"Yes fucking way. He was really handsome back in our mommies' day and he could sing, too. That's why he got all the girls."

"So the bad-ass one, what, he's our uncle?"

"No relation."

"Not even a second cousin or nothing?"

"We come from the singing janitor, Bobby, not the legendary criminal. I sorry, but it's true."

I wanted for call up Doreen and confirm what I heard but I was scared. Doreen would know the truth about our father but she would kill me if I called and reminded her I'm still alive. Maybe I'll call when my legs work good and I can run if she snap. Or maybe when I get some settlement money and can pay her back little bit, maybe then I go her house, drink coffee and ask questions about our alleged father. I just couldn't believe what Taysha was telling me. The singing janitor? And not one of us can carry a tune for save our life.

But somewhere in my gut, I had doubts. I used to look at the man I thought was my father in prison and I would think wow, I going grow up to be just like him. And the voice in my head would go, yeah, braddah, you full grown and you still six inches shorter than Pops, so try figure that out.

So there, in just one big swoop, Jesus wen give something and Jesus wen take something away.

I found out going get money for lying on my broken ass and doing nothing. That's good.

The guy I always thought was my father, the man I admired my whole life, turned out to be just another prisoner with a fat nose and a fantasy that his sown seeds made kids he didn't even know about. That's not good. That's sad.

Talk about a broken heart, but. I always did think of my father as this bad-ass ladies' man with a dick the size of his nose and the power to reload over and over again three, four, seven times a night.

So wait, Taysha, where you got the upepe nose from?

"You ever seen my mother?"

"Oh. Yeah. Right. Wait, what about my nose?"

"That's just bad luck. Sorry."

Man! Well, at least I get my big money coming my way.

Honest Steve said he would be in touch and that it shouldn't take too long. Like maybe a year.

A year?! Shet, I gotta wait one year? What I supposed to do while I waiting with no money.

Tony said Jesus will provide. Jesus always provided for him and I just needed to believe that the dude will be there for me, too.

I told him, "Yeah, while I waiting for Jesus to provide, maybe you can provide a little bit on his behalf."

Tony thought I was worried about the time-on-my-hands waiting part. Fuck that. I can wait for the rest of my life, no matter. But waiting without money and the comfort money provides, that sucks shet.

Tony had this great idea that I can help him in his ministry. I can go with him to people's houses during one crisis and pray with them. I can counsel people going through hard times. I can lead the youth group in car washes and sing-alongs.

And I was like, shet, you cannot score me a gig with the cell phones in the mall?

Tony thought I was just joking around about that. That's the junk thing about being such a funny guy like me. When you like be serious, everybody still think you playing around. Sometimes being hilarious no work in my favor.

So I got stuck doing all the Jesus jobs during the day while Tony was cruising in the mall talking to people about how much minutes they get on their plan.

I couldn't drive yet because my leg couldn't bend and Taysha not supposed to drive on account of the missing toes because she doesn't really have feeling in her feet. I guess you cannot drive too good if your feet don't feel.

So instead of actual home visits, I had to answer Tony's church line phone and if get members that like get counseled or prayed on, I gotta talk them down off the building and tell them come to my crash pad in his garage.

How bad can that be, right? All I had to do was lie down on the couch, tell them take a seat on the pulley bed, they tell me their troubles, I tell them Jesus cares. It was like having visitors. I like visitors. I am a people person. I'm a good listener.

Except nobody was calling, so Tony told me get the church phone list and start reaching out. He wrote me a script. All I had to do was remember to put in the person's name in the blank part so that I don't say, "Hello Mr. or Mrs. Blank" because then they could tell I was just reading from a card.

I remembered to say "Mrs. Robello" instead of blank, but she still wasn't into my action.

"Yeah, what you like?"

"I'm Brother Bobby from Pastor Tony's church. I was calling about your prayer request from the other week."

Big pause . . .

"Why, what?"

"Well, I thought maybe you'd like to talk about the request you were praying for."

"No, I no like."

"Didn't you put a prayer request card in the box at the church service last week?"

"Yeah, and I put twenty bucks, too, but what I praying for is between me and the Lord. I don't need no nosy buggers praying to Jesus on my behalf."

She hung up on me! I couldn't believe it! She better not let me see her in church on Saturday or she gonna need some prayers, I tell you that.

The next three calls didn't even answer. Only answering machine. I hate talking to those things. I always mess up and end up going, "Fuck. Never mind. I call back later," and then I too shame to call back later because I said fuck on the recorder.

I never did in my life have one answering machine. Maybe when I get my big money, I'll buy me one. Not like I get plenty people trying to get in touch with me but you never know. I no more phone now, how do I know who like call me? I want to make a message that says, "I'm sorry but Bobby can't come to the phone right now." Is that cool or does it make me sound like I'm taking a shet? See, I don't know this kind stuff. So many things yet to learn in this big free world.

The number seven call I made was the jackpot. I was calling for one guy name Caesar Munoz but a chick answered and could tell that she was crying.

"You OK?" I was hoping, hoping, hoping.

"No, not really." All right, she was nibbling on the bait.

"What's wrong?"

Big sigh. Oh yeah. Come to Bobby. I mean, come to Jesus.

"Nothing really."

Coy chicks piss me off.

"No for real, you can tell me. I'm Pastor Bobby from the church."

"Oh. From the church? I never did go to that church. I know Caesar and his mom go, but I always work on Sunday."

"We get our church on Saturday."

Ho, that broke the floodgates.

"Every Sunday he go out dressed all nice and he tell me he going church!"

"Maybe he fucking another chick on the side," I said, all helpful.

Ho! Cry! Scream! Cry some more!

And then stop.

"Wait, you a Man of God. You not supposed to say 'fuck.'"

Ho, I liked the way she said "fuck."

"I'm sorry. What you said?"

"I said you not supposed to say those kind words, right?"

Damn it, she was teasing me.

"What kind words?"

"Swear words."

Come on already! Don't lead me on. You said it one time before, say fuck again. Oh please oh please say fuck. Say fuck!

"What particular swear word you thought I said?"

Pause.

"I pretty sure I heard you say 'fuck.'"

"What was that? I didn't hear you."

Long pause.

"Hello? Hello? Ma'am, what did you say you thought you heard, please?"

Pause.

"Fuck you, weirdo. I ain't playing your sick games. I'm not stupid."
And she hung up the phone.

That night I told Tony I helped a young woman work through her anger issues that she had from her rocky relationship. I told him yeah, by the time she hung up the phone, she rediscovered her self-esteem. Good, eh?

Tony told me I did a good job.

I told him no ways, was Jesus.

Tony told me, "Amen."

Next day, same thing. I called a bunch of people who no like talk to me. I talked to a bunch of people I no like listen to, then I called Caesar Munoz's chick to see how she doing.

"This not that freak from the church, right? Father Bob or whatever?"

"Bobby. Just call me Bobby."

"Yeah, well, go to hell, Bobby."

"Can I ask you something?"

"No"

"Can I ask your name?"

I cannot explain, but I felt a connection to this chick. I could listen to her tell me to fuck off all day.

Just then, a miracle occurred. I heard the boyfriend's voice in the background calling her name.

"Sonya! You busy? You can come scratch my back?"

"Miss Sonya?"

Long pause.

"Bobby from the halfway house?"

Ho! This was the best coincidence of my whole life!

"Yeah! Sonya! It's me, Bobby! Wow, this is unreal. I gotta tell you, I think about you every time I take my pain pill. I really do."

Got pretty quiet on the other end. Keep going, Bobby. Keep it flowing.

"You always took care of me, even when you was mean. I know you really cared about me and that's why you was the way you was, all cold and hard and mean and stuff. And I tell you what, the way you used to yell orders at me and make me sit up, beg, and roll over like a dog, wow, that got me so hot."

Very quiet. Only breathing.

"You probably heard about my accident that day and maybe you feel responsible because you partly are, but let me tell you my ass is almost totally healed and everything works good. Real good. I would be happy to show you if you like come on down and check it out."

Deadly quiet. And then a deep breath.

"Bobby, do not call me again."

And she hung up.

When she said no call her, she said it in that voice that I had to obey. Was a total kill-joy. I would love to see her again, have her check out my wounds, show her the ropes on the bed. But she spoke and I must do as she says. She probably planted some kind mind control device in my head when I was sleeping. Yeah, and I was blaming the mental guy for shaving my head with a potato peeler. Was Sonya the whole time! Oh, she better watch out because I telling Honest Steve to add her name to the top of the list of people who owe me money because she the one who was forcing the pills.

Get some alimony from Caesar while you can because you going be paying my broken ass for what you done.

Doing God's work was so fucking lonely.

Couple days of working the phones and I finally found a sucker willing to come over. Barry Izuka just lost his dog and was at home crying and yes, he would love to come over and share about it.

Share don't mean share when you talking about crying over a dead dog. Share means they talk and you just gotta nod and nod and look like you give a shet.

So there was Barry talking and crying and there was me, Bobby, nodding and making sad "I understand" eyes and after about two hours of this crap, I felt my meds wearing off and I ask him if he don't mind getting me a glass of water. I guess he took this as a sign that I tired and like him leave already because he stood up and apologized and said it's time for him to leave and I'm all no, no, please stay. I am so enjoying your long, long, very long-ass story about your stink dog who was shetting and puking all over your house for the last six months and oh yes, I do agree, that is totally unconditional love when your dog has some mean dog shets and you let her sleep in your own bed. Yes, Barry, you are one kind motherfucker, I give you that.

But Barry said no, no, I should be going. I've cried on your shoulder enough.

And I was thinking fuck yeah but I'm saying oh no.

And then—you wouldn't believe—I didn't believe—Barry pulled out a hundred-dollar bill, pressed it in my hand and told me I'm doing God's work.

And then he split.

And I was like holy crap, all I gotta do is listen to loser sob stories while I'm lying on my sofa and people will actually pay me to act like I interested? Bring it fucking on!

I mean, not like I would ask for donations. That would be different. That would be wrong. All I was going do is listen and help. Listen and help.

So I made more calls. I booked my days. I had people telling their friends and referring me to other losers. Sometimes I had hard time stay awake, but I would think about the money coming to me and I would say 'Bobby, wake your broken ass up. You have a job. You have a calling.'

Pretty soon I had a line out the door. I not even joking. The word got out around town that I had the gift of comforting the broken-hearted and I was drawing crowds. I was making bucks.

People would come in with all their heartaches and sob stories and I would listen and pray and give them my special healing blessing and they would leave so calm and happy. I never ask for a damn thing and they was piling money on me.

I heard all the stories of the husband cheating, the wife cheating, the daughter pregnant from the neighbor. Sometimes at the end of the day I would be so tired because all that negativity was going inside me like poison and if I never take a huge dump that day, I would keep their sad stuff inside me like a cesspool.

One day Taysha came in the garage hobbling with one cane. She had another toe threatening to go bad on her.

She started yelling and screaming and kicking people out and threatening to call the cops.

I was like, "What, Sister Tay?"

And she was all "No fucking 'Sister Tay' me! You selling drugs in Tony's house!"

No, see, I wasn't actually selling drugs. Taysha saw it all wrong. Some of my peoples, they was so upset I decided to share some of my pain pills with them. What you gonna do when somebody in front of you need help? You gotta help, right? That's what Jesus would do.

I was only doing what Jesus would do.

And yes, sometimes they gave me money, but that wasn't for the pain meds. That was donation for the church and as mahalo for my ministering. The money was for Jesus, Taysha, not for drugs.

Fine, Taysha tell me. Then give me all the money you made ministering and I'll deposit it in the church account.

"But . . ."

"Since the money was for Jesus and all."

Crap.

Whoever our father was, Mr. Jail or Mr. Janitor, he had some smarts that he gave Dori and Taysha but didn't bother handing out to me. I am just not as quick as those wahines sometimes and that sucks. That just sucks.

So that's how Tony's church got the new sound equipment so he no have to use the old karaoke machine to preach in the cafeteria on Saturdays. And now they can make extra money renting out the sound system for parties and high school dances and whatnot.

So was a win-win situation for everybody, even though I kinda lost out.

But I worried about my peoples sometimes, out there without any comfort from their troubles. It made my heart hurt to think of them. It made my heart ache.

So I took couple pills and went sleep. Amen.

Chapter 16

TONY AND TAYSHA WENT OFF TO VEGAS and left me in charge of house sitting their house. I never did hear of a house sitter. I guess so that's like a baby sitter for a house, except a house cannot steal six slush floats, lock you out, and barf all over the fucking creation. So this should be an easy gig.

I could walk pretty good by then. I wasn't hotsteppin' or break dancing, but I could get around without the walker and the crutches. Pretty much. I had to hold on to the walls sometimes and I was so addicted to the high toilet and the handlebars in the shower. That should be standard equipment if you ask me, especially if you're a heavy drinker or a recreational drug user. It makes the morning-after piss much less dangerous.

Taysha looked all pretty before she left. She lost all her weight on a cheese diet. Cheese is good for diabetics. She read that somewhere. Tony was always trying to make her eat, what, like vegetables and crap, but she told him she wanted to fit into her size 14 wedding gown so she was going be disciplined. Cheese and only cheese. Tony, he supportive and strict but when it comes to Taysha, he know when to fucking drop it so I got the vegetables and shet that Taysha didn't eat. Thanks, sister Tay. I got so fucking regular I could go through a roll of toilet paper in one day. Lucky thing got the handle bars by the toilet because my thighs were getting sore from all the squats.

I told Tony no worry, I take care his house like it was my own. Tony said he prayed on it and Jesus told him to trust me. And I was like, eh, thanks, Jesus. But why you had to pray for an answer, Tony? Don't you know me by now?

Taysha told me Jesus forgives and so does she, but she don't forget nothing so I better watch what I do.

After they left, I decided I should do a thorough assessment of the property. Tony showed me around before he left, but I wanted to do some deeper checking. See what's what.

So I went inside the house. Checked all the rooms. Made sure everything was secure. Open the fridge. OK, that's secure. Open the bathroom cabinets. Yup, secure. Look under the beds. Ho, that hurt my pelvis crack. They should be grateful to me for all the pain I endure to keep their house secure. Under the beds is secure. Check.

I was on a chair digging in the back of the top shelf of the hall closet when I heard the doorbell ring. I never did hear a doorbell ring for real in my whole life, only on television. The thing was loud! It scared me so bad I little bit more fell off the chair. I almost had recrack my pelvis. Shet. I don't want no pelvis replacement surgery. No ways.

I carefully got off the chair and went to answer the door. I thought might be the neighbors asking why Tony's car wasn't parked on the lawn or maybe even Honest Steve with my money, though nah, probably too soon.

I opened the door and I couldn't believe who was standing there, pissed-off look on her face, hand on her hip, little hand-made paper tickets fanned out in her other hand.

"Jorene!"

"Oh fuck. Do I have to run into every psycho on the whole island? Shet, I have the worst fucking luck."

I was so happy to see her mad little self I almost hugged her. But then I remembered that any reinjuries at this stage could mean permanent disfigurement. I saw that on TV recently and it was as if the soap opera doctor was talking straight to me.

"Hey, little girl, how are you?" I didn't try to hug her but I sent her an uncle hug with my mind.

"Fuck you, Uncle Bobby. I not nobody's little girl. I gotta sell cottage bread tickets. You gotta buy. You still owe Mommy money."

Not like she wanted to hang out and shoot the shet with me, but I did get her to tell me that she was selling this stuff for cheerleading so they could go to a special cheerleading camp and cottage bread is something they make on Molokai and ship over for sports teams to sell for fund raiser.

Wow, she said all this like it was common knowledge, like as if I was asking retarded questions.

"Everybody sells cottage bread for fund raisers for school stuffs. If you actually went to school, maybe you would know this."

"So who lives in the cottage? What, like Molokai elves?"

She looked at me like she was going yell.

"Are you fucking nuts?"

Wait now, me, I don't know too much about cottages and elves and bakeries. Seems like I saw a cartoon like that once. Is it something else? Fairies or some shet? The little guys with the pointy shoes and the saggy hats?

"Just go get money and give it to me."

Anything for my sweet niece. Jorene, she the best. She going college one day and I going watch her graduate and I going be so proud.

I had some trouble finding money. Tony left me little bit cash for "incidentals" but I didn't think cottage bread tickets was incidental, more like accidental because was an accident Jorene came to this house because if she knew I was here she would probably just keep going. My niece, she love me, but she don't like me too much.

So I had to do some digging around Tony's house. I already knew where there wasn't anything. I started on the places I didn't search yet. The crawl space in the ceiling, the vent above the stove, the toilet tank because I not going make that mistake again. Or did I take Doreen's toilet tank money? I still cannot remember.

I found Tony's stash in a shoe box at the top of the guest room closet shelf.

Oh my goodness.

Clearly I did not know the man.

He had stacks of $50s in there wrapped like a total drug dealer. He had some watches and jewelry, a nice jade pendant, some old coins, and wait, what is this in the small box?

Teeth!

OK, put that back. Worry about that shet later.

I went to the door and gave Jorene a handful of cash and told her to keep her paper tickets. This cottage already get enough bread. Heh heh heh.

Jorene told me her school don't want no drug money.

I told her fine, then give 'em back.

She told me no, she going to keep 'em and give 'em to Mama Dori for all her pain and suffering she went through being my sister and my cousin.

I told Jorene no worry, when my three big checks come in, that right there gonna buy Mama Dori a brand new house, a brand new car, and send all three kids to college, though Kennison get as much chance in college as I get in the Miss Maui pageant.

Jorene was about to tell me bullshit, I ain't getting no three big checks coming in and then she stopped, cocked her head like she heard something in the wind, and looked at me different. Yeah, who was whispering in her ear that I was really and for true going get rich? Gramma? That's you? Eh, no go telling nobody else, OK? I gotta see how much I getting and make up a budget before I go play Santa Claus around Wailuku with all my family and friends and ex-girlfriends. Because you know I get plenty of those. Speaking of, I wonder how Corina is doing? Every time I think of her my bite scar gets a little throb. I miss that girl.

Jorene got all serious. Doreen-kind serious. I got little bit scared.

"How much?"

"I don't even know yet."

"When?"

"The lawyer said might take a year."

"From where?"

"From the lady who runned me over with her car and the restaurant that made me wear the big taco and the halfway house that put me on the street all loaded."

Jorene, the future lawyer, was doing the math in her head. I so proud of that smart, salty girl.

"You get permanent injuries?"

"Gee, let's see. Rods in my legs, screws in my ass, one foot is shorter than the other."

"You could get half a million."

For real? I was thinking couple thousand would be 'nuff. Shet! I am so set!

Jorene was thinking so fast I could see smoke coming out of her ears. She pushed me out of the way and ran inside the house. I little bit more fell down and broke my ass and I was going yell, "Hey, chicky, watch it!" but me, I don't talk hard like that to my niece and my nephews. They like my own kids sometimes, that's how much I love them most of the time.

Jorene was in the kitchen and she was on the phone. Ho, her fingers work as fast as her mind because I didn't even see her press no numbers.

"Mama, this Jorene."

Holy shet! She was calling Doreen at work! Is she crazy?! Crap, I was thinking fuck, I disowning this fucking kid right now because I ain't going down for this action. She KNOW you never call Mama D at work. Not no reason, not no how, not even if the sky is falling, the dog is on fire and there's snow in Sand Hills. I was thinking if I should lock down the house and hide or just run for the mountains already.

"This is the biggest family emergency ever. You gotta come pick up Uncle Bobby right now."

I could hear the screaming from the other end of the phone and I was on the other end of the kitchen trying not to listen.

"For real, Mommy. He going be rich and if we don't have him locked up at our place, you know he's gonna fuck around and spend all that money and we not going get nothing."

I couldn't hear Doreen's voice anymore. She wasn't screaming anymore. She was talking. Talking soft and kind of secret like. And Jorene was going, "Uh-huh. Uh-huh. Yeah. OK. Yeah."

A cold chill ran over my nuts.

Jorene hung up the phone and turned to me super slowly. It was like I could hear the spooky music like in the movies right before somebody pull out a knife.

"Mama says you staying with us from now on. She coming to pick you up after work. She says I have to stay with you to help you pack your stuff. So where's your stuff?"

That stinking little brat locked me in my room and sat by the door. She watched me so hard I thought her eyes was going pop. How someone can go hours without blinking is scary to me.

I figured I had to create a distraction so that I could run away.

Not that I didn't want to live with Doreen and the kids-them, but the way they were making it, just like I would be their prisoner there until my three big checks came and then they would kill me in their sleep, bury me in the sand next to the building, and go buy a big house in Wailuku Heights next to Mrs. Fujinaka and leave my bones there with the kiawe beans and the bees' nests.

I was so sad for myself. See, money ruins everything. You only know your family really loves you when you don't have money. When you get rich like me, you don't know if they really like having you around or they planning to kill you off to get your stash.

I told Jorene I had to take a shower before we go. She said go right ahead, not like I don't stink or nothing. She already checked the bathroom and figured no way I could escape.

The window above the toilet was about two-and-a-half feet across, big enough for me without the cast, but I still had the cast.

What the hell. I had take off the jalousies. Hemo the screen. Got in the shower, ran the water all down my cast. Pretty soon the thing was melting like slush float in the hot sun and I scraped off strips of gauze and chunks of plaster and padding and all the various shet that fell there. I found one pen. I found some peanuts. I found a quarter.

I left the shower running and crawled out through the window bare-ass naked with my skinny hairy white leg and my fat hairy brown leg limp-running as fast as I can.

Ow! Fuck! Ow! Fuck!

OK, OK, OK, OK. No bend the knee yet. Do not bend that knee.

So stiff and sore, like a three-hour hard on. Story of my life.

I ran by the perfect lady's house. She always get her laundry hanging so perfect on the line, like a small army, all the pants one side, all the shirts together, all the underwear in the back. If I take some of her laundry, guarantee she going notice something missing. She organized, that's why. She has her system.

The other lady across the street, but, she hang her laundry any old kapakahi way. She don't have no system. All she has is clothes hanging all over the place on the line, pants mixed with shirts, panties facing the street. Go for it, Aunty. Do your thing.

She not going notice the khaki shorts and T-shirt I small kine borrowed from her clothesline.

Kind of too tight the shirt, but that's OK. Said something about a club or something, but I couldn't read upside down while I was limp-running.

The shorts was elastic waist, so the thing fit good. I was little bit worried was wahine shorts but naked guys limp-running down the street cannot really be fashion experts, was how I figure.

Jorene spotted me going down the subdivision road heading for the highway and she came running. She would have caught me but just then one car came around the corner and—see, now, this is how I knew I learned my lesson—I jumped on the hood before the thing could mow me down. Lucky thing Mrs. Fujinaka was going pretty slow or else I could maybe have gotten reinjuries. But she was cruising, driving to her friend's house to drink tea and eat cake and shoot the breeze about the Hongwanji cookbook fundraiser so she wasn't in no hurry.

Eh, when she got her license back? Who did the repair on the Dart? Look nice. No can even see all the dents she made with my body. Maybe wasn't even Mrs. Fooj. Maybe get more than one old lady in Wailuku mowing down ex-con drug dealers with their Dodge Darts. You never fucking know.

This Mrs. Fujinaka was screaming and driving around trying to fly me off the car. I held on to the windshield wipers as she drove through Waiehu, Waihee, turn around, Paukukalo, Beach Road heading to Kahului. I rolled off when she got near Kahului Harbor.

Maybe I won't be getting my Mrs. Fujinaka check after all. Then again, she never have no witnesses except for Jorene, and Jorene want me to have money so she can take my money so she going keep her damn mouth shut about what she saw.

So there I was in the bushes on the side of the road by Kahului harbor wearing ladies' elastic waist pants and a too-tight T-shirt that said "Wailuku Seniors Garden Club."

I kept walking more and more into the bushes until I got to the ironwood trees part. Had all kinds of junkalunka cars in there, dirty diapers, used paper plates, broken beer bottles, and all the rest of the garbage dump inside there. It pretty much smelled like shet. It pretty much smelled like prison.

That's when I heard the voice of my past calling out to me.

"Son, that's you or what?"

I looked inside the cab of an old Datsun and there he was. My father. My jail father, not my janitor father. He was lying down on one old pareau and smoking a meth pipe.

"Daddy?"

He made like he was going to get up to give me a hug but he was too relaxed.

"Come in, son. Welcome to my hale."

See, I knew he was my daddy. My daddy push drugs, not one broom.

"So what, you jumped the fence?"

"Nah, son. Parole."

"Get the fuck out!"

"Did my time."

I was so proud of my old man. Even though he got super fat and really old and living in a Datsun at Kahului Harbor.

"So why you living in one truck?"

He took a while to answer.

"Son, I think you will come to learn that life inside is easier than life out here."

That was fucking deep, I tell you. My old man is The Man.

". . . And that the real prison is within your own mind."

Wow. I needed to have whatever he's smoking because I wanted to come smart like this man.

We hung out the whole rest of the day. He shared with me his pork and beans, I told him about my big money that was coming, we laughed about old stories about my mother back in the days. Not like my father really knew her except for that one time, but she stuck in his memory all these years. Or else he was a good bullshitter.

Nighttime came, I thought he was going let me crash in the truck next to him. No, sorry, son. The cab is for me, the back is for Rusty. Rusty is his latest wahine, and let me tell you, they didn't call her Rusty because she get ehu hair. They called her that because she is rusty. She squeaked when she walk. She look about 200 years old. Poor Rusty. She needed a frame-off restoration.

So my sorry sore ass was on the hard sand with the toads and the mosquitoes.

I found my father. I missed my sofa.

Chapter 17

MY FATHER AND RUSTY DISAPPEARED DURING THE DAY. Those two was like cockaroaches. They never come out in the light.

My father and his chick didn't go out of the shade of the ironwood trees or the little cardboard house they had on the side. Too many years in prison and he no could enjoy the sun. I don't know what Rusty's story was. Maybe prison, maybe she was like a creature from a spooky movie where if she goes out in the sun she would melt or turn to dust. She was already pretty much dust as it is. Dust and rust. Same smell. Bad smell.

I was craving that sofa. Takes a lot to miss that fucking piece of fucked up furniture, but when you sleeping on rocks, you miss the hard sand. When you sleeping on shet, you miss the stink dog cushions. Something like that. Life is that way sometimes. For me, at least. I miss the bad when I get the worse.

Cannot go back to Tony and Taysha's house now that Doreen know what kind money coming my way.

So I went through my list of friends.

Barry Izuka would be perfect. He only sitting at home crying about his dog. What else he get to do?

And Chala. Chuck. Whatever my mango-headed best friend is calling himself these days. Chuckla would help a brother out if he still get his strength. Who knows how he doing after the pineapple field poison we drank to get high? Maybe he all brain damage and weird. Ah, not like he was all that with-it before. But he's strong as a truck. And I knew where to find him.

So I dug around the bushes to try put together a pair of slippers for me. I found one big kalahopper size 13 black rubber slipper with a mean fish design on the foot part. Right on! Perfect! OK, little bit too big, but can handle. Only about two, three inches extra by the heel part. He go.

Only the left side, but. I couldn't find the right. Crap.

I went through the bushes and what the fuck? Every forgotten, lost, and runaway slipper was left foot, left foot. Like was there a band of one-leg druggies hopping around the bushes at Kahului Harbor at night or what? Fuck!

Finally I found one right-foot side but was a chick's pink sparkle girlie slipper with a flower in between the toe part.

Shet.

Fit pretty good, but. That chick must have big feet. Or else this slipper no belong to one chick.

Shet again.

So there I was slip slap slip slapping up the road with one slipper the size of a boogie board and the other side all dainty like Cinderella. Mahu Cinderella.

When my three big checks come in, first thing I going do is buy me some good slippers.

I went Tony and Taysha's house first. I thought Doreen and Jorene would have gone through the place but no, all they wanted was money from me not money from Taysha-them. They rather be poor than rip off somebody's house. They rather jack brother/cousin/uncle Bobby than hurt sister/aunty Taysha. That's Doreen. She get her code of behaviors.

I found Barry's number in the church address book, the book I no longer supposed to have access to anymore but I going erase my fingerprints after, so long as I remember.

I called him up and told him come on down, pick me up, we got a job to do.

Barry still sounded all depressed. He been crying about that dog for months.

"I don't know, Bobby. I kind of busy."

"Bullshit you busy. You sitting around watching video of your dead dog. Turn off the TV and come pick me up."

Busted. I could hear him turn off the TV.

"So what are we doing?"

"It's a special mission. I tell you when you get here."

"A mission for Jesus?"

Ay, this guy. True believer, him.

I told him, "Oh yeah. We helping Jesus out. We going be doing His work."

Oh, Barry liked that one. He was up Tony's house in five minutes all excited about the mission for Jesus.

I got him to drive me to Chala/Chuck's place. Corina's place. Same place as Doreen's place but downstairs and more stink. This was a risky operation, this one, and I was scared but was daytime so hopefully Doreen working, the kids were in school, and Corina was out getting chicken lunch for Chuck/Chala while he watching TV at home.

I told Barry go knock on the door while I hide in the truck but he no more the balls for door knocking in a strange place. Something about traumas selling cottage bread tickets for T-ball when he was a kid. Barry is such a panty. So I tell him wait for me in the truck and keep the engine running just in case we gotta dig out fast.

Doreen's truck was gone. That's good. The windows at her place were all closed. That's good. Corina answered the door with Chuck/Chala right behind her. Crap. That one not so good.

Her eyes was on me like she was trying to place my face. Maybe she no even remember. She made fast-glance down to my elastic waist khaki shorts like she was looking for ID but if she no can see my dick I no think she can remember me.

I was sad. Relieved, but sad. How could she forget our night of passion, the promises we made, the way I begged her to stop biting me and then begged her to never ever stop.

"I looking for Chala."

She moved to the side so he could see me. Well, at least Chala recognized my face. He smiled super big and came and gave me the huge man hug-back slap combo.

And then he stepped back and started Samoan slap dancing. Swear to God I thought that's what it was. I was like, trippy, you working luau these days or what?

Corina told me the whole story.

Chala's mango grew. He don't talk like a Haole anymore. He don't talk at all.

So what about the slap dance?

"That's his sign language. He made his own. He telling you, 'What's up, asshole, long time no see. How come you didn't come see me when I was in the hospital after we drank all that shet?'"

"Tell him I was more fucked up than him is why I didn't go see him in the hospital."

Corina's hands were flapping around. No look so much like slap dance when she do 'em. Look more like slap ass.

Ay, shame on me with my Corina fantasies slipping out when I standing there talking to my best friend, her boyfriend. No class.

Now Chala was slapping his thighs and arms and making chops in the air.

"What Chala said?"

"He told me I no need tell him what you said because he can still hear."

"Oh."

Chala flapped and Corina watched. When he was pau, she turned to me.

"Chala says what the fuck you like."

"Tell Chala I need his help."

Flap, slap, flappa-flap flap.

"He says dumb-ass, you can talk to him directly. He can still hear."

He made one more hand motion in the air. Eh, I got that one.

"Fuck you too, Chala. It's good to see you."

Chala didn't even need to know what was up. I told him I needed help and that was it. That's how it is with best friends. No questions asked. Or maybe he was asking questions in Barry's truck because his hands was flapping hundred miles and hour and I had no fucking idea what he was trying to say.

We got to Tony and Taysha's house and I took Barry and Chala into the garage. As soon as Chala seen the sofa, he start laughing and shooting me the "fuck yous" with his hands. Barry was all nervous already. This was more action than he seen in years and there wasn't even no action yet.

"OK, so you know, eh, Chala?"

Chala nodded for "yes."

"Um, I don't really know, Bobby," Barry with big eyes, worried.

"We just gotta move the sofa, Barry, that's all."

I was thinking knock it off with the crazy flapping hands already, Chala. Look like you saying we gotta rob a bank or hunt for whales or some crazy shet. Just put your fucking hands in your pocket until I tell you to lift the sofa.

"So how is this helping Jesus?"

Chala made the international sign for "what the fuck??" which is pretty much palms up, eyes wide, head forward.

"Jesus doesn't need a sofa, Bobby."

I was thinking I should just cold cock him and steal his truck. Give him something to cry about besides that damn dog.

"No, Barry. You right. Jesus don't need a sofa. He got one nice cloud sofa up in heaven. But there's this guy who live on the beach and he need one sofa."

"Like 'the least of my brothers,' right?"

"Well, get my father over there, at least I think that's my father."

"No, like the least of Jesus's brothers."

"I didn't hear the part where Mary had more kids."

Me and Barry was going round and round. He knew his Bible, that's for sure. Me, I don't know shet but I know a twitchy fucker when I see one and I needed twitchy Barry to help hapai the sofa, tie it to the back of his truck and haul it down Kahului Harbor for me. So I was all into the philosophical discussions with him.

Chala, he was just enjoying the crazy conversation, lying down on the hospital bed, smoking a cigarette, pulling his leg up with the rope, down with the rope, up with the rope, down with the rope.

My Fujinaka shirt was lying on the bed right where Chala was putting his cigarette hand. I should have told him eh, try move your hand, that's the shirt I wear to go Mini Mart eat my slush float next to the gas tanks and I think so the thing is small kind incendiaries already. But ah, what are the chances?

And me and Barry was talking up, shooting the holy shet, him checking to see if my story about Jesus and the sofa was for real. Me, working all my brain muscles to convince this fucker to shut the fuck up and lift the damn plaid cushions already, we wasting time.

Chala was flapping and flapping and going like a fricken chicken but me, I was kinda tuning him out. I knew he was going help me with the sofa. No gotta work hard to win him over.

By the time I finally took notice that the garage was in flames, Chala was out the door and grabbing for the water hose. My Fujinaka was fully engulfed. I felt my heart pinching. My favorite shirt. I grabbed it and shoved it in front the stream from the water hose. I was so into saving that shirt that I kind of let the fire spread before I started to think about trying to put it out or calling 9-1-1 or whatnot.

Well, at least I saved my shirt.

I gotta save that sofa.

Barry saw me struggling to push the sofa out of the garage. He was totally frozen with panic. He little bit more pissed his pants, I could tell. I yelled at him and he came and started helping me push. I took notice when get something big going down, helps to have something to focus on. Me and Barry focused on that sofa.

Chala stopped trying to beat down the fire with his hands and jumped in to help with the sofa. If only Chala had a truck, he would be the perfect friend—super strong, funny, silent and with a hot chick who likes some action on the side but doesn't remember it afterwards. But Chala plus Barry plus Barry's truck equals perfect friend. For me at least.

While Barry and Chala were loading the sofa on the truck, I ran back in to get the stash of money I found in the closet. I took the whole thing, the cash, the jewelry, the little box with the teeth. Worry about that one later.

Then I took the water hose and sprayed down the flames as much as could. Just like when I killed the fire in one spot, the thing would pop up even higher in another spot. Chala and Barry was yelling at me to hurry up get out hurry up get out but all I could think of was shet, Taysha and Tony's house. But me and the water hose was like trying to piss out a hibachi. I dialed 9-1-1 on the melting plastic phone and ran to the truck.

By the time me, Chala, and Barry took off down the road, the whole house was totally on fire. Thank God I got my sofa, my Fooj and my money, Ay Jesus. I hope Jesus remind Tony and Taysha about that part about Him providing because they don't have nothing left. Shet. I hope to hell He provide.

Barry took us down to Kahului Harbor and we put the sofa next to the buss-up Datsun where my father sleep at night. I had all that cash with me so I told the boys eh, we go splurge. We go drive up Pukalani, find a pineapple field, and drink the weed poison. Chala was cracking up with that one. I mean, his hands was cracking up.

Barry said no, he had to get home and start with his chores.

I bet you this fucker still lives with his mother.

So we just went Kahului Minit Stop. (Not Theresa's one, and even though the girl working there was named Theresa, was a different Theresa. I think. I dunno. Maybe she got her teeth fixed.) We bought booze, all the potato wedges they had, and cigarettes to wash it down. Then we cruised around Kahului and picked up some other essentials. We went back to the sofa and partied until the sun was coming up over Haleakala and Barry said he had to go work.

Bye Barry. See you next time I need a truck.

Wow, did I say that out loud? That was rude.

Chala flapped his hands at me for "You always rude, motherfucker."

"I not. I get compassion."

"Bullshit," Chala signed with his Chala hand signs.

"Fuck you, Chala. If wasn't for your mango, you wouldn't even be interesting."

Chala thought this was the funniest thing he ever heard in his life and he laughed his ass off with his hands.

I crashed out on one end of the sofa. Chala took the other end. The two of us woke up sore neck, sore back, smelling like smoke and booze and everything.

Then Chala flapped me his big idea.

"Why you never rent one hotel room for sleep last night? You had the money!"

Shet. I don't know. I not used to having choices and when I get one choice to make, I figure it's my job to pick the wrong one.

At least I have the plaid sofa, a cardboard roof over my head and my favorite Fujinaka shirt, burned but still can wear.

And Tony's money. And the teeth.

Chapter 18

ME AND CHALA PARTIED SO MUCH that the whole next day was a blur. I think somebody brought us pizza. I think my father told me his life story. I think I found a right-side slipper.

Me and Chala partied so much that the whole next week was a blur. I don't think I slept for a couple days. I don't think I woke up for a couple days.

Me and Chala partied so much that the whole next month was a blur. I was so loaded I started to hear Chala talk in his old Chala voice every time he flapped his hands. Chala was so wasted his mango shrank down to a lychee and he started talking like Chala again. Which was cool and trippy and fucking scary.

Me and Chala partied so much that the whole next year was a blur.

During that time, I got to know my father real good. So good, in fact, that I figured out he couldn't be my father. For real, what the chance get three fuckers named Delbert Pacheco living on Maui? This guy wasn't the bull of the jail, this guy wasn't the bull of the broom, this guy was just some chubby druggie loser from Honolulu living in a rusty Datsun with his rusty chocho chick. His rusted chochick. Something like that. And all the time he was playing like he was my daddy, giving me advice, saying he proud of me, telling me stories about him and my mom when they was in alternative learning school together. Motherfucker. Except he wasn't. At least not with my mother.

Was Ginger Lei Bonafacio that tipped me off. I was dropping names from prison and he was making like yeah, yeah, oh yeah, that guy was so funny, that guy was so stupid and when I got to Ginger Lei he made like oh yeah, that mahu was so pretty and I knew right there he was bullshitting me because Ginger Lei was nice and kind and all that but even if you into ugly mahus, Ginger Lei was too far off the charts.

"Wow, fucka, you not even my dad."

"Of course I am. Son. Pass me that joint."

"OK, then, if you my father, where you was when you poked my mom and got her hapai?"

That's one question no grown man should have to ask, but I had to know and I was too fucked up to care about racking up more personal demons.

"Uh, Kanaha Beach Park?"

That fucka wasn't even from Maui. Could tell right there. Kepaniwai is the default impregnation place for every teenage parent in the central valley. Dumb-ass Honolulu asshole. Failed the basic question.

He told me was just a big misunderstanding. More like he was leading me on so I would share my stash.

I was so sad that the asshole lied to me. I was feeling all kinds of love for my daddy. Sometimes when he was talking, I was pretending I was a small boy and he was reading me bedtime stories and shet. He was talking about some crank he scored or some house he ripped off and it was like fairy tales to me. Mother Goose and whatnot. I had my head on his shoulder during story time and everything. Fuck, he broke my heart.

A broken ass can be fixed. A broken heart is forever.

Fucka.

During that time, I thought about Taysha coming to cry by my hospital bed when she was the one in there getting toes cut off. Fat beautiful Taysha, now not-so-fat beautiful Taysha, coming home to a burned up house to start her new married life. I thought about Corina carrying that box of chicken she had to work so hard to remember to a guy she already forgot. I thought about Kenji having to give up that sofa for me, because truth be told, that dog could stretch his fuzzy ass out from one arm rest to the other if I wasn't there. I thought about Barry cutting his partying off after one night and going in to work the next day while me and Chala just kept on going and going. Not Barry. Barry knew he had to go to work to pay his rent so he could keep the house where his dog was buried. I thought about Theresa and how pretty she was without gauze hanging out of her mouth and how hard she worked to keep the potato wedges always stocked. I thought about potato wedges, my chubby little friends, and slush floats, nectar from heaven. I thought about all the good things in my life, same like I used to do in prison, wishing I could hold on to them all and thinking, shet, I not even locked up. Why the hell am I so fucking sad?

During that whole time, I tried not to think of the teeth in the box. What the hell did Tony do? Torture some guy to get his watch and rings? What, was Tony gonna melt out the gold fillings? What kind of sick shet is my brother-in-law up to? He ever try pin the house fire on me, I got him on murder. Or at least torture. I get the proof. I get the proof in one little box and it's freaking me out.

I don't know how long I was living on that couch doing all the kinds of stuff I promised I was never gonna do no more. I don't know how long I was on that couch doing all the kinds of stuff I only used to dream about doing when I was on the inside.

All I know is that I woke up one day and Chala was beating the crap out of me.

"What?! Fucka! Get off! She never tell me she was your chick!"

And then I looked again, and it wasn't Chala, was Warren.

"What?! Fucka! Get off! I going get a job as soon as I can find somebody to hire a guy with no education, no job skills, and a steel rod holding his ass together. We'll fucking work it out!"

And then I looked again and was Tony.

"What?! Fucka! Get the fuck off me! Who told you that leaving a guy with a prison record in charge of watching your house was a good idea? Jesus? I don't think so. Jesus too smart for that. Jesus told you to forgive me but he sure as hell didn't tell you to trust me with your house."

And then I looked again and it was a big pink glitter slipper with a huge flower between the toe part and it was slapping my head the way you pop a cockaroach and I was the cockaroach trying to run with my skinny legs and hide underneath the kitchen cabinet and I could feel the slipper whacking my brown shiny roach back and my antennas were letting out little roach screams of terror.

And then I woke up for real. Chala was looking at me like he was scared of my roachiness.

"You was screaming like a freak," he told me with his hands.

"How long we was out?"

Chala made his hands kind of slow and loopy for "I don't know, but I get one beard down to my ass and I gotta piss super bad."

"Yeah, me too."

We went behind the Datsun so the splashes wouldn't get on the sofa. OK, not like some piss would ruin that sofa, but habit already. Try take care my loyal friend Mr. Plaid with the fold out sleeper that never did fold out.

We was both mid-stream when we heard someone come up behind us, feet crunching on the ironwood pine cones.

Corina!

We both turned around same time and she saw. She saw everything, bite marks and all. Her face was all excited. Chala! Bobby!

Chala's face got all cloudy mad. He saw Corina's face. He saw my bite marks. He figured everything out. He was zipping up, hand-swearing, and charging for me all at the same time.

Corina was looking back and forth, back and forth, like trying to choose the best 4-H calf at the Maui County Fair and I thinking no ways, I not entering into no dick contest with Chala. Shame if I lose.

But I promise, I could see in her eyes and I knew in my heart that she was about to pick me when the sheriffs showed up with the dogs. My dick won! I was so proud.

I was ready to go back to jail already. Mostly because I was hungry and needed a shower super super bad to scrape off one whole year of partying from my stank-ass body. So me, I gave up without a fight.

Chala gave a fight. He took all that ass-kicking that was meant for me and went straight for the German shepherds, who put up a good doggy fight before backing off and letting the guys with guns and clubs do what they got trained to do.

Poor Chala. He was yelling with his hands, "Owwee! Sore! Enough already! Shet!" but they must have thought he was still fighting with all that flapping so more they were hitting him. Somewhere in there he cracked a deputy's jaw and things got serious. Corina was crying and screaming for them to get off, looking at me like she wanted me to do something. Just like she forgot she just picked me in the dick contest. Just like she forgot she even knew me now that I pulled my elastic waist shorts up. All she cared about was poor mango-headed Chala getting his ass broked. Finally, he gave up fighting and lay down in the sand, ass kicked, hands silent, charges pending.

So the sheriffs weren't there to take us to jail. Well, they took Chala to jail because of the assault on the deputy, and then to the hospital when they realized he was the guy with the mango. The rest of us little mongooses living in the bushes by Kahului Harbor all got rounded up and dropped off at a big warehouse in Puunene. The place was filled with Army cots. They served us stew and rice and bread with butter and told us we could take shower.

Come to find out it's a homeless shelter.

And I told the social worker, I not homeless.

He says yeah? Where you live?

I show him the small plaid cushion I brought from the couch. My security cushion. My lovey.

He told me find a cot and help myself to some clothes. They got stuff from Salvation Army for us homeless people to wear.

And wouldn't you know it? I looked in the box and there was another fancy reverse-print Reyn's aloha shirt with the name "Fujinaka" written on a small piece paper from the dry cleaner stapled onto the neck tag.

I didn't know I was homeless but in the homeless shelter, I'm home. I got me another chance after all my chances ran out. Ay Jesus.

Corina was on the cot next to me. We go sleep holding hands between the cots, but pretty soon my whole arm was pins and needles and I had reel my hand back to my own cot or else was going fall off.

She was on her little cot, ass hanging off both sides, rocking her legs and licking her lips like she wanted something and I know what she like but honest to God, I was so fucking tired I couldn't even think of that action. I took a shower from a water hose, shaved with a plastic razor, ate canned stew for dinner, and now I lying on one hard, stiff Army cot instead of my warm, squishy sofa. I was bone tired. I was so tired from sleeping for a year. I was so tired from partying for a year. Or maybe it was just a week. It all kind of ran together. I was tired down to my cracked pelvis and my ass rods holding me all together. I just wanted for sleep.

I woke up in the middle of the night and one crazy looking menehune with a big hedge of hair was sitting on my bed grinning at me. He turned his head and smiled at me with side-eyes. I could see he had a weird median strip of fuzzy hair going from one side ear over the top and down to the other side like a headband.

"Ricky?"

Big smile! "Bobby! You remember!"

Yeah, motherfucker, like I'm gonna forget one guy who shaved me blind with a potato peeler and left me looking like a fricken lolo for how many months.

"What the hell you want?!" Like I really wanted for know what this fucka wants.

"You get anybody you no like inside this place? Ha?"

I looked around. I didn't know nobody yet except for Corina, sleeping all round and drooly in the cot next to mine. I liked her just fine.

"Why, what?'

"Anybody give you trouble, you let me know." And he held up a rusty potato peeler and made like he was going cut somebody's throat.

My stomach took a huli like I was going barf right there. That canned stew from last night was saying, "Let me out! Let me out!"

"Thanks, Ricky."

"You go sleep now, Bobby. I watch your back."

I was awake almost the whole night after that. I kept my plaid pillow protecting my head. Never know with that fucker. You just never know.

I woke up in the morning and first thing I did was check my head. My hairs was still there. I spotted a guy on the other side of the shelter looking like he all bald with a fluffy headband going across his head. I was all glad Ricky made a new friend.

A church group showed up with breakfast. I was all ready to get up and make a pig of myself when I seen Taysha and Tony coming with a huge pot of coffee and a wet box of doughnuts. Quick I had hide my head underneath the plaid pillow and made like I sleeping. I heard them come over to the cot next to me, not the Corina cot but the one on the other side. I heard them talking with their nice Jesus voices and asking somebody if they like a doughnut and a blessing.

I heard Tony's voice going, "Ma'am? Ma'am? Excuse me, ma'am?"

And then I heard Taysha's voice going, "Hey, I know you! You're my brother's mother!"

Holy crap, Mama Trinette?

Can't a guy enjoy a wet doughnut after a year of hardcore partying without running into his long-lost drug head mama first thing in the morning? How come everything gotta be so fucking complicated?

I heard my mama talking to Taysha. She didn't sound like my mama. She sounded kind of normal. She recognized Taysha right off the bat and they was talking all nice, like as if my mama didn't hate Taysha and Taysha's mama's guts for the last thirty-something years because they oofed the same guy on the same night in the same car. Hate like that is hard to heal. Maybe my mother was growing a head mango.

But no, she was asking Taysha all kind ohana kind questions, like "How's your mother?" and "So what have you been doing lately?" and "Is that your husband? So handsome for a midget!"

Yeah, and he manly for a one-nutter, too. But don't get too close to old Tony because he has a freak side he hides from the world. You never know when he going come out in the night, yank your teeth, dump your body, and take your stuff. Or snitch you out to your mean sister. So watch out.

Taysha asked my mama if she like pray and my mother, she get this sound in her voice that I never did hear before in my whole life of seeing her one weekend a month or going to visit her at the inpatient day room.

She sounded all happy and peaceful.

My mama told Taysha that yeah, she would love to pray together because she did recently accept Jesus as her Lord and Savior and that Jesus turned her life around. All the stuffs that she threw away, Jesus had grabbed back from the garbage dump and saved for her, waiting for when she got her head screwed on straight, and now that she was clean and sober and born again, he was giving her stuff back to her one by one. She said she waiting because she know one day Jesus going give her kids back to her, even the ones she don't remember having, the ones that went directly into foster care after birth.

Ho, how much kids you get, Mama?

She was telling Taysha that she pray one day she finds her first-born Bobby again. She get some things she like tell him.

Taysha told her yeah, she get some things she like tell Bobby, too. Tony thinks Bobby died in the fire but no, Taysha said, she get the super Jesus vibes that I alive and well and crashed out on somebody's couch somewhere. Tony prays for Bobby's eternal soul, Taysha hunting for his sorry ass.

This going bad for old Bobby.

I was thinking if I can just slide off the cot, run to the bathroom, and escape out the jalousie windows like I did when I ran away from guard dog Jorene.

Nah, my legs too jelly from all the time I spent passed out on the couch. I cannot run the way I used to, even though that time I was running with pins in my ass and the metal rod holding my ass to my body. I was even slower after all I went through that lost time at Kahului Harbor.

So I just had lie still like one rock and listened.

Taysha was leading the prayer and my mama was doing the Ay Jesus part.

"Dear Jesus, we ask a blessing on your dear child, Trinette. A woman who has suffered from the choices that she made that brought her away from you."

"Ay Jesus."

"And we ask you Lord to turn her thoughts to thoughts of you, Lord, not thoughts of drugs and booze and selling her body for dope."

"Ay Jesus."

"Because you know she been a fucking whore a long time, Jesus, and she need your help to come straight."

"What kind prayer is this, Taysha? You not supposed to say 'fuck.'"

"Be with her Jesus as she starts this new life. Turn her hands to your work, Jesus. Turn her heart to your love. Turn her eyes to those around her who need her help as much as she needs you."

And I was thinking, oh no, don't turn no eyes to nobody around you because then you might take notice of me and I not ready for this family reunion, that's for damn sure.

"And please let her find her beloved firstborn son Bobby, who needs very much to be found right now. For his mother's sake, for his sake, and for various insurance purposes. In your holy name we pray . . ."

"Ay Jesus, yes, yes."

"Amen."

"Amen."

"Amen."

That last Amen was me. Like a fucking trained dog, I said it without even thinking. Maybe was all that praying Taysha did over my bed after surgery. She implanted the Amening when my subconscious was vunerable. I was so fucking weak.

"Bobby?"

The two of them were on me like flies on dog shet.

My mama: "It's a miracle!"

Taysha: "I knew you was alive!"

My mama: "Ay Jesus!"

Me: "Oh, hi you folks."

Taysha: "I gotta tell Tony."

Me: "So what you up to, Ma?"

Taysha went waddling off to find Tony. I took notice she put on some of her ass pounds back. Maybe she not pissing as much as she eating or maybe she get one toe acting up, making her all bloated.

My mama was sitting on the edge of her cot facing me with a sweet mama-ish smile on her face that I only seen on other people's mama's faces. She kept saying this was a miracle and I was thinking hell yeah, the miracle is that you're sober and nice and happy to see me. I been praying for this one so long already I gave up praying.

Mama told me stories about all she been thinking about for her new life. She leaned over and patted my shoulder or my knee when she was talking like she was so happy to see her boy she cannot stop touching to make sure I'm for real.

Mama told me she went through a Christian drug treatment program and for the first time in her life, she love herself and that made all the difference in the world.

She told me she like go college now, maybe get her associate degree, learn some skills, maybe come back as one counselor to help other womens get their life together. She not sure. She gotta keep working on her recovery to where she feel she on really solid ground.

She told me her sister, Doreen's mama, is sick with wahine cancer and not going be around too long. I thinking, so what is wahine cancer? Chocho or chichi? By the way my mama talking, I was thinking it's something in between, but what wahines get in between those two places that mens don't got? That one, I not too sure. I was sad for Doreen and sad for Doreen's mama. Not like they were close but Doreen, she get her way of loving people from a distance. Her love is like an arrow, and the thing can fly far and stab you in the ass when you not looking.

Mama told me stuff about how she thinks of me all the time and how she missed out on my childhood. She told me about the time she took me and her other kids to the beach and then went off in the bushes with some of her work furlough friends and left us alone all night and the cops came the next day and bought us slush float and took us back to our gramma's house. She said she was so messed up then she cannot believe she abandoned us like that and she sorry, she so sorry and she hope I know that she love me so much now that maybe that can little bit make up for all the no-love she gave me when I was a kid.

She told me she wanted to come to my high school graduation and she bought a double carnation lei and everything but her counselor told her she didn't have enough credits at the time for a day pass so she so sorry she couldn't be there. I didn't tell her that nah, no worry because I didn't grad anyways. I never like make her feel like a failure that her kid didn't finish high school. Because I did. Pretty close. I just gotta take that equivalency test again and try pass this time.

My mama told me she sorry she never did make it to my birthday parties even though my birthday parties wasn't really parties, just excuse for Gramma to drink with the neighbors.

My mama told me she sorry she never did take me Disneyland or Sea Life Park or movie theater or any of that stuff she promised. She felt so sorry for herself she was such a fuck up mama. She felt sorry for me, too.

"You never got a chance, Bobby," she told me. "You was always a clever boy. If you had a good childhood, wow, maybe you wouldn't have ended up such a loser. Or maybe you'd still be a loser, but not this bad."

And me, I was just sitting there listening to all that thinking one, is Taysha bringing Tony here to show him I still alive so he can kill me? And two, I gotta take a piss really bad.

My mama closed her eyes and was praying that I can forgive her and I took that as my sign from Jesus to run to the bathroom, take a major piss, and check out my escape possibilities.

The window was pretty small and pretty high up. Me, I didn't think I was in shape for climbing toilets at the moment.

Besides, as my bladder getting empty, my brain was thinking clearer. If Taysha was in the spirit to kill me, she would have taken me out already and not wait for her goody-two-shoes Tony to come yank out my teeth and toss my body in the rubbish bin.

Come to think of it, maybe Taysha was the murdering teeth-yanker. She always was a sweet girl but she get one kind of snappy temper every so often. What if one day she snapped all the way and yanked somebody's teeth out of their head?

Maybe was Tony's teeth. I never did open up his head and do an official count. Maybe he missing some on the back and the sides. Maybe that's how she got him to marry her. She left some in his head so she could threaten him more later. Sneaky Taysha. That explains so much stuff.

So OK, if Taysha was going to kill me I would already be dead. Maybe they just going hurt me for revenge. I can handle that.

My mama was clean and acting like she sorry she fucked up my life and she didn't even try to bum a cigarette from me, so everything there was cool. Weird but cool.

Corina was eating doughnuts for breakfast and she was so happy. Doughnuts from Tony's church. Doughnuts from Jesus. Holy doughnuts. Hey, I was getting my funny back!

Chala was in the hospital getting his head checked waiting for them to tell him he going die so he can go home and start partying again.

Me, the sheriffs asked me my name and I told them and must be they ran a warrant check and I came out clean because I ended up in the Homeless Hilton over here.

Ricky the weirdo found me and left me the fuck alone. Somebody else woke up mohawked this morning, not me.

So all in all, things was good. Shet, was great. Bobby came out on top once again. I stood pissing in that bathroom feeling grateful.

I was thinking maybe I don't gotta split. Maybe I just pull up my elastic waist khakis and go right back out there and have a doughnut. Take my licks for burning down the house, say I sorry and get forgiven. Everything is good. Nobody chasing me down. I am home. I am sheltered.

Plus, since I got Mama here and she all lucid and shet, maybe I can find out once and for true who my daddy is because all of a sudden seem like get couple contenders.

So I went out to see my mama, Corina, Taysha, and Tony, my family, the people who accept me for who I am and how I am no matter what.

Except Taysha called Tony and Tony called Doreen and Doreen had come flying just like she had a magic broom.

Just my fucking luck to get busted on a Saturday and wake up on a Sunday when Doreen not working, just sitting at home re-tiling the bathroom and waiting for the phone to ring with news about me.

She was on me like a fat man on doughnut day. She was all over me like stink on a sofa.

"Come on, Bobby. You going home with me."

"Please, no, Dori! No make me go home with you! I scared!"

"You better be scared, ass wipe. Get your shet and let's go."

"No, Mama! No, Taysha! You don't understand! I scared go with Doreen!"

My mama made all wide-eye, like suddenly I one six-year-old kid saying please don't make me eat the ice cream. I hate ice cream. Oh please don't make me!

"But Bobby, Doreen offering to take care of you. You so lucky she love you so much!"

"Yeah, Bobby, you really lucky I love you so much." Doreen was grabbing me by my ear and carrying me to her truck. Mama and Taysha and Tony was waving good-bye, see ya, see you later. Corina was going back to the big plastic table for another doughnut. Good-bye my love. Good-bye my chunky little rat-bite girl.

Doreen threw me by my ear into the cab of the truck. No sitting in the back with the camper shell and dog pillows. The dog had to sit in the back. Me, I had to sit in the front next to the passenger door with the broken handle so cannot open from the inside. Doreen cranked the key and we burned rubber out of the dirt parking lot around the Second Chance Fresh Start Homeless and Houseless Drug Free Temporary Shelter and Housing Assistance.

The first thing she said to me when we hit the main road came with her hand choking my neck: "Where's that fucking sofa?"

Chapter 19

HONEST STEVE WASN'T RETURNING DOREEN'S CALLS and she was pissed. She called in sick to work to go track him down at his office, which was something she never ever did before. Not the track-him-down part, because she know how to find somebody who trying to be lost and don't I fucking know that. But the call-in-sick part, she never did before. First time in all her four years driving the courtesy van that she missing a day of work on account of illness. Even when she sick she don't call in sick. She just load up on cold pills and drive that courtesy shuttle like a pro, white knuckles on the wheel, glazed eyes on the airport loop, one wet piece of Kleenex tucked inside her bra strap.

She said she just like know how much longer she gotta keep me locked up in the bedroom until my checks come.

Doreen so smart. She made sure she told Warren I was back staying with her so that all my mail and other correspondences come to her house.

Correspondences. Big word, Doreen.

"Shut the fuck up," she tell me. "I going community college as soon as I get your accident money so I improving my fucking vocabulary."

If she not home, she make sure Jorene catch the mail when come to the crooked mailbox hanging off the pole by the street. Everybody in the building supposed to have their own slot but the spacers inside the box are so rusted the letters fall all over the place. Doreen taught the daughter to go through everybody's little mail cubby to check for the checks every day.

Me, she got me locked up in the bedroom. And I mean for real kind locked up. Had one padlock on the outside of the door. How's that?! She gave me food and let me go bathroom twice a day and she let me watch a small TV she got from Corina's apartment before the Goodwill truck came and took everything else that was left behind.

So she was keeping me fed and quiet. She was keeping me alive for the sake of the money and because deep down she love me because I'm family. And to keep me in line, she got the broken toaster.

Kennison tried to fix the broken toaster with a fork and now the thing shocks you couple good volts when you press the toast button down. The fork is still stuck in the coils, but Doreen figured out if she held the toaster by the plastic parts on the side with her hands in oven mitts, she wouldn't feel the shock but she could zap the hell out of me when I did something she didn't like.

Ask for cigarettes. KZZT!

Say one dirty word. KZZT!

Look too long at the jalousie windows like I planning my escape. LONG ZAP! Like KZZZZZZZZZZZZT!

I was quickly learning how to avoid the toaster.

I tried talk nice to Doreen's kids through the locked door. Develop strong bonds.

OK, so not like Doreen's kids was all that nice to me, but I figured going take us some time to come close again after all the trust issues I had put them through.

Jorene, she had good fun insult me. She liked to make her cat claws sharp on old Uncle Bobby and I let her go for it because doesn't really hurt. Not really.

I told her through the door, "Hey, Jorene!"

She told me, "I cannot hear you."

I told her, "If you cannot hear me why you answering?"

She told me, "I not answering. I just letting you know I ignoring you."

Hoo, she so swift that girl. That's college materials right there. She going be one doctor or one lawyer if she keep going like that. And a good kind lawyer, not like Honest Steve. The kind lawyer get one office, not just one post office box.

Kennison, he no talk too much, but when he walked past the door, I would say stuff and I could hear him listening.

Walk, walk, walk, going down the hall.

"Hey, Kennison"

Stop.

"Hey, if you not doing nothing, you think maybe you can run down the street and get your old Uncle Bobby one strawberry slush float?"

Scratch, scratch.

"I get some money here in the sofa. If you open up the lock, I give 'em to you. You can buy whatever you like for yourself, too. I don't even care if you use my money to buy cigarettes. Just no tell me about it and I don't know about it, right?"

Quiet. He was trying to think this through but he think so slowly he forgot the plan already.

"So just open up the lock and come inside, let me give you the money and you can go store for me, OK?"

Tiptoe down the hall. I lost him. But for a while there he was sniffing the bait.

They all ratted me out to Mama Doreen and I got the toaster for all what I was trying to do. After that, I only said hi to them through the door and I didn't get them to try to do nothing. I scared talk to them too long.

Liko, he would sit in the hall outside my door and ask plenty questions. He went from quiet and sneaky to junior interrogator. That's no way for a kid to grow up. Made me nervous.

"Uncle Bobby?"

"Yeah?"

"How come the air coming out from under your door is so stink?"

"That's cuz Uncle Bobby is detoxing and I had kind of plenty tox inside my body."

"Uncle Bobby?"

"What?"

"What is tox?"

"It's like dirt."

"Uncle Bobby?'

"Yeah, Liko, what?"

"So why you eat dirt?"

"Eh Liko, you don't have homework or something? Maybe some cartoons on TV?"

He no let up, him. Question, question. I had fake sleep to make him go away so I could for real sleep.

Doreen made me sleep on the plaid sofa. Never have much left of the sofa. The thing was down to the sofa skin and bones. Doreen thought maybe I still had some money from her and from Tony still stashed inside somewhere. She took me straight to Kahului Harbor from the homeless shelter and she made me load that sofa all by myself in the back of the truck and make 'em fit underneath the camper shell, which it didn't, so I had to sit in the truck bed on top the rotten sofa holding onto the camper shell so the sofa didn't fly away while Doreen floored it up Beach Road to her apartment. Me, I wasn't in danger of flying out of the truck. Doreen tied me to the bumper with Kenji's rope leash. Lucky thing the rope was long enough to reach otherwise she would make me run along behind the truck.

She made me carry the thing by myself up to her place. Up the stairs on my back. My ass rods felt like was going bend in couple places, but not like Doreen gave me choice. I had to haul that sofa up or else. And with Dori, I don't ask, "Or else what?"

When I got the sofa inside her apartment, I put it in the living room where used to be before Doreen sent me and Corina sailing out the window on our plaid airship of love. Doreen tell me oh, no, no, no. I gotta take it into the back bedroom. I was like gee, thanks, but where the kids gonna sleep? She told me no worry about the kids. The kids will be fine. Me, I wasn't going nowhere for a while, so she told me just get comfy on my orange plaid friend and take a nice long nap. And when I get up, take another one. Take as much naps as I like because I didn't have nothing going on except waiting for the mail, and she was going do that for me.

The sofa was just about dead. Doreen pulled it apart thread-by-thread looking for my stash. Then she sprayed the whole thing down with Raid so no bugs could get into her house from that filthy thing. Then she sprayed it with bleach water to get out all the diseases. Then she tried to vacuum it but the vacuum was smoking and had hard time to suck so she stopped. The cushions weren't cushiony anymore, and where they still had a little bit of stuffing, it was all wet and moldy and stink. The plaid threads were frayed and worn away and the whole thing looked kind of fuzzy now. Kenji wouldn't even lift his leg on it anymore. But I tell you what, that thing was like a part of me already. That plaid went everywhere with me. Good times and bad. And just like that ugly orange sofa, I was frayed and broken but I am still here. Ay Jesus.

And the sofa told me, "Hey, Bobby, been meaning to mention, I'm not orange. I'm burnt sienna."

And I'm like what the fuck? The sofa talking to me now? I thought the toilet singing show tunes was bad, but I was drinking old cold medicine at the time. If I hearing the sofa talk I must have seriously damaged my brain with all of that shet.

And then I seen Kennison standing there with my dinner tray looking at me funny and I think, "Ay, am I thinking out loud?"

Kennison gave me the eye and nod his head all serious like "Yeah, Uncle, you acting fucking scary so knock it off."

Thanks for the feedback, braddah Ken. Not like you not too spooky yourself. But whatevers. You play football and you get tan skin and light eyes. That's enough to catch all the chicks even if you little bit creepy.

Kennison lifted his eyebrows at me again and said, "Fuck yeah. I score all the time. But you still thinking out loud so shut the fuck up."

Doreen put the kids' beds in the living room. Well, she made me put the kids' beds in the living room. Liko still slept with her, which if you ask me is not too good for a boy. If he feel all safe and loved, how he ever going learn to take care of himself out in the world? But me, I kept those thoughts to myself.

Doreen put me on one strict program. Everything had a rule. Every little thing. Hundred times more rules than before, all enforced with the toaster.

First thing she did was break me from my swearing.

I was like, shet, that's not even in my top 25 bad habits.

She told me she don't care and she zapped me with the toaster for that shet I said. She don't wanna hear no more shet, fuck, dick, mother-fucker, asshole, or goddamn coming from my mouth no more, not ever, never again.

I was all, "Can say crap?"

She told me, "No fucking way."

I said, "You can say fuck but I cannot say fuck?"

She told me, "Because you trying to get your life on track and I am not a fuck-up like you." And then I got zapped for the fucks.

I told her, "Eh, you trying to get your life on track, too."

Doreen had her oven mitt hand on her hip, the other one holding the toaster. She was just about all out of explaining her reasons to fuck-up cousin/brother Bobby. "Look, I trying to get my life on track, too. You right about that. But compared to you I am a fucking saint, a community leader and a pillar of society. So you just keep your fucking trap shut and no more fucks or shets or nothing out of you. You got it?"

I almost said, "Fuck yeah," but I caught myself in time and said, "Yes, Dori."

She unplugged the toaster.

"Well all right then."

I was thinking going be kind of easy not to swear when you don't talk too much. I was home by myself all day when Doreen was working and the kids were at school, and when they home, not like they knock on the door to come in and have long chats. But Doreen no like me even think in foul language anymore and I swear to God she could hear my thoughts.

"Yes, I can," she told me. Swear to God.

"Hey, can I say 'swear to God'?"

"No, Bobby. You cannot. No dinner for you tonight."

"Sh— shucks."

"That's better. But still, no food."

Darn it.

Through the next few days I got to where I could tell when I was thinking quietly to myself and when I was blabbing my thoughts to the whole world like a crazy man.

If my mouth was moving, that was a pretty good indication that I wasn't keeping my thoughts to myself. I tried to remember that. It got easier. Sometimes, but, I slipped.

I guess I kind of went through a lot and recovery is a slow, ongoing process.

Oh, but Doreen was making sure I was processing every day.

Next she told me I giving up cigarettes. I was like, what the heck?!! She told me no ways she letting me smoke inside her place and damage her kids' lungs and no way she letting me out on the balcony where with my history of behaviors, who knows what I might do.

Oh, that's not fair.

Hand on her hip, she told me, "Brah, where's my list?"

Shucks. She got me. I guess I did do some crazy stuff over the years and yeah, I guess some of it did involve her balcony.

Then she started reminding me of stuff I did from way before.

The time I was sixth grade Iao School and I went to the top of the County Building and dropped rocks off the top to see if I could make a puka in somebody's head. (I did.)

The time I tried to climb the roof at Wailuku Dairy Queen so I could ride on top the red spinning spoon. (I could.)

The time I barfed slush float off the Wailuku Bridge onto oncoming cars because I was mixing vodka in the ice cream again.

Eh, I don't remember that.

"Bobby, you lucky you remember your name at this point."

Sh—shucks. She was right. I guess I kind of have a thing for high places.

"Bobby, you have a thing for high. You don't even care what is the places."

Right again. Gosh darn.

So yeah. Doreen and her toaster made me quit smoking. I thought she was going torture me the whole time by going outside to smoke on her balcony, then come back inside and make me smell the cigarette smoke on her. But no. Doreen didn't smoke no more. She was on a program, too. She was on a self-improvement program for years now, working on one thing at a time, but now she was kicking it in high gear. She was eating tomatoes, she was exercising after work, she was reading big books. I gave my sister/cousin credit. Just when you thought Doreen is all the Doreen she'll ever be, she dug deep and came back stronger. And she didn't even need toaster therapy to make it happen.

I tried use her as my example and my motivation but quitting the cigs was the hardest thing I ever did in my life. My hands was shaking the whole day. I ended up sucking on my knuckles. One time I tried to light a magazine with two piece of plaster I knocked out of the wall. I figured was something like rubbing stones together. That's cave man style, right? I think I seen that on a commercial.

Doreen told me after a while, the urge going pass. And golly gee, she was right. The urge just about killed me, but right before I was going die, it let up and left me alone. I never even like smoke anymore. Cigarettes, I mean.

Then Doreen got me trying to lose weight and get healthy. She came in the room every day and made like drill sergeant, telling me do push-ups and sit-ups and run in place. First day I could only do like five push-ups and stuff but after couple weeks, I was up to ten and I was feeling like Maui Muscle Man.

She was teaching Kennison to cook for the family and she make him make healthy kind stuff. She figured Kennison need culinary skills to fall back on in case the college football thing didn't pan out. Jorene, she smart and she skinny. She'll have a career and eat out so she don't need to learn how to cook, plus she not too interested in eating. But Kennison, Doreen got him making vegetable omelets and tofu loaf and all kinds of food with stuff she made him get at the farmers' market. At first I was like, hey, he cannot start with the basics, like Spam musubi and chicken cutlet with brown gravy? Doreen said I get two choices: I can shut up and eat or I can shut up and don't eat and get the toaster. Up to me.

I shut up and ate and after a while I promise, I wasn't even craving no Spam or cutlet or even—and this I could hardly believe—slush floats wasn't calling my name every morning noon and night. That was an addiction I thought I would never ever overcome.

Doreen said I broke my carbohydrate and glucose habit. I told her wow, I didn't even know about those ones. I do know I will never eat toast again my whole life.

Couple months of Doreen kicking my okole and making me eat salad, I didn't even recognize myself when I look in the bathroom mirror. I looked like I looked in high school, except my eyes not stoner red.

One day, Doreen came home with a new aloha shirt for me that she found at Goodwill when she was looking for jeans for the kids. And I mean this was a new aloha shirt. Nobody's name was on the inside neck tag. This shirt never been worn by anybody but me. Even had the tags from the store still attached by the underarm part. I didn't ever want to cut them off, those tags were so special to me. Doreen told me no act like a lolo and she cut off the tags with her teeth.

Doreen told me the next step in her Mama Dori's Rehab Program was I gotta get a job.

Uh-oh. This step never did work out too good for me before.

Oh but this time, she set me up at the rental car place down the Kahului Airport, same place where she work. That way, she was going keep a close eye on me and she was going be there to slap my head if I wander two inches away from my path or take one minute too long on my breaks. She was going bring the toaster to work if she has to.

She told me I was going clean cars, pick up stuff people leave behind in the back seat and whatnot.

She seen the look on my face and she told me, "Not that kind stuff in the back seat. Stuff like snacks and slippers and whatnot. Not everybody in the world oof in the back seat of cars. Some people actually use a bed."

Or a sofa, but I kept my mouth super tight so that one didn't slip out and get me the toaster treatment.

Doreen told me I could keep the little things people leave behind in the cars, but the expensive kind stuff, like cameras and jewelry and cell phones, we gotta take to the lost and found. Sometimes we might even get a reward from the guy who left his watch or sometimes we get a certificate from the company for good service award.

I wanted a good service award.

So I caught ride with Doreen and the kids in the morning. When Jorene and Kennison got dropped off at Baldwin High School all the cheerleaders made like they waiting for their cheering co-captain Jorene but really they waiting for her handsome younger brother, backup quarterback Kennison with the light color eyes. This made Jorene super mad and it was the best part of my day to watch her face when the girls ran past her to flock around her silent younger brother.

Next Doreen dropped off Liko at his preschool. He took his own lunch from home. A healthy sandwich made by brother Kennison. A box of raisins. An apple. Doreen wasn't taking no chances with no mean diseases over there, and she knew at least Kennison always wash his hands before he touch food. She was training him good.

She was trying her best to train me good. Go work same time as her, pau work same time as her, get lunch same time as her. I couldn't go nowhere unless she take me. I didn't do nothing unless she tell me to. It was the most brutal program I ever been on and I gotta admit it was nothing but a relief. Having a wahine like Doreen thinking for you, making all your decisions, telling you what is right and what is wrong takes so much pressure off a man's mind.

I still was worried she was going kill me for the money, but probably she going kill Honest Steve first. No money to kill me for. Those three checks was still pending. What is pending? Doreen told me that's fancy word for it's coming. The checks is coming, that's what Honest Steve told her when she busted into his house and told him what the hell and he better get off his ass and make this happen because her brother/cousin been in his pains and sufferings so long without nothing restitutions for his injuries from the responsible parties.

"Ay, Doreen, should go law school. Or work corrections."

"Shut up, Bobby, you just concentrate on vacuuming the sand."

That was pretty much what I did all day. Vacuum sand. The cars was dusty outside because all the people sign the paper promising they not going drive the rental car off-roading but then they all drive the rental car off-roading and pretend like oh, was really windy in Kihei and that's why they picked up the dust. They just ran the cars through the car wash for the outside. The brushes scratched the paint but didn't really matter because the cars only have to last like a year before they get new cars in the fleet. Nice, eh?

But inside the cars, had so much sand, surprising still get some left on the beach. Sand under the gas pedal, sand under the back seats, sand in the trunk compartment, sand all in the floor mats. Everybody who sat inside these cars must have been carrying couple buckets of sand in their cracks because it all emptied out into the upholstery.

I found some other little stuff, too. Chips, macadamia nut candies, bottled water, beer. I put all that stuff in the employee breakroom. I found part of a slush float in the cup holder of a Corolla but was lime flavor, not my strawberry, and just looking at it made my mouth sore from all that sugar.

I was a changed man.

And speaking of, I was finding lots of spare change around the cars, too. That, I pretty much pocketed. We not talking hundred dollar bills, we talking nickels and quarters. I figured nobody going miss that kind stuff and money is healthier for me than chips and slush float. I gathered up all the coins I found and at the end of my shift, I gave everything to Dori.

The night we came home from my first day at work, Doreen told me come eat dinner at the kitchen table with her and the kids. Me, I didn't say nothing the whole time. I just chewed my lean chicken and green salad with my mouth closed and listened to Jorene talk about the girl she hate, the guy she like, and the teacher she turned in for unprofessional conducts.

After dinner, I helped wash dishes until Jorene yelled at me that I was only getting in the way. When she was pau washing, I helped wipe dishes until Doreen told me stop it, she no like me break her stuff even if everything is plastic.

I went to the sofa in my room to lie down and think about stuff and get out of everybody's way. Soft knock on the door. Doreen came in. She never knocked. She usually just opened the padlock and walked on in. Spooky. I was scared.

"So what, you going kill me?"

Doreen sat down on one end of the couch. Changed her mind. Dusted off her shorts and sat on the floor.

"I thought about it. Probably not."

I could tell she was telling the truth, but then Doreen always tell the truth. If she say she going kill you, she going kill you. She tell you probably not, you get a good chance to live.

"You like know why?"

When Mama Dori asked you that kind question, you had to say, "Yes." That is the rule. That is one of the rules. One of the many, many rules. Even if you no like know why.

"Yes."

"Because you making progress."

I let that one go down slowly, like soft rain on a hot day.

"For real?"

"For real, Bobby. You working hard and you doing good."

"You proud of me, Dori?"

"Oh hell no, you're still a screw-up and one good day at work doesn't take away all the mess you made out of your life and anybody else's life that was unlucky enough to get near your life. So no go thinking that you paid no dues because you owe me and the kids and Taysha and Tony and Chala and Corina and Warren and Theresa and Sonya and Kenji so much for all the crap you pulled."

"Kenji?"

"You owe Kenji his whole sofa! Poor baby only get the small futon now, poor baby. Don't you ever forget what that dog gave up for you. You owe this whole world and don't you ever forget it. You been a user and a loser and abuser. You never did nothing for nobody, not even yourself. When I found out you was going get all kind crazy money coming your way, all I could think of was how much more people's lives you was gonna mess up while you was busy messing up your own. And now maybe, MAYBE if you stay on this path of the straight and narrow, maybe if and when those checks come in—but mostly if because I don't know if I trust that lawyer you hired, Bobby, he no smell right to me—but if those checks ever do land in the mailbox, maybe that money won't take you and everybody around you down to the bottom past dead."

My eyes was full of tears and my voice was stuck in my chest. I didn't know what to say. That was how much my sister/cousin loved me. She loved me enough to electrocute me with a toaster and give me another chance.

"Doreen, I promise, I going work so hard and do so right."

Doreen whacked my head harder than she ever whacked my head before. My teeth all rattled like dice. The health food was making her more strong. She could probably bench press a car.

"Don't make me no promises. You the most full-of-crap person that ever walked through my door, and believe me, I seen some full-of-crap men in my life. Just know that you're the only full-of-crap guy I know who has big money coming his way but I just might change my mind about killing you if you piss me off."

I cried myself to sleep that night. I felt so valuable. I felt so loved.

Chapter 20

IN THE END, CHALA DIDN'T HAVE A MANGO NO MORE. His tumor came so big was like a jabon or one of them upcountry seedless watermelons. Come to find out his mango days were his best days and when the thing grew to a bigger fruit, things got rough and he suffered. He couldn't talk. He couldn't flap. Poor thing.

I told Doreen about the whole talking-like-a-Haole thing. She told me you don't need no head mango to pull that one. Doreen said plenty people know how to do that, turn it off and on. I was like, "No ways!"

She was like, "Yes ways. No tell me you don't know nobody else who bilingual."

I told her I thought I not supposed to talk about sex stuff like that in front her kids.

She slapped my head for acting stupid. She was right, but. I knew what she was talking about. Busted again.

"Why you act stupid on purpose?"

"Because it's funny," I told her.

"It's not. It's just stupid."

Wow, I never did think of stupid not being funny. I always thought was the same thing. Doreen was so smart and she was getting smarter all the time. She blew my mind on a regular basis.

"For real, but, you know get plenty local people who can talk Standard English, right?"

"Like who?"

"Like me, for one. Like Jorene."

"You kidding!"

"You don't hear me talk like that because you don't hear me in the van at work. I talk perfect English in the van. When I yelling at you, I gotta talk pidgin because it sounds meaner."

"Try show me. I like see."

She cleared her throat.

"Bobby, don't ever do that again."

"Wow! OK, now do 'em regular."

"Bobby, you fuckin' ass wipe piece of shet, you ever make like that again I going fucking kick your alas so hard they going end up in your ears!"

"Oooh. You good."

"I know. And get Haoles that can talk like us, too."

"NO WAYS!"

"Like that's news to you. Fuck, Bobby, sometimes you act lolo but sometimes you really are lolo. And none of that is funny."

And that kind of broke my whole world because I thought at least some of it was funny, even the parts when I was faking like I didn't know better but I knew better. I didn't know that stuff wasn't funny, but.

Chala was funny, no matter what language he was talking and even if he wasn't talking at all, just making his made-up sign language. Chala was hilarious, even to the end.

He got to die in the hospital, which was way better than dying in jail. Corina came from the homeless shelter to be with him and she squeezed her big ass onto his little hospital bed and nibbled on his ears all night long. Say what you like about Corina being a whore and all that, but that girl, she was loyal when it counted.

Corina stayed with him all day and night at the end, cuddling his shaky body, the long part of her mullet covering him like a blankie, the short part itching him by his face. But then her legal husband Paco got paroled. Unreal timing. Not like they couldn't keep him couple months so Corina could be with her dying boyfriend in peace. But that's always how it happens. Paco got paroled and he went looking around for Corina and somebody told him oh, she's at the hospital with her husband and he was all no ways, I'm the husband and the person told him wow, you cannot even see your bite marks and that was it. After Paco beat up the guy who knew about the biting thing—because only one way he would know about the biting thing—he went straight to the hospital to look for Corina and her frosted mullet, tight jeans, and restless teeth.

Paco didn't have to threaten no nurses to find out where Chala was. They just pointed to the room and got out of the way. Somebody called hospital security, but security took a look at Paco charging down the hall and decided they should wait for the cops.

Paco busted in Chala's room and saw Corina lying there sadly chewing on Chala's IV tube. Paco screamed and Corina jumped straight out the window, and lucky thing was only the second floor and lucky thing she was at the hospital because they put her leg cast on same day, no waiting.

Paco grabbed Chala by the throat and told him he was going kill him.

Chala, big smile on his face, took a deep breath and looked Paco in the eye and told him, "Sorry brah, you too late!" and then he died. Chala died laughing.

I got all this from Taysha who was in the hospital for another toe removal at the time and heard the story from some of the nurses who saw it firsthand.

Taysha said it was a miracle that Chala had the gift of his voice back in the last moments of his life, even if what he had to say was just a big "fuck you" to the guy whose wife he was poking. Still, Jesus was at work.

Taysha said had plenty miracles going on in that hospital that day. Come to find out that her toe, which didn't end up needing removing, was swollen because her feet was swollen because her whole body was swollen because she hapai!

Ay, Jesus!

She said Jesus made her diabetes-wracked body fertile and Tony's one-nut shot potent and created a new life in a barren land. It's a miracle.

Amen to that.

Taysha working on forgiving me for the fire and stuff, not because of me but for her child's sake. Now that she carrying a life inside her, she don't want to influence the baby with all her hatred toward me. So she letting it go.

Hatred?

"Oh yeah, Bobby. I hate your fucking guts. I would kill you right now with my bare hands, but I wouldn't want to subject my unborn child to my evil rages. Praise Jesus for keeping me from ripping your heart out of your chest even as we speak."

Amen to that, too.

Taysha came to see me at Doreen's apartment. She wanted to make sure she knew how to find me for when my big checks come in. Not like they not getting insurance money for the house, but still yet, she wanted to make sure justice has a chance to work its miracles. Amen, she says.

I didn't Amen back on that one.

Taysha and Tony living with one of the families from Tony's parish. They going crazy sharing a small house and they pretty much all hate each other but Jesus helping them all work it out.

I had questions in my mind that Taysha's baby probably is from the husband of the family she living with because Tony might be a nice guy, but he little bit light in the manly man department. If the baby come out short like a big midget with two different color eyes and one blond Afro, I will forever shut my mouth and never doubt Holy Tony again.

Tony was the nicest guy I know but I always had my doubts about him. He too perfect. Nobody can live like that.

OK, so turned out the teeth was nothing. Nothing like I thought was, because I was pretty sure was something.

That stuff in the box was all from Tony's mother. Her jewelry, her money, her teeth, and whatnot. Taysha told me sometimes wahines get sentimental and they keep one ponytail of their hair when they cut 'em short. Tony's mom kept her teeth to remind her of her younger days when she could eat whatever she like, corn on the cob, steak, tako poke, whatevers. It was her connection to her good old days, Taysha said.

OK, I could see that.

My connection to my good old days would be the teeth marks on my dakine, but I not supposed to reminisce about my substance abuse hazes like was something good.

Even though was.

OK stop it. There I was at Chala's funeral and all I could think of was all those happy days and weeks and months spent blasted out of my head with this guy. Lucky thing Doreen didn't bring the toaster with her to the funeral services because I swear she can read my mind when I'm thinking thoughts I not supposed to think.

Sometimes I got like flashbacks to stuff me and Chala did when we was loaded but I wasn't sure if was a memory or a dream or some crazy movie I watched on the blurry halfway house TV. Like, did me and him really swim across Kahului Harbor before the sun even came up and then get fished out by the tugboat or did I imagine that? Or the time we broke into the kitchen at the halfway house and ate all the soda cracker packets out of the boxes? Making contest like on the kids' TV show where you eat the cracker and then see who can whistle first. How about when we jacked a couple of kids parked by the breakwater having sex in a beat-up Sentra? The boy was so scared he was telling us more stuff we could take, like, "Here, take my stereo. Here, I get forty dollars in my wallet. You like my chick? Here, take the girl. She's pretty and her necklace is a real diamond."

Yeah, that last one really did happen because I found part of the girl's necklace in the sofa cushion. I remember the chick being so mad at her boyfriend for giving up her small diamond necklace that she kicked him out of the car and drove home alone. The guy was cool, but. He hung out with us for a couple hours thinking she would cool down and come back to pick him up. But after a while, he gave up and called his friend. And there he was all that time partying with us and bonding like a brother and he didn't even mention the cell phone. Offered up the girlfriend and her jewelry before his own cell phone. Kids these days, no?

Me and Chala did all that kind stuff together. We had adventures like two kids, like how friends supposed to do crazy stuff together. I never going find nobody like him again in my life. He was like my father figure even if he was only couple years older and I slept with his chick sneaky kind on the side. He was the guy who taught me what it means to be a man, especially how a man should live on the outside. He taught me you gotta enjoy life to the fullest, be there for your friends, and remember that what you mean is more important than how you say it.

I going remember you for always, Chala. If I wasn't a reformed man, I would be drinking to your memory right now.

Doreen looked side-eye at me and I probably had the "I was thinking of alcohol" look on my face because she reached over and pinched under my arm with her fingernails and whispered, "KZZZT!" Made my nuts shrivel.

Corina was standing in the front of the cafeteria looking sad. Tony was doing Chala's services as a favor to the family, plus it's good advertising when people hear how awesome his praising is. Make them want to come back for more during a happier occasion, like Saturdays. Chala's first, second, and third wives was in the front row sitting at the fold-out tables with all his kids. Corina was on the side by herself. She was the closest to him but she don't rate no spot on the family cafeteria table. The three Chala exes all seemed like they was ganging up against Corina. Whisper, whisper, point, point. And every so often they made the international gesture for "dick biter" so I knew that they know. Chicks can be so mean. You would think they would all hate each other but no, they all united in their hatred of poor Corina.

When came time for me to go up and pay my respects, I tried make my mind as clear as possible and my voice as soft as possible so only Chala can hear what I saying. Those exes of his looked like they get big ears and they was straining to hear every little confession.

I leaned way, way over close to his face. He smelled stink, just like always. That made me even more sad and sorry for all the stink days we spent together.

I went in real close to his ear and was about to make my confession and my goodbyes. Ay Jesus but he had plenty ear bites on his ear. Look like the edge of a McDonald's apple pie already. Flakey and everything. Oh Chala, you lived a full life.

And then this huge monster man came in and pushed me out of the way. He had on ankle chains and there was two sheriffs standing behind him in their brown polyester sheriff suits. Monster man had on a nice suit with a Fujinaka-looking shirt but Fooj didn't have no clothes that big. Nice clothes and jailhouse slippers. Typical funeral clothes for an inmate.

Come to find out was Chala's son, the oldest one. Ay-ya, Chala had a kid as old as me! How early he started out making babies, third grade?!

The guy told me, "Sorry, I only get ten minutes to talk to my old man. The ACOs taking me Dairy Queen after."

"Dairy Queen is something else now," I told him. His face looked all panic. "But they still get slush float."

He smiled. "Right on."

I moved to the side so he could talk to the father fast-kind. If you get chance to be outside and pick up lunch, you gotta go with that opportunity. I can understand that.

I was trying to make like I not listening so I was looking around at all the people. The exes was trying to make like they not listening so they was looking around at Corina. Corina was not listening and not looking around at anybody. She was so lost. Chala was her soul mate. All the rest of the guys was just snacks. He was the main course, always.

The son made the sign of the cross, but fancy kind, like when they kiss their thumb and point up to the sky five times. Then he leaned over and told the father, "Daddy, I gotta tell you something. I banged your chick. She was hot. But I sorry."

Ho! All the exes' heads turned to Corina and their mouths was loud-whispering back and forth. Corina was wiping black eyeliner tears from her face with the fringe-edge of her mullet. She didn't recognize the big guy in his prison slippers and leg chains.

But then she did.

Braddah pulled down his pants and whipped it out, bite marks and all.

Corina leaned in close to look good. She gave a little gasp.

"Brandon?!"

Brandon looked down at himself and sadly told the father, "The scars on my dick is nothing compared to the scars on my heart. I sorry, Daddy. I going be sorry every time I look down and see how I betrayed you."

He zipped his pants, wiped a tear, and turned to one of the sheriffs.

"Get time or what?" And he nodded with his head to Corina.

"Not if you like stop get slush float."

Brandon looked all bummed.

"Sorry," he mouthed to Corina, who nodded sadly and went back to her crying for beloved Chala.

The oldest ex, Brandon's mother, was standing up from the cafeteria table like she was gonna throw blows with Corina. The other two exes were holding her back like, "Don't do it, Erlanda! She ain't worth it!"

The sheriffs was getting nervous, putting their hands on their gun holsters. Brandon was telling them hurry up, he didn't want to miss out on the snack stop.

And then Erlanda jumped up on the cafeteria table and launched 20 feet, sailing, flying over the other exes' heads, to grab Corina by the mullet tail and tackle her to the ground.

Was full ultimate fighting smack down super brawl action after that. The other two exes joined in and fists were flying, fake plumeria hair picks were popping out, fake fingernail tips were raining on the concrete floor, shorty muus were ripping, blood was dripping, and Tony was calling on the Lord to intervene.

Me, I wanted to jump in and save Corina, but like all guys know, you don't get involved in chick fights. I thought Doreen would jump in too. She loves a good scrap, but she just sat there and gave me the eye like, "Don't you dare. Don't you fucking dare, Bobby. Think of the toaster."

I would not dare.

Taysha jumped in to tear the wahines off of Corina, but when one of the exes caught her on the chin with a left hook, Taysha stopped Ay Jesusing and taught those girls a lesson in girl fighting. First lesson, wear your hair in a bun so nobody can pull it. Taysha can seriously pull hair. By the time the cops came, Taysha had the exes too tired to resist arrest. Taysha got more strong with her pregnancy hormones. I told myself I better watch my mouth around her until she hatch.

Corina was arrested, too, and I seen her going away in the back of the police car. A couple of her teeth were lying on the cafeteria floor in front of Chala and the portable Jesus statue and the new sound system. I picked them up to save for remembering our happy times.

Doreen was like the wise old lady shaking her head at the stupid things kids do. She leaned over to me and said, "See? Aren't you glad you didn't get tangled up with that chick? She's trouble."

Doreen forgot about good trouble because she was working so hard to get all the bad trouble out of her life. Maybe some wahines can forget about how a good life is one good trouble after another, but a man always get that somewhere in his mind. Maybe someday I'll talk to her about the difference between good fun trouble and screw-up-your-life trouble. Because get difference, even though when I in the middle of it, it all feels good fun to me.

After the funeral and the arrests, Doreen could tell I was sad because I lost my best friend. She asked me if had anything she could do. I wanted for tell her, shoot, we go eat slush float. Slush float and fries. Slush float with little bit vodka inside and fries. Maybe a teri burger on the side. Cigarette after the meal to wash it all down. Beer chaser with the cigarette. After that, let's just see where that takes us. I get some sorrows to drown.

But no, I just told her nah, I like be alone with my thoughts about Chala and our years of friendship.

Doreen said no, no good be alone. We should all stick together at a time like this.

I told her, "Wow, Doreen, that is super nice of you."

She told me, "You think I nuts or what? You get that look on your face like you going start at the liquor store and keep rolling down the hill to the bottom of meth mountain so I ain't letting you out of my sight, fuckhead."

Sometimes I wished Doreen didn't care about me so much.

She said would be good for my healing process if I made a memorial. Like when somebody die in a car accident and they put flowers and stuffed animals on the side of the road. I told her Chala didn't die in a car accident, it was the big mango that grew into a watermelon. She told me she know, stupid ass, she just giving example.

So that's how come get one rock in an old Pukalani pineapple field with an empty jar, some plumeria flowers I ripped off from the school and a sign with white road striping paint that says, "Chala 4-eva. Rest in peac." I ran out of room for the "e." Doreen said that's OK. Chala wasn't going to ding me for spelling.

Before I went back in Doreen's truck, I walked back to the rock and looked for the bottles of weed poison we left behind. Just checking. Aw yeah. Was still there. Not like I was going come back and do that stuff again, but just good to keep track of my options. Even though I was a changed man. Even though I was clean and sober four months.

I took a leak in the bushes before the long ride down to Wailuku. I was thinking about long talks me and Chala used to have about all kinds of stuff. I wish I could remember what we said. I looked down and I saw the evidence of my betrayal. I felt so bad.

"I never got to say sorry, Chala. I sorry I banged Corina."

And I zipped up fast and ran to Doreen's truck before a lightning bolt could hit me or a bee could sting my dick.

He was dead and I was still thinking he could kick my ass. That's how great a guy Chala was.

Chapter 21

HAD THIS GIRL THAT WORK AT MY WORKING PLACE, she was kind of cute.

OK, not really, but I liked her anyway.

First time I saw her I thought she was a guy. Second time I saw her I thought she was a guy. Third time I saw her, we ate lunch in the back room and talked story for 20 minutes and I thought she was a guy. I told her, "Laters, Braddah" when we went back work.

Then I heard one of the other guys talking to Braddah and calling him "Shantel" and I was thinking, eh, that's not a girl's name?

It is a girl's name, stupid ass.

Oh wow. Come to find out I am straight. I was having my little doubts for a while there. I thought I was checking out a soft dude, but really I was checking out a butch girl. Cool.

Shantel wasn't my usual kind of chick that I liked.

For one thing, she wasn't passed out in vomit on somebody's living room floor. I met couple of my girlfriends that way.

For another thing, she single. Before time I loved to tap into some-body else's woman because easy, right? Don't have to pay their rent or buy their dinner or support their babies. Shantel didn't have no husband or no boyfriend.

For another thing, she had a job. And she was going school. And she was past 20 years old already and she didn't have no kids.

OK maybe she could be into chicks, but if she was, I don't mind. I could be her side-order man. Her man fries. Whatever she needs.

For the first couple of weeks at my job, she wouldn't even make eye contact. But pretty soon, I was telling her my Bobby jokes and making her laugh, saving her my box raisins from lunch. Stuff like that. And I could tell she was falling for my charms.

One day Shantel was going to vacuum out the same Corolla back seat as me and her hose caught me right between the legs and she sucked on my nuts through my pants part. She was all embarrassed and I was all shocked and kinda sore but the more I thought about it, the more I liked that suckin' girl.

After that, I tried to make sure me and her work on the same car at the same time. I try go for the vans because if I chasing her down on the subcompacts would be too obvious I was trying to squeeze in close to her and her hose.

Was a big game. I had to run for the vans first so I could get to the door, open it up, and spread my legs fast so she can come behind for the hose sucking. But cannot get there too fast or else going look obvious I waiting for my nuts to get sucked.

But her, Shantel, my little suspected lesbian, she always played along. She timed her run to the van or the SUV so she got there right after me so when she sucked my balls with the hose, looked like it was an accident. Looked like she was just rushing to get the job done.

I dreamed of the day she get the job done. And you no gotta rush, Shantel. You don't gotta hurry at all.

I was thinking maybe she's like a vegetarian who eat a juicy steak every once in a while when her blood need the charge. Let me be your steak, Shantel. Let me be your meat.

Other stuff happened too, stuff that let me know she was interested.

One time she found a box of condoms in a car. She brought it over to the lost and found box.

"I'll take that," I told her. "I might need 'em."

And she said, "No, you don't."

See! She was telling me I could be free with her! She was ready to take that chance with me!

One time I was watching this old dude trying to take his wife's wheelchair out of the back of the SUV and he was struggling and working and sweating and then he had try take the wife out of the car and put her in the wheelchair and I was watching that and thinking wow, some vacation and Shantel came up to me and said, "What you looking at?" and I told her, "The man having hard time." And she told me, "So go help him." And I was like, "OK, then. I will." And I went over there and helped the guy hoist his old lady and I dropped her all gentle inside the chair and when the guy wanted to give me a dollar I told him, "Nah, that's OK. Keep your dollar. She not that fat."

Shantel watched what had happened and when I went back to where she was by the trash cans, she told me, "Nice."

See! She inspired me to be a better person!

Shantel is my soul mate.

I just had to find out if she's a full-on lesbian or just part-time.

My first pay check came after two weeks. The paper was burning my hands, but I gave the whole thing, envelope and all, over to Dori. "This for my rent," I told her.

I was wondering if she was going give the money back and tell me that nah, I earned it, the money is mine to spend as I wish so long as I don't do nothing stupid with it. But no, she told me, "About fucking time," and she made me sign the back part over to her.

Two more weeks passed, I got another check. By then I was hanging on to the spare change I found in the car just to buy stuff like a boiled egg from the airport snack bar. Sad when your big treat is boiled egg. I handed my check over to Doreen and I was so hoping I get the "Nah, Bobby, you buy yourself a little something special." But no. She made me sign the back, then she looked at the front and told me, "You should offer to work overtime. You ain't making shet."

Two more weeks had pass. I was flirting with Shantel like a dog in heat but was hard to make any moves when I cannot even take her out after work.

So then I had get my big idea.

When my check came, I waited until we was all eating dinner at Doreen's table and I made my play. I told Doreen I like use my check to take her and the kids out to a nice restaurant for dinner. To show my appreciation. To give the kids a little treat. To practice my social skills, because I remembered they did that in the Alternative Learning Center in high school—they took all the drop-out kids to go eat at a nice restaurant so they could learn to do more than shoot pool, get high, and punch walls.

Doreen was amazed. She didn't think I had this generous, thoughtful side in me.

The kids was on my team right there. Jorene was all excited for the chance to get dressed up. Kennison wanted for pick up some cooking tips. Liko was so bored in his small little life that a trip to the garbage cans down the road is a big adventure.

Doreen said I wasting my money, but she couldn't come up with too many reasons to shoot down my idea because she like eat something that wasn't cooked in her own kitchen, too.

So then, was on. I was going take them out to a nice fancy dinner at a place up the street where every Friday night they have all-you-can-eat crab legs.

Oh, and I had throw in there, I taking my friend from work.

Doreen sat up straight like she just heard a burglar alarm go off.

"What friend from work?"

"Oh, Shantel, you know, the chunky one with the tattoos. Her."

"Oh, the lesbian? That one? I didn't know you guys was friends. What, you two checking out the same chick or what?"

"Nah, Doreen, I kind of like her."

"Her who?"

"Shantel."

Doreen's eyes was popping out of her head.

"Mommy, what is a lesbian?" Doreen wanted for slap me for that but I wasn't the one who said that word in front the small boy.

"That's a chick that likes chicks," Kennison told the small brother.

"Oh, like Miss Suzi at the preschool," Liko said. Kids these days, they no more hang-ups like we had. They pretty right on.

Doreen was turning purple.

She sent me to my room and locked the door on the outside. After the kids was in bed, she opened the lock and came in, no knock, toaster in hand.

"Bobby, what the hell you doing?"

"I promise Doreen, was just one small Twinkie. Didn't even taste good. And right after that, I was back eating healthy the whole rest of the day."

"No, I mean going out with a lesbian."

"I didn't say it, you did."

"She is!"

"How you know for sure unless you one too?"

She swung fast but I ducked faster. All this healthy eating was building my defenses inside and out.

"She not into guys. She not into you. Why you wasting your time?"

"She's cool."

"Yeah, OK, so why you cannot just be friends, why you gotta fall in love with somebody who not going love you back?"

"We is friends. And you don't know if she cannot love me back. Maybe she get feelings for me. Every day, she sucks my nuts."

Doreen toastered me hard after that comment. I thought I might not have nuts for Shantel to suck after that toastering.

When I could breathe again, I asked and Doreen said no, wouldn't have been better if I said that Shantel uses the vacuum hose on my testicles. It wasn't the words, it was the action.

But I like the action.

She zapped so hard she burned out the toaster. Now she has to shop for another faulty appliance.

No more getting anybody to suck my nuts with the vacuum hose at work. Or after work. And no sucking my own nuts with the vacuum hose at work. Or after work. Or ever.

"Frick, Bobby, that is so sick! What the hell is wrong with you?"

Maybe if Doreen had nuts she would understand. Doreen get balls, but she don't have no actual nuts.

But few days later, Doreen saw me all love drunk and dreamy at work and she get the idea that if I spend time with Shantel after work, I going realize that it will never work between us. Doreen wanted me for hurry up and find that out so I could move on to someone else. Someone who likes guys. Someone who likes guys like me. And hopefully somebody who could take me off her hands once she get her hands on my money. So we was on for the dinner.

Lunchtime at work, Shantel was coming out of the break room while I was going in. I figured that was my chance. I told her, "Eh, can talk to you for a second?"

She said, "Yeah, but your second is pau." And she just had keep going, back to the vacuum hose and the blue paper towels.

I love a chick that play hard to get.

Pau work time, I tried meet her at the employee locker. She looked like she seen me coming and was trying to run away. I had try get between her and the door and she was going side to side like a basketball forward hustling to the net with me blocking her shot.

"So Shantel, you like go out eat or what?"

Her eyes was panic like she was trapped. Probably never been asked out by a man before. Probably a man-virgin. I was getting all excited just thinking of the stuff I can teach her.

"Why?"

"Me and my sister and my sister's kids going out to eat Saturday at one nice restaurant and I was thinking if you like come with us."

"No."

"No, for real. Just come. No pressure. Get all you can eat crabs."

That caught her by surprise.

"For real?"

"You can meet us there."

"Crabs?"

"All you can eat!"

"OK."

"OK!"

"Right on."

"Right on!"

"So, can bring a friend?"

So that's how I ended up paying for two all-you-can-eat crab leg dinners for Shantel and her girlfriend Shatrisse plus food for Doreen, Jorene, Kennison, who ordered steak, and Liko, who ordered dessert. My whole pay check went up in that one dinner and all I ate was salad bar. Doreen was way too happy, laughing up big with the lesbians like they was old friends. She was looking at me with the big "I told you, stupid ass" Doreen eyes. She looked like she was digging on those crab legs too even though the crab legs in the all-you-can-eat bucket was the small legs of the crab that they couldn't serve on one expensive dish, the kind get more shell than meat and you end up sucking on that bony straw trying to find some kind of seafood taste.

The whole dinner idea sucked. The whole Shantel idea sucked.

Dori was so happy that I was so shame, she let me walk Shantel and Shatrisse home to their place in Happy Valley. Just to rub it in. Doreen wasn't even thinking, "Eee, Happy Valley, drug dealers, meth labs, bad action . . . maybe Bobby should just go home with us." She just wanted me to face up to my bad judgment about Shantel. She wasn't thinking about my bad judgment in other stuff.

I got them to their apartment door and told them OK, laters, have a good night doing whatever it is you ladies do after you spent three hours sucking on crab legs. See ya.

And they was like hey, Bobby, thanks for inviting us to dinner. We had fun. Wanna come in for a beer?

And I was like, wait a minute. This scenario never even cross my mind, and I usually pretty good at letting all kind naughty party action cross my mind any old time it felt like it. Heck yeah I wanted to come inside, ladies. Get two of you but get plenty Bobby to go around so share, ladies, share.

But they wasn't interested in me that way. They just wanted to shake me down, see if I had more cash, some stash, gift certificates, anything. Anything but my manly charms. They wasn't even interested listen to my good stories. And me, I get some good stories. But nothing. They gave me a beer and turned on the TV and stopped paying me attention.

And that was pretty much the end of everything.

Eighteen beers, four joints, some coke, some meth, and a pack of cigarettes later I was roaming the low-income apartments looking for my mother's old friend Uncle Georgie hoping he/she could explain the world to me and mix me one of them Bloody Marys with the cough syrup inside.

I found couple wahines I thought was Georgie but wasn't. I found couple guys I thought was Georgie but wasn't.

I found couple guys I thought was Corina and I got the bite marks to prove it.

Me, looking for love in all the fucked up places. Me, fucking up every time I find love. I only feel good when I cannot feel nothing.

I got the idea that I should go back upstream, like a salmon or whatever the fuck fish live in cold water, back up to where my eggs was laid. I started up the Iao Stream, up, up into Iao Valley. Most of the stream in Happy Valley was dry but once you got closer in the valley, that fucker was running like a giant taking a major piss. The smell of ripe guavas was thick with mosquitoes. The roar of the water was so loud, I couldn't even hear myself talking to myself, not even in my head.

People was on the bridge by the park yelling at me asking me what the hell I doing trying to swim upstream in the rushing current that was blasting fast but was only four inches deep over all the rocks. Iao Stream was all rocks and all blasting at that point. Pretty hard to swim, but I was stroking. I think I was stroking. Maybe I wasn't swimming. Maybe I was just flopping from rock to rock. I don't know, but. Seemed like I was bleeding but couldn't be because I didn't feel my body.

All I could think of was if I go up to Kepaniwai Park, maybe I could live in one of the houses in the ethnic village. To tell the truth, the Haole house is the nicest, but that's probably because it's locked all the time. The Hawaiian house is dark and get mosquitoes. The Chinese house get too much people taking wedding pictures. The Japanese house get too much noisy kids throwing bread to the fish. I guess my choices is the Filipino house with the lumpy bamboo floor or the Portuguese house with the spooky oven. Maybe I can live in between, make my own halfway house.

Fuck, I am hilarious when I am my normal unhealthy fucked-up self.

I got to the part of the park where have the picnic pavilions and I hauled myself out of the water. Had some families making barbeques and some kids with a keiki first birthday party. Hey, every keiki first birthday party needed the good fun silly uncle. I know how to do that. I was thinking I should kokua, help out those families, give them the gift of my fucking hilariousity. However you say that.

Nobody wanted to share their teri chicken. Or their chow fun. Or their shoyu hot dogs. I went from table to table and nobody told me, "Hey, good fun uncle! Glad you showed up! Here, let us make you a plate! Grab a cold one and join the party!"

Nope. None of that action. Some kids pointed and laughed at me. Some of the small girls ran screaming. One of the daddies told me to get the fuck out of there before he broke my ass. What happened to the aloha, I like know? What happened to ohana and everybody getting along? I thought this was Hawaii? When did stuff get so crazy and mean? Can't a naked, loaded, crazy, bleeding man find a place at the picnic table anymore? I mean, really, what's a guy gotta do for a shoyu hot dog these days?

I fell into the koi pond, the same koi pond that I fell into when I was a small kid, the koi pond of my worst nightmares.

That's OK. That's OK. That's OK. Just float. Just deal. Just handle. You a grown man now. You not scared of no fish bumping your face with their cold hard fins. You not scared of no tadpoles swimming in your mouth and in your ears and up your nose. You not going freak out. You just going relax and relax and relax.

After a while I was pretty sure I turned into a fish, sleeping with my eyes open, breathing through the water.

My gramma was on the little concrete bridge smoking a cigarette and standing by a bucket and scoop net.

"Hey, Gram!"

She threw the cigarette butt in the water and it made a fhtttt sound when it hit.

"What the hell now, Bobby? What the hell you did now?"

"I think I'm dead."

My grandma rolled her eyes as she rolled another cigarette.

"You not dead. You just fucked in the head. I would kill you myself but I no like you come over here disturb my peace in the next world."

"I know I messed up, Gramma. I sorry."

My gramma took the bucket, turned it over and sat down.

"You the type only sorry when you end up ass deep in frog water and your dead gramma show up in your hallucinations."

"That's true."

"You're like these stink fish in this stink pond, swimming in the same circle all day every day, eating shet, shetting shet, eating the shet you just shet."

"I could be a fish. Turn me into a fish."

Gramma scooped the scoop net into the water and snatched me up in the red strings. She turned the net over and dropped me onto the cement walkway.

"You gotta start back from the beginning, Bobby. You gotta start yourself all over and do it different this time. That's your only choice. Your other choice is more swimming in circles and eating shet. And if you wasn't so loaded right now, you would take notice that eating shet don't taste so good."

Gramma took her bucket and her scoop net and disappeared. I flopped around on the sidewalk for a while until the kids started pointing and laughing. I looked over in the bushes and I could see something sticking out behind a junked car and some rusted construction equipment and some bags of garbage . . . the edge of an abandoned sofa. Not Doreen's sofa, but close enough. Maybe it was plaid, hard to tell because it was so rotten from the rain and the sun. The sofa called to me with its big sofa mouth. "Bobby! Bobby! Come home! Come home!" I crawled through the park, crawled through the weeds and buffalo grass, crawled up to that beckoning sofa and went to sleep until the sirens woke me up.

And of all the charges I get against me now, the one I don't understand or even remember is "operation of a heavy equipment vehicle while under the influence of an intoxicant."

How the hell did I get that backhoe to start? The thing was more fucked up than the sofa. More fucked up than me, even. Unreal. I would never think a backhoe that rusted out would do so much damage to a parking lot full of cars.

Chapter 22

DOREEN CAME TO SEE ME ONLY ONE TIME, only to get me to sign the power of attorney paper for her. I didn't mind her getting all the settlement money from my accident. I was going give it to her anyways. Most of it.

"Doreen, I just wanted to say I'm really sorry I let you down and I know you want to kill me for this and when I get out, you can strap me to a faulty electrical appliance and turn on the juice for a month if you like. I know I deserve it. That's how sorry I am."

Doreen gathered up the legal paperwork and the checks I signed over to her and walked out without even looking at me, like she don't even care no more, like I not even worth hurting or killing.

That's what hurt me the most.

I wanted her to want to kick my ass again. That's how I knew she cared.

Tony is the only one who comes to visit me. Well, actually, he just says hi sometimes when he's doing his rounds of his prison ministry. He pray for me and I try get him to tell me what's going on on the outside. Him and Taysha built a two-story house with their fire insurance money and when I say I can't wait to see it, Tony starts praying. Taysha had the baby, a girl with two green eyes and a brown Afro and a wide upepe nose to beat all upepe noses. Tony let me see a picture. They named her Tonysha, and she is cute, cute, cute. I was secretly hoping for the name to be BobbyLynn or something, but maybe next one because Taysha is pregnant again. Ay Jesus.

Corina comes every so often to see her husband Paco, who is back in prison for attempted murder of Chala even though Chala was going die anyways. Corina, but, she don't even notice me. Half the guys in the visiting room trying to catch her attention by waving their dicks under the table. Her face is a blank. It's only about Paco when she's with Paco and now that Chala is gone. Me, I'm just a dick in the crowd.

One of the guys in my unit told me he was delivering furniture for Sears when he was on the outside. Buss-ass gig but then he could case all the houses and come back later and take stereos and shet. What a racket. Anyways, he told me he delivered one nice fat Sears sectional to my sister/ cousin's new house she bought in Lower Wailuku Heights.

I was like, "Sextional? Ho, what is that?"

He told me one sectional is a massive sofa the size of a SUV that you can move around any kind ways so that your whole living room can be filled with wall-to-wall sofa if you like.

I was like, "Shet, Doreen still get that dog or what?"

He told me, "Shet yeah. And that fucker bit my leg when I tried to go back daytime and lift the TV."

"And what about your neck. The dog bit you there too?"

He touched the scar on his neck and smiled. "That was a different dog. A big-ass dog with long shaggy hair."

This bastard sure had some bad luck with dogs, eh?

After that I was all dreaming of Doreen's new sectional, a sofa that stretches from wall to wall, all ass-warm and snuggly.

I wrote Doreen letters telling her I'm happy for her. I put in little lines in the end about how I looking forward to getting out and coming to live again on her bountimous sectional sofa. Even just one section sound like would be enough for me. One section for the dog, one section for me.

She never write back yet, but she will. Me and her is family. I can wait.

Acknowledgements

Thank you to Darrell H.Y. Lum and Eric Chock for teaching, leading, encouraging, and keeping it real. Thank you to Wing Tek Lum, Gail Harada, Nora Okja Keller, Micheline Soong, Michelle Cruz Skinner, Jean Toyama, Brenda Kwon, Mavis Hara, Juliet Kono, Joe Tsujimoto, Lisa Kanae, Marie Hara, Milton Kimura, and Fuku Tsukiyama for generous honesty, sharp eyes, and fabulous dinners. Thank you to Joy for always seeing the bright side, to Xander for his artistic vision of plaid and feet, and to Wayne for transforming that idea into a book cover. Thank you to Krista, Aoi, and my mom for watching the baby while I wrote.

Lee Cataluna won the Elliott Cades Award for Literature in 2004. Her book *Folks You Meet in Longs and Other Stories* received a Ka Palapala Poʻokela Award in 2006. Her plays have been produced in theaters around Hawaiʻi. She has been a journalist in Hawaiʻi for 20 years and is nothing like Bobby, though she is somewhat like Doreen.